The Chronicles of Ratha: Book Two A Lion Among The Lambs

Erica Lawson

Affinity
eBook Press
NZ
2014

The Chronicles of Ratha: Book Two A Lion Among The Lambs
© by Erica Lawson 2014

Affinity E-Book Press NZ LTD.
Canterbury, New Zealand

1st Edition

ISBN: 978-1-927328-09-5

This is a work of fiction. names, character, places, and incidents are the product of the author's imagination or are used fictitiously and any resemblance to actual persons living or dead, businesses, companies, events, or locales is entirely coincidental.

Editor: Nat Burns
Proof Editor: Alexis Smith
Cover Design: Irish Dragon Designs

Acknowledgements

This story began its publication journey in the hands of Blue Feather Books. Since they closed their doors, Affinity picked up the mantle and have allowed me to continue Jordana's story. I thank them very much, especially Julie, Erin, Irish, and Nat for their support and encouragement.

I'd also like to thank my two "families" – my personal family who have supported my writing career from the beginning, and the sisters of my heart, who have accepted me with open arms. I appreciate their support and kind thoughts over the last few difficult months.

Dedication

To my two families—one of my blood and the other of my heart

Table of Contents

Other Books by Erica Lawson

Out of Retirement
Miss-Match
Reflected Passion
Possessing Morgan
Chronicles of Ratha: Children of the Noorthi
Soulwalker

Prologue

It's been nearly three years since I last had a chance to contemplate my life. Three years since someone's thirst for vengeance had thrown me in the path of the Noorthi. Three years since my life changed completely.

And what's happened in those three years?

The most important thing was probably the birth of my child a little more than two years ago. No, I didn't have a child but the little girl is my baby. Confused? Imagine how I felt when I found out that I'd become a father. And I hadn't even touched the woman. I'm still trying to figure that one out. So far I've just put it down to one of those mysterious things the Noorthi are so good at. After all, they're holy women and a mystery to the rest of us.

Little Rice has been both a joy, and a real pain in the ass, as toddlers tend to be. They are so adoringly cute as they cause mayhem in their wake. But I knew her namesake so knew what this little tornado would be capable of. Then again, she was my kid. Enough said.

And Beri? I've stayed with her despite our celibate relationship. Now, I didn't say it was easy. Far from it, but I don't know who to blame. I'd like to think it's the Noorthi ochre flowing through my veins that's responsible for my predicament, but it could be Beri's enigmatic smile that keeps me coming back, or maybe I just like the idea of having a kid. Beri has always said that I could go and... what was the old saying? Ah, yes, go and sow my wild oats. But how could I do that to her? For the past few months I've been living nine-tenths the way to insanity.

1

However, I've made some progress with Beri. It's taken nearly three years but she'll kiss me now, at least not without throwing up. I'm kidding. She seems to enjoy it because there have been times when she'll kiss me, and not the other way around. In the past few months she's even held my hand in public. I've seen Fen chuckle in my peripheral vision. She certainly seems to know more about this relationship than I do. Maybe I should be asking Fen when I can make my next move instead of trying to read Beri's body language.

I've sobered up permanently, courtesy of the ochre, and I don't particularly like it, but no matter what I do the taste never changes. Everything is just awful to drink. Once or twice I even forced myself to get drunk in defiance, but in the end it just wasn't worth it. I'm sure my dad, if he were alive, would be happy I've settled down. I hate it. Well, not hate exactly. There are parts of it that are great, but I'm still fighting it.

I still work off-world from Heaven. After all, a girl's got to bring in the income for the family, right? The boys are still here on Heaven and do the same thing. Work off-world then bring home the credits to the family who are now living with them. I suppose I do it more to keep in touch with the outside world. To realize the universe is still out there and I'm still part of it.

Not long after Vel's death, everyone made a pact, and so far it's worked very well. No one knows that Heaven exists. We jealousy guard the untouched virginity of the moon, keeping it safe for our families and the Noorthi. No drinking, fighting or carousing is allowed on Heaven. After all, that's what Arcus on Telgan is for. One or two of the locals know of us, but they're sworn to secrecy. It's a matter of necessity to have someone know of our existence in case something catastrophic happened and we needed to be contacted.

Construction is finally finished on the landing bay and a tunnel had been added to connect it to the healer's cave on the other side. We can now move from one side of the plateau to the other without having to go over the top.

Of course, Grit and her cronies quickly ordered that a new Great House had to be built for the Noorthi, which became a bone of contention between the settlers and the Noorthi. One had one priority while the others had another. I pointed out to all concerned that if a compromise wasn't reached, nothing would be built. They soon settled their differences.

And what about Malt, I hear you ask? Well, she's changed. She's blossomed quite a bit, not only in her self-confidence, but also in her looks. That gawky, fourteen-year-old is now gone, and even with four arms she's turned out to be quite a looker, if I say so myself. She hasn't found anyone yet, but she has plenty of friends to make up for lack of companionship. She used to come with me when I worked, but lately her responsibilities have lain on Heaven, especially after the death of Floric.

I'm sitting in my usual spot on the plateau and looking out over the village that's sprung up. The huts sit under the canopy of trees and are hidden from prying eyes overhead. In the far corner is a small patch of open ground. Next to Floric lay half a dozen more graves belonging to Noorthi women who have died of old age.

Damn, I miss the old man. When I first met him he was a real pain in the ass, but as time wore on he became a great asset to us. He taught Malt many things, for which I am eternally grateful. A year in from his employment, he even mellowed, his grumpy attitude waning as he grew to love the new life on Heaven. Although Malt never talked of it I knew she was hurt badly when he fell sick. Even Grit's extensive knowledge of medicine did little to improve him, until finally his body just gave up. Malt stepped into Floric's large shoes, not only as inventor but also as teacher to the children of our little village.

And Sasha? She's still working a lot but she's made a point of coming home more often and spending some quality time with Rales. It's been good for them both. Even though he's been busy with all the construction work, I know he still misses his little girl. I think Sash has finally realized that.

We made a salvage run to Juno right after Vel and Grimm's demise to see what we could find of the Noorthi Great House. It was necessary to use Floric's cloaking device to get inside and rummage around because the Consortium forces had taken up residence after they defeated Grimm's soldiers. I can still hear

Grit's disgusted snorts as she observed the rampant disregard for religious artifacts. We could only soothe her indignation by recovering something of use to the Noorthi sisterhood.

What I didn't know was that three of Rales' boys, Dorin, Wakes and Hagan, had hacked into Grimm's computer and emptied his bank account, transferring it across half a universe into an account that had just been concocted a minute before. They had also discovered a secret alcove and promptly emptied that too. The only thing that saved them from my wrath was that they offered it to our community. It seemed that it was common knowledge that our funds were getting low, and they pleaded that they were doing it for us all. Besides, they pointed out logically, if we didn't take it, the Consortium would. We took it.

So that's it. Three years on and life goes on like the first day we arrived. A little more comfortable maybe, but we work, we eat and we sleep. Heaven has sure lived up to its name.

Chapter One

In The Beginning

It was nearing the third anniversary of our arrival. The rising sun was shining brightly and the air was fresh. I observed my little piece of Heaven from the old landing site while I savored my early morning coffee synth. Life went on, as always. Our little village had continued to thrive, and the Noorthi were, well, the Noorthi. Despite their close proximity they still remained mysterious.

I studied the scar on my wrist. How could one little flower change my whole life? Since the tattoo the Noorthi had given me, my life had been turned upside down. I was once a carefree, booze-drinking, hard-fighting space pilot for hire. Now I'm an administrator. Not literally, of course. I wouldn't be caught dead in such an organized position. But the Noorthi had backed me into a corner and if we wanted Heaven to work, then someone had to make the decisions.

My finger ran across the raised skin, tracing the delicate lines of the Noorthi symbol. It had been kind of exciting at first to carry such an exclusive tattoo. Lately, I've taken to wearing a wristband over it because the incessant questions from people I'd met annoyed me.

"Raa!" The tiny squeal put my teeth on edge. Little Rice scampered up the hill toward me, her mother trudging along behind her. The tiny bundle of limitless energy threw herself into my arms and I barely got rid of the cup I was holding before her squirming body hit me.

"Raa, high! High!"

Rice wouldn't be content until I threw her up into the air. It used to be easier a few months ago but Rice had been adding weight, and inches, to her little frame. "What have you been feeding her?" I asked Beri.

"Same as always." Beri finally sat down next to me, her face firmly fixed on her daughter as I threw the toddler into the air. "One of these days you're going to drop her."

"Nah! Unless she's seventeen, of course, then I might have a bit of trouble."

Beri chuckled. "You? Admitting you can't do something?"

"Shocking, isn't it? Maybe at seventeen she'll be throwing me around."

"Considering who she's a part of, it wouldn't surprise me."

Surprise couldn't begin to explain how I felt when Beri told me she was pregnant and I was responsible. Me. That's right. I'm her father… err, mother… err, co-conspirator. Whatever. You get the picture.

"Raaa!" Rice was wriggling around and complaining because I'd stopped tossing her in the air. She swung her legs and kicked me in the arm, and I nearly dropped her.

"Hey, squirt. Stop that! Do you want me to drop you?"

"Yessss," Rice said with a cheeky voice.

"Come here." I wrapped my hands around her tiny waist and put her on the ground. I tickled her and she squealed with delight. The more I tickled her the higher the squeals got, until they reached the pitch that sent both of us covering our ears.

"No screaming," Beri said in her 'stern' voice and Rice stopped, blinking once or twice as she looked at her mother. I wasn't sure whether Rice was going to cry or laugh. It was that sort of expression.

I looked down into Rice's blue eyes. "And what have you been doing? Running your mother ragged?"

She stared up at me and answered as only she could. "Yes."

"Figures." I turned my attention to Beri. "Has she been behaving?"

"What do you think?"

6

I heard the weariness in B's voice. "Do you want me to take her for a while so you can get some rest?" When Beri didn't answer I looked over my shoulder at her. "What's wrong?"

She bit her lip and I just knew it was about me. "You're here to give me some bad news."

"It's time."

"For what?" I gazed at Beri. "Spit it out, woman."

"Rice must begin her tutoring." Beri tried to look at me but couldn't. She found the grass underneath her very interesting.

"Tutoring?"

"Noorthi tutoring." Beri said nothing more, as if those two words said everything.

"Okay. So what does that involve?" I asked warily. My stomach was churning because of Beri's expression. It was something that she didn't want to tell me.

"You won't be able to see your daughter for quite a while." Beri's eyes finally met mine with some sadness.

"And how long is a while?" I felt myself getting agitated.

"Adulthood."

"Are... you... trying... to... tell... me....," I enunciated each word clearly and succinctly. "That she is going into the Noorthi stronghold for the next..." I mentally counted. "Fifteen years?" I hadn't realized that I was shouting until Beri winced.

"Something like that."

"I *hate* that phrase. You use it to cover the hideous truth. Why can't you just say what you mean?"

"Raaa!" Rice cried, her hands covering her ears. "No!"

"It is our way, Jordana, you know that. She must be instructed in the ways of the Noorthi."

"I thought you weren't Noorthi, but the *Children of the Noorthi*," I emphasized. I was scrambling for any kind of argument I could find because B was telling me that little Rice was going away for a very long time.

"We are in some things, but not in others. This must be done, J. She must know her heritage."

"At the expense of mine," I said flatly.

"She is my child—"

"*Our* child—"

"—and she will be Ashaltea one day. She must be prepared for that. Would you deny Rice her destiny?"

"And my influence on her will ruin all that?"

"That's not what I said."

"No, but it's what you thought." I stood and paced restlessly. Suddenly Heaven didn't quite live up to its name. "What about my position in the Noorthi? Doesn't that count for something?"

"Maybe I should have sent Fen."

"Maybe you should have!" I snapped back.

Beri stood and reached for Rice. "Come on, Rice."

The child looked from Beri to me, then back at her mother, meekly taking the offered hand and allowing herself to be led down the path back to the Noorthi village. At the bottom of the hill, I saw Beri pick up Rice and disappear under the canopy of vegetation.

Little Rice's voice started to wail. "Raa! Raa!" It broke my heart to hear the tiny squeals of anguish and it took everything I had to stay put. I slumped to the ground defeated. Who would have thought that one tiny child could break me?

I was tempted to jump into Bessie and fly to the nearby planet of Telgan to get drunk and find a fight. I so wanted to hit something right now.

"Am I interrupting something?"

I glanced at the woman stepping onto the plateau.

"What do you want? Come to give me more bad news?"

"Well, hello to you too." Fen stood there, calmly watching me.

"Beri ask you to come and smooth things over?" I asked harshly. Fen was the voice of reason and the buffer between Beri and myself.

"Beri doesn't know I'm here. I could see she was upset."

"No kidding? Imagine how I feel." I struck out with my foot, collecting a clump of grass with the tip of my boot.

"It has to be done."

"No, it doesn't! Why is it I'm always the one who has to sacrifice everything, huh? She's asking me to give up my child. I can't do that."

"She's Beri's child. Our future Ashaltea," Fen explained patiently, "Rice's future had already been set before she was even born."

"I don't object to her being Ashaltea, Fen. It's the not seeing her for fifteen years that's the obstacle. According to you, I'm a Noorthi. Doesn't that buy me visitation rights at least?"

"You will be a distraction to her." Fen took the last few steps toward me then rested her hand on my arm. "Let's sit down." She motioned to the piece of ground that overlooked the valley.

I resisted at first but finally took my seat next to her. She wanted to discuss this calmly and I wanted anything but. I was angry. I was frustrated. I was disappointed. The Noorthi wanted everything from me but would offer nothing in return.

"And how am I a distraction?" I think I already knew the answer to this one, but any other question eluded me.

"You see how Rice is when she sees you. She becomes wildly out of control. You give her excitement and play—"

"She's a tiny kid, Fen. She deserves fun and games." I leaned back on my hands, trying to relax.

"But she's a Noorthi, J, and one day she will lead us. There is a lot of responsibility with this position."

"And a lot of power," I added.

"Power? No. Order. We need order to survive. We need order to be who we are. Without order we are nothing."

"Do you really believe that?"

"Of course. It is in our very fabric."

"And what of family, Fen? You're asking me to give up family."

"You have Malt."

"But Malt isn't my flesh and blood."

Fen's gaze shifted to the path leading to the village. There stood Malt. I looked but I wished I hadn't. She'd heard me.

"Craz!" I hissed. "Malt!"

9

As expected, she turned away and disappeared from my sight. What else could go wrong?

"I gotta go." I didn't wait for Fen to acknowledge what I said. I stood and ran after Malt. "Malt!" Hey!" She increased her pace down the hill and I had to slow down or lose my footing. Damn it! Why did she have to hear that? By the time I reached the village Malt was truly out of sight.

Denneck's wife passed by. "Jeeka? Did you see Malt?"

"Sure. She went that way." She pointed to the cave in the wall.

I looked up and saw Malt disappear inside. "Thanks." I jogged up the path, but I was reduced to a slow walk by the time I reached the cave mouth. "Geez. She's making me work for this."

I suppose I should have expected that she wasn't there. Malt was truly hurt. I continued along the tunnel until it reached the landing bay. Malt was on the other side of the hangar sitting at the rim of the cave.

"Malt?" She glanced at me over her shoulder then returned to her inspection of the view. "Honey?"

"I'm not your honey." Malt said it quietly, but I heard it clearly.

"Yes, you are."

"I heard every word."

"No, you didn't. Fen was trying to get me to accept something I didn't want to."

"You mean that I'm not your family? I got that." She refused to look at me as I sat down beside her.

"I consider you family."

"You said I was not your child."

"Which is true. But you are family of my heart, Malt." I tentatively reached for one of her hands. Would she take it? "The Noorthi are about to take Rice away from me. Fen was telling me that you were enough."

"I'm not." Malt looked at me with tears in her eyes.

"You listen to me." I gave up waiting for Malt to make the first move, so I grabbed her hand. "You are more than enough, but they're telling me I can't see her. Rice has to go to Noorthi school, and that means no outside distractions."

"And for how long? A month? Two?"

"Until Rice is your age, Malt. They want me to go without seeing her for fifteen years."

"That's stupid!"

"Tell me about it." I tugged on her hand. "You hold a special place in my heart, kid. But there's also room for Rice."

"And Beri." Malt wiped the tears away.

"Beri?"

"Oh, come on. You had a child with her."

"I held her hand! As Carn is my witness, that's all I did!"

"Uh huh." I had a feeling that whatever I said was not going to be enough in her book.

"Believe me when I say I wouldn't give you up for... for..." I scrambled for something that held special meaning for me. "Heaven. Our home. You are my home, Malt. You're the one I can count on to be there for me. I've run out of fingers and toes for the number of times you've saved my life. And I don't trust just anyone with my life."

As I spoke Malt's sadness began to wane. I had done another monumentally stupid thing and my ochre-tainted words were healing an emotionally open wound. This was one time that I was glad I had the tattoo.

"So what are you going to do about Rice?" She voiced my fear.

"Anything I can. I'm not giving Rice up without a fight."

"Maybe you can strike a deal," Malt suggested.

"Yeah, a deal. But what can I offer them they don't already have?"

Malt sat quietly for a moment, her gaze roaming over the view from the hanger bay. "It's not the schooling that's upsetting you, right? It's the no contact." I nodded. "How about a certain time of the day is your time, while the rest is Noorthi time?"

I had already thought of that, but I wasn't going to let Malt know. If she was going to offer advice I'd take it. "Sounds interesting, but I'd like more time."

"But you're not going to get it. You'd be lucky to get them to agree to that."

"I know."

"It's better than nothing."

And I knew that was my only option. It was either see Rice for a little bit each day or not see her at all. Now all I had to do was to convince Beri that it was a great idea.

We sat together looking at the scenery spread out below us. It was a very pretty landscape, with blue skies, lush vegetation and a temperate climate.

"This moon is really great," Malt said.

"Yeah, a hundred times better than Rigeus."

"What was Rigeus like?"

"It was certainly not for the likes of you, my sweet Malt." She smiled as I murmured the endearment. "It's a penal planet, full of dust, sweltering hot days and no water. Then there were the nasty women prisoners."

"Sounds pretty scary."

"It was." I leaned closer. "Just don't tell Beri, okay?"

"There you are." Epi trotted across the floor of the landing bay. "Grit is all worked up about one of her predictions."

"She makes predictions?"

"All the time."

"How come I didn't know?"

Epi grinned at me. "Because they didn't concern you?"

"You are such a smart ass."

"So you keep saying." Epi extended her hand to help me up. "I think you need to talk to her."

"And do what? Beat her until she forgets what all the fuss was about?"

"We can't oppose her visions. You can."

"Why not? You've got as much right to tell her she's wrong as the next Noorthi."

Epi's gaze dropped to the floor and she scuffed her boot.

"What?"

"She cannot be questioned on this. It is our way."

"Is this another one of those secrets that I'm only going to find out about when there's an emergency?"

"Yeah…"

"Something like that. Yeah, yeah, I know the drill." After three years you would think the expression would have worn out its welcome. It appeared not.

"Excuse me, Malt. It seems I have another small Noorthi catastrophe to avert." I let my hand ruffle her shaggy hair.

I walked alongside Epi across the hanger bay floor to the corridor leading to the cave. "What's so special about Grit that her word is law?"

"She is *hedera*."

I didn't understand that word.

"*Hedera*," Epi repeated, as if I was supposed to be impressed. "She is our spiritual leader."

"I thought Beri was that."

"Beri is Ashaltea, leader of the Juno Noorthi, but Grit is *Hedera*. She is our connection to all things, seen and unseen."

"You mean something like a high priestess?" I'd read that somewhere.

"It may be, if a high priestess is the gateway to our spiritual well being."

"A high priestess is a woman who offers prayers up to the god or goddess of whichever religion they represent. They can supposedly converse with the spirits on the other side."

"The other side of what?"

Sometimes it was just easier to keep my mouth shut. "Between two planes of existence." Epi stared at me. "Between the living and the dead, dummy."

"That's not quite it, but close. Grit has the ability to sense the ebb and flow of nature in all its forms in the universe. It is an elemental harmony that we seek, so that we are able to live life peacefully within the boundaries of space, time and the various existential planes."

Epi's explanation was going way over my head, so I opted for high priestess. "Then why is she your healer?"

13

"We lost our healer on Rigeus to Vel. Grit had some knowledge so she took up the mantle of healer as well."

"I'm grateful that she did." After all, Grit was the one who saved me from a grisly death by brain burnout. If she wanted to play medtech I wasn't going to stop her. "So, is that topknot on Grit's head too tight?"

"Huh?"

"You Noorthi have no sense of humor. What is she so upset about?"

"Maybe she should tell you."

I grabbed Epi's arm and stopped walking. "I'm asking you. What's wrong?"

"She has had a vision."

"And?" I had gotten that much information already. "Tell me something that I don't know."

"There will be a great upheaval."

"Oh, Carn!" I started running through the corridor. "Sasha!" I yelled.

"What?" I heard Sasha's faint voice from the other end.

"Get everyone out into the open. There's going to be a cave in." I was about to say earthquake but I didn't have time for explanations. Whatever I wanted to call it, I needed to get as many people to safety before the moon swallowed them up.

Chapter Two

The Great Upheaval

"What are you doing?" Epi stood there and looked at me.

"We have to evacuate everyone before the earthquake."

Epi laughed. "I didn't say that."

"Yes you did. A great upheaval, you said."

"I think you need to talk to Grit."

"I think I do." I left Epi in the corridor and went in search of Grit. I found her bent over a mortar and pestle grinding some leaves. "You better explain why I just sent everyone running into the forest in panic."

"What are you talking about?" She looked up from her work.

"A great upheaval."

"Who told you?"

"Epi. What great upheaval?" I just wished Grit would get to the point. Maybe she got some perverse pleasure from making me squirm. "What was your vision?"

"It was not clear to me. The Noorthi, Ratha, something will happen to the Noorthi." Her voice was unsteady. This news obviously scared Grit.

"Good happen or bad happen?"

"I cannot see."

"How convenient," I mumbled, earning a pinch from the old woman. "Ow!" I rubbed my arm.

"Do not take this lightly, Ratha. I have never been wrong."

"But you can't tell me what's coming. How am I supposed to react if I don't know what it is?"

"Why must you know? Even if I had said nothing, you would do what you do best. You protect. You defend. You save us. All I can see is a great upheaval within the Noorthi. Something that is going to change everything."

My mind was already filling with ideas, both absurd and unbelievable. "Are we talking universe-changing or Noorthi-changing?"

"Both."

"So, just the usual, huh?" I suppose I was due for a hard time. After all, I'd been slumming it for the past three years.

"So it seems."

"I better go and tell Sasha to call off the evacuation."

"Ah, it seems I am not the only one who cannot see the future clearly all the time."

"Hey! All I heard was great upheaval. What would you have done?"

"Checked with me first?"

"One of these days, *memesh*...." I took a swipe at the air above her head. There was nothing worse than a smart ass holy woman. I turned to leave, but stopped. "I have something to ask. It's about Rice."

"Her time has come."

"I know that, but I can't see her."

"That is our way."

"She's also my kid. She will be my only legacy for generations to come. Help me, *please*."

Grit grabbed my hand and closed her eyes. She smiled. "Ah, how delightful!" She giggled. The woman actually giggled like a little girl.

"What?"

"Do not dismiss this yet."

"What's going on? Please, just tell me and stop these games."

"Rice will not be your only legacy."

"There's Malt"

"No, not Malt."

"Beri will have another child? Is that possible?"

"There will be another child. Have you not learned by now that anything is possible?"

"Wow!" I couldn't stop the smile on my face. "Am I involved?"

"Yes, you are."

"So I'll have another kid. I should tell—"

"No! Say nothing or this could change the outcome. This is a secret that is yours and yours alone." She looked me in the eye.

I'm sure she was pulling my leg, but I reluctantly agreed. Let her play all the games she wanted. I withdrew my hand and turned to leave. "Sheesh."

I stepped to the edge of the cave and looked out over our little village. People were milling around on the old landing plateau. Sasha spotted me and waved her hand.

"False alarm!" I yelled. Not sure whether my voice was heard or not, I trotted down the path to the valley floor then up the other side to the plateau. "It seems I got it wrong."

"You? You're never wrong!" I noticed Sasha took a step back as she spoke. She was obviously expecting a poke from me.

"Ha, ha. It seems the great upheaval Grit was referring to concerns the Noorthi and not a landslide."

I turned my attention to the gathered crowd. "Sorry, everyone. It was a good practice though, don't you think?"

The looks I got told me in no uncertain terms what they thought of my sudden scare. It wasn't my fault.

"Next time, give us warning," Dax muttered.

"That's the whole point, Dax. There'll be no warning." He just glared at me.

"What?" I asked Sasha. "I try to save their lives and I'm to blame."

"You *are* to blame, J. Next time, check your facts." Sasha followed the last citizen down the trail to the village, leaving me alone on the plateau.

I sat down in my usual spot. "What did I do?" I lifted my hands and let them drop. When would the day end?

I heard a cough behind me.

"Hey there, Delica. Are you still here?" She looked at me dazed. "Are you all right?" I stood up and made my way to her. She was sweating profusely. I lay my hand on her forehead. "You're burning up. Go and see Grit." I gave her a gentle push toward the rim of the plateau and the healer's cave. I watched her carefully as she stumbled down the path. When she disappeared into the cave I sat back down to try and find some peace in the view before me. I had a bad feeling that things were going to change around here, and not in a good way.

†

The next two days passed without incident, which was worrying in itself. Knowing that something was coming had a way of putting me on edge. That, plus Rice's dilemma, had me short-tempered and frustrated.

I took refuge from the day's activities at my usual spot on the plateau, absently sipping a coffee synth while I watched the breeze stir the treetops. My daydreaming was interrupted by the arrival of Grit. It looked like I didn't have to wait long for that something to happen.

"Bad news or worse news?" I asked as she struggled up the path.

"Why do you have to live up here?" she wheezed. "It is too hard for this old woman."

"Then I won't ask you to sit down."

"I may fall down." She struggled to sit, falling the final few inches and hitting the ground with a thud. I caught her arm but I doubted it did much to slow the fall. "Ugh."

I waited patiently while Grit moved herself to sit next to me. It wasn't pretty. "So this is going to be a full-fledged speech, is it?"

"What are you talking about?"

"Since you took the effort to sit down, I assume that you're going to be here for a while."

"I am tired, cheeky, and I want to rest." She frowned at me and I couldn't help but laugh.

"That only works on the Noorthi kids, *memesh*." If Grit was taking the time to sit then it must be serious. "The bad news."

"There has been a second person who has become ill."

"Like Delica?"

"It appears so. She is showing the same signs."

"Where's Delica's husband?"

"Working I believe. He will not return for another four days."

"And what about Delica?"

"I have given her a potion. There has been no improvement yet. It may take another two to three days before we can tell."

There was no point in asking if the second patient had come in contact with Delica. We were a small community and it was near impossible to avoid someone in those circumstances.

"What do you want from me?" I asked.

"We only have a few leaves left. If we have more ill people we may not be able to manage."

"Do you want me to find a sertech?"

"No, but I thought it wise to let you know."

"Good idea, not that I can do much to help."

Grit laid her hand on top of mine and patted it. "Just being here is help enough."

"You are such a smooth talker." I smiled at her.

I half expected Grit to get up, or at least ask me to help her up, but she just sat there.

"Is there something else?"

"Are you in such a hurry to get rid of me?" She sounded nearly insulted.

"Of course not, but I thought you had things to do."

"I was looking at the view. Very nice."

"Yeah, I like it up here. I found it helpful to stop once and a while and just look at the view. It reminds me how lucky I am."

"Lucky?" I had no doubts she thought I had the opposite view of my life.

"Sure. Just look out there. It's beautiful. I never took the opportunity to just enjoy nature in all its glory before. Despite what I say, meeting you has been a good thing." I laughed. "Never thought I'd admit to that, did you?"

The look on her face gave me her answer. "No."

"You caught me on a good day. Ask me tomorrow and I'll deny it."

Grit leaned her head back and laughed. I think that was the first time I'd actually heard her laugh like she meant it. It wasn't a cackle but an almost delightful musical melody of humor.

"What did you give me when I was dying?" It was a question that had niggled at me for some time now. I didn't have a burning need to know, and maybe it was foolish to ask, but it was something that I was curious about.

"You have died more than once. Which death are you talking about?"

"Stop delaying. You know very well what I'm referring to. The time when my brain was about to go into meltdown."

"Ahh."

"What are you not telling me? What did you do?" Suddenly I felt very vulnerable.

"Nothing bad."

"But good for who? Me? You?"

"I had always said you had a great purpose. The special root we used was already yours before we had even met."

"Grit, I don't believe in divine intervention, or destiny, or karma, or anything else you want to call it. You put me in a position I didn't want to be in."

"You do not?"

"Not now, no, but you forced me into something I wasn't ready for. I don't know if I am now."

"If I waited for you to decide, young one, I would probably be long dead."

"Which brings me to another point. Just how old are you?" A twentieth century saying came to mind, *never ask a lady her age*. I chose to ignore it.

"How old do you think I am?" she countered.

"Oh, no. If I guess wrong I could get into a lot of trouble." The way she carried on sometimes I thought she was around two thousand years old.

Grit watched me for a moment then answered, "four hundred and thirty eight years old."

"That's impressive. Do Noorthi usually live that long?"

"Not in our House. I am the oldest by far." I heard the pride in her voice.

"Your secret is safe with me." I had to draw the conversation back to my original question. "What did you give me?"

"Does it matter? It saved your life and that is all you need to worry about."

"Yes, it does matter because you're not telling me everything." I just knew it was bad news.

"It was the gulacca root and you have been the only one to use it. I cannot tell you how it will affect you because I do not know."

"And yet you did use it. You could've killed me."

"But you did not die." Grit was right. I didn't die.

"Just what is going on here?"

Grit sighed and gazed out over the treetops. "Our future had been foretold by the Great One. She had seen our exile and your return."

"Return? I've never been to Rigeus."

"No, but you were our protector in a past life."

Past life? "I don't believe in reincarnation either." This was like one big adventure story.

"You were the Great One's protector thousands of years ago. She had seen your return in our time of need. The scar is proof of her Word."

"This is nothing more than a souvenir of Vel, and you know it. There's nothing mystical about it." I looked at the scar in question and remembered how I got it. As if reminding me, there was a twinge of pain in my wrist.

"Why do you think I did not tell you? I knew you would react like this. You are not ready to believe what the signs are telling you."

"I'm just a gal who happened to be in the wrong place at the wrong time. Nothing more. You're trying to make me something that I'm not."

"You do not believe you are a hero?"

"I neither believe it nor want it. I had a life before all this."

"And yet here you are. You could have left us at any time."

That was true. "I take my commitments seriously, *memesh*. I said I would look after you, and here I am."

"There are others here who could take your place."

It made me wonder why I didn't go back to my old life. The settlement was safe and running smoothly. I wasn't really needed any more. What kept me here? Beri? Rice? Now Rice was going to Noorthi school, there was no need to stay.

"They'd mess it up." It was a lie, and I think we both knew it.

"I think you want to be a hero, but you fear believing in yourself. Believe that your destiny is with us. Believe that you can make a difference. Believe that you are *the* Ratha and that you are walking the path only you were meant to walk."

It was a pretty speech and I knew Grit was using every bit of eloquence she had to press her argument.

"Think on it."

"I'm not going to suddenly grow wings or anything, am I?"

Grit struggled to stand, so I rose and extended my hand to her. She grunted as her aged body protested. "Who knows?" Her hand patted my cheek before turning to walk slowly down the path. I watched after her as she picked her way across the valley floor and ascended the path to the cave.

"Who knows?" Suddenly, I was scared of what I had become.

†

Three days later a delegation of Noorthi sisters approached me as I worked on Bessie. When they moved in packs the Noorthi were a dangerous species. I had hoped that they would pass me by, but my hopes were dashed when Grit stopped in front of me.

"May I help you?" I said casually. I didn't feel casual. In fact, I felt downright terrified.

"We need to speak with you."

I looked at Grit and the gaggle of elders who followed her. "So I can see. What's up?"

"The sickness is spreading. We do not have enough *casidium* leaves to treat everyone."

"Then we get some more." Grit stared at me. "What?" I felt my stomach drop. Maybe I should be asking the most obvious question. "Where are these leaves?"

Grit glanced around at her cohorts. "I know of only one place to find what we need. Alengola."

"Alengola? Never heard of it."

"It is the source of our sisterhood."

"You mean there really is a heaven?" I kept a straight face as I said it, which did nothing to add to the humor of the statement. Grit leaned and pinched me. "Ow! You know, for a holy woman you sure like to pinch a lot."

"Only when someone tests my patience." I was being scolded like a child. "This is serious."

"Fine. Where is Alengola?"

"We do not know."

"That makes it so much easier." Grit leaned in again and I held up my hands. "Okay, I get it. Leaves on Alengola. We just have to find out where it is."

Grit stood up straight and led her group away from me.

"When do you need them?"

"Yesterday."

Just great, now all I needed to do was travel back in time to yesterday to find leaves on a non-existent planet. Was Grit calling me a hero or a miracle worker? There was only one person I knew who I would occasionally call miracle worker. "Malt."

I finally found her on the trooper ship at the computer. "Hey, Malt. I've got a job for you." But Malt's expression was not happy. "What's wrong?"

"I think I found out what the sickness is. You're not going to like it."

"You have to tell me first before I can decide whether I like it or not."

"Monolial disease."

"Oh, craz. How the hell did it end up here?" Then I remembered. Delica was sick the day of the evacuation exercise. Delica's husband worked off-world at… where did he work?

"Where does Egran work?"

"I was just checking that. He works on Tuolon. They've just reported an outbreak of Monolial."

"Crud! What's the cure?"

Malt scrolled through the data on the screen. "Fluextron, but it's only available from Consortium medical stations."

"And what if we don't have it?"

She looked at me gravely. "Death around fourteen days from first symptoms, and it's highly contagious."

"First thing we need to do is isolate those who are sick and those who have come in contact with anyone sick in the past twenty-four hours."

"That's just about everyone."

"Does it say how it's contracted?"

Malt returned her attention to the screen, looking for the relevant piece of information. "Like a cold. Contact by body fluids and touching something the victim has touched."

"All right." My mind raced to formulate a plan. "Isolation. Get a cleaning crew and disinfect everything. Those not sick at present will need to wear gloves and a mask for the time being. Ask for volunteers to look after the sick, and make sure they understand the risks."

"And what are we going to do?"

"Grit has asked for some leaves for her potion." I glanced at the screen. "I have an urgent job for you. Find Alengola."

I didn't wait for Malt to reply. I left in a hurry. There was so much to do with very little time to play with. First I needed to find Beri.

It didn't take much to find her because I went to the most obvious place. In the Noorthi compound, I found her sitting cross-legged watching Rice's first lesson.

"What are you doing here? You know you're not—"

"We don't have time." I pulled her up and moved her away from earshot. "There's been an outbreak of Monolial."

"And that is…?"

I had forgotten that she had been in isolation from the rest of the universe for most of her life. "It's a very contagious and deadly disease. It can sweep through Heaven in a matter of days and kill everyone." I was being a little melodramatic but I didn't have time to tiptoe around the subject.

"What do we do?"

"I've ordered those sick into isolation. Everyone else will have to wear masks and gloves to avoid catching it. I want you and your sisters just to do what I ask for once. No questions. Keep an eye out for anyone who isn't feeling well. Move them to the isolation area quickly." I was about to leave when I said. "And please, *please*, keep yourself and Rice safe, okay. For me?"

Beri smiled gently at me. I hesitated, waiting for the inevitable question that would come, but it didn't. She looked into my eyes and just nodded. I shook my head and headed off toward the cave to report to Grit. Just when I had Beri figured out, she actually did something I asked her to. Would wonders never cease?

I walked up the path from the Noorthi compound to the cave and waited at the entrance. Grit stood off to one side, content to let her healer underlings attend to the sick. She saw me and approached. I started back down the path to the valley floor and hoped she would follow me. When it seemed that we were alone I turned around to talk. "We've got a big problem."

"I already know that, Ratha."

"You know about the Monolial?"

"Whatever it is called, I can see that it is spreading, and fast. We have a further five sick since I last spoke to you."

"Untreated, these people have about two weeks before they start dying."

Her brow creased and she inhaled deeply. Her hand rose to her mouth and she tapped her lips as she contemplated the news.

"How sure are you that the leaves you want will work?" I suppose I should find out whether this trip was worth the risk.

"Delica is on the mend. While I have given the next two the same potion I just don't have enough for everyone."

"Will one of the other herbs work in its place?"

"I am not sure, but I will try."

"I've got Malt working on locating your planet. We still have to get there, get the leaves and return. There might not be enough time."

"There will be time."

"How do you know?" It was stupid to ask the question because I found that Grit never said anything she didn't mean to.

"I know."

†

During the next two days Malt and Grit worked feverishly on their respective projects. Malt scoured all known databases and then some, trying to locate Alengola. It seemed the Noorthi home planet was as much of a secret as Heaven was. She searched anecdotal evidence and bedtime stories, news articles and hearsay. I saw that she was frazzled and ready to give up. On the eve of the second day she found what she was looking for. While it wasn't the exact position at least we had the neighborhood and what to look for. We all hoped that it was enough.

Grit, meanwhile, tried various combinations of her potion on the sick. Up to dusk on the second day there had been no improvement, except to those who were treated with the original potion. Despite Grit's protests, I ordered her to use the remaining leaves on the healers and those helping the sick. I begged Beri to take it also. After all, the Noorthi needed their leader. Reluctantly, they all took it before returning to their duties. I know it was selfish of me to insist Beri and Rice took it, but that was my prerogative as Ratha.

Unbeknownst to me, Grit had also given the potion to Malt, Rales and Sasha. She later explained that if they were sick the whole community would grind to a halt. As Grit put it, I would be off gallivanting around the universe looking for her leaves and they needed someone to make the decisions. I pointed out that we did have a thing called a comlink, but she seemed to think I needed to be actually present to make a decision. I think it was because she knew how much they meant to me that she did it. Grit was getting all mushy on me, not that I'd say it to her face.

I gave Grit as much time as I could before deciding to go on the quest to find Alengola. Time was fast approaching where I couldn't delay it any longer.

The simplest solution was to just go by myself, but it wasn't as easy as that. Alengola was the heartland of the Noorthi sisterhood. Unless it was completely deserted there would be the sisters to contend with. There was no way they would take my words as the truth.

Grit would have to come. She was the *hedera* and therefore someone of high stature. Of course, she would need one or two of the elders to accompany her to help with the leaf gathering.

And Beri? I knew she was apprehensive about meeting her fellow sisters, but could I risk leaving her behind? I certainly didn't want Rice in the middle of the sickness and mayhem.

I suppose I already knew the answer even before I asked her. Beri would put aside her fears and come. She was Ashaltea. Surprisingly, Fen also volunteered for the trip. Was it to support Beri or the chance to come face to face with her heritage? No, knowing Fen, she would be there for Beri. That was how she always was.

So I had my little band of adventurers ready to go. Malt would be my co-pilot and at the last minute we added Sasha and her ship to the crew. Sasha would transport the leaves back to Heaven as soon as we could get our hands on them, while I brought everyone else home once the Noorthi rituals had been completed. How did I know? It was the Noorthi. How could there not be rituals, or at least a lengthy discussion or two?

I gave them two hours to be ready or said I'd go without them. Despite my idle threat, two hours later they stood assembled next to Bessie.

"Are you sure you don't want me to come along?" Rales looked disappointed he was going to miss out.

"My friend," I said, but I think he already knew what the answer would be. "It's a group of women. I don't think they'd accept you readily."

27

That would be an understatement. I wasn't going to tell him that men had become extinct around them. Even the most basic instinct of survival of the species was a thing of the past. The male was dead and buried in their eyes. "Besides, I need you here to keep things running smoothly. If panic sets in, it could get a whole lot worse."

"Do you think that's a possibility?"

"Not really. The Noorthi will just pray and we have a small community that will probably all be ill by the time we reach panic stations."

"You really are an upbeat person, aren't you?" He stared at me.

"Just telling you the facts."

"And why am I staying here again?"

"You're a man."

"Oh." What more could he say. It was true. "Have a safe trip then." He pulled me in and hugged me tightly. "Come back in one piece this time."

"I'll try."

He moved to Sasha and hugged her even longer. He whispered something into her ear, but I couldn't hear it. It was probably to take care and keep an eye on me. Why is it no one believed I could look after myself?

One of the cooks brought me a parcel, which I assumed was food. I was just thankful the Noorthi didn't offer. There would be no way I could not accept it if they did, and considering we were going into Noorthi territory, my expectation was that the food would simply be awful. Time would tell if I was right.

Chapter Three

Hi Mom, I'm Home!

The flight took about thirty-eight hours, with four hyperjumps negotiated before we were in the system where Alengola supposedly existed. If Malt was wrong then it was a wasted trip. Malt was hardly ever wrong. As Sasha had the newer ship, she would already be stationed in orbit around Stareng, the primary planet in the Aster Duo system, when we arrived.

"What took you so long?"

I just knew she was going to say that. "We took the scenic route."

"Figures. I thought we were in a hurry."

"We are." I glanced at Malt in the co-pilot's chair. "Okay, Malt, where to now?"

She had been studiously reading the references she had accumulated and had been poking holes in my holomap as she eliminated the planets one by one.

"It's either this one." She pointed to a small point about a hundred thousand miles from Stareng. "Or this one." Her hand shifted to a small object farther out from the hub of the system. "Logically, I think it's this one." She pointed to the furthest choice. "If they were closer to Stareng, there would be more sightings."

I couldn't argue with that point. Besides, the first place she pointed to already had a name, and it wasn't Alengola. Maybe it was Alengola disguised as Alpha Nexus. No, my gut was telling me Malt was right.

"You take the distant one," Sasha suggested. "I'll take Alpha Nexus. If either one of us finds their choice is wrong, then head to the other one."

"And if we're both wrong?" I suggested.

"Then.... oh."

"Just contact me and let me know what you find."

"And if you're not on board?"

I don't think Sasha liked being seen as a fool. Funnily enough, I didn't either. "Malt will be here to take your call."

"What? Why do I have to stay?" Malt asked.

"Because I say so, that's why."

"But, J...."

"Good luck." I heard Sasha chuckle on the comlink.

"See you in a few." I signed off and pushed the ship into drive. It would be another jump to the far reaches of the system but at least it wouldn't be as long as the first part of the trip.

I was so glad when we dropped out of hyperdrive because Malt had been whining the whole trip about why she had to stay on board. If I thought it would do any good I'd send Malt in my place and I'd stay on board, but I knew it would be a fruitless exercise. No, I had to face them as Ratha.

Once through the stratosphere, we checked out the planet. Bessie's sensors told me the air was breathable and the vegetation lush. In fact, it was a lot like Heaven. That, in itself, made this speck of dust the end of our search.

"Scan for life signs."

Malt activated the scanner even as I said it. There wasn't anything immediately obvious, except for small critters that lived under the mass of what was loosely called trees. Small pools were dotted here and there, feeding streams that meandered through the lush covering.

We were half-way around the small planet when the scanner alarm went off. I moved Bessie down closer to the planet and skimmed across the tree tops.

"Can you see anything?"

"Not yet." Malt pushed her face against the window in an effort to see downward.

"Wait, I think I see something." I lifted my finger and pointed forward. A white spire rose from the greenery like some silent sentinel. "What do you think?"

"It could be."

"Let's see if we can find somewhere to set down."

That was easier said than done. There was barely a break in the trees and it looked like there was going to be a decent walk to see if the spire actually was attached to something more substantial.

"Over there." Malt's finger pointed to the right, and I saw a patch of bare ground where we could land. I was glad that I had brought Bessie because the space was small. While it took a fair bit of concentration on my part to maneuver her, my Bessie slipped easily between the trees to the ground as if she was shimmying into an old fashioned twentieth century corset. It was a tight fit, but damn Bessie looked fine!

I shut down the engines and climbed out of my chair. "Stay here."

"But—"

"Malt, please. Just stay put." She was still trying to plead her case and I'd had enough of it. "I need you to watch my back on this one."

Malt's mouth opened to argue but she stopped. Her mouth closed and she sunk back into her chair.

"I'll be back in a minute." I left her in contemplation. Beri and Fen stood next to the exit and were ready to go. "Let me check this out first."

"But—"

They must have heard my teeth grinding because they backed away and let me go. Then again, it may have been the scowl on my face.

I opened the hatch and waited for the ramp to lower to the ground. I breathed deeply. The air was fresh and clean and it seemed good, almost too good. Maybe a more thorough look was needed. I walked down the ramp and stood on the ground. I don't know why, but I had an uneasy feeling about the place. Maybe it was my natural suspicion that set off my internal alarm, but something felt wrong.

I went on a small foray into the surrounding vegetation. I don't know what I was expecting to find, but I didn't find anything, or at least nothing dangerous. Maybe it was all in my mind.

When I arrived back the Noorthi were congregating around the hatch. It seemed they were eager to start. Rice was wriggling in Beri's arms and once she caught sight of me she screamed. I don't know who she inherited her set of lungs from, but Rice sure was loud.

"Everyone ready?" Everyone was ready except me. I grabbed a bag and stuffed a couple of items into it. If I didn't say goodbye to Malt she'd give me hell about it.

"Are you all set?" I said as I leaned against the cockpit doorway.

"I suppose so," she said grumpily. "This is going to be so boring."

"Malt. If I need you in a hurry, it's going to be anything but boring."

"But where do I land?"

"You don't. It'll be a pickup and run."

"Trouble?" She looked uncertainly at me.

"Maybe. I don't know. I can't blame it on the food this time." Malt came up to me and threw her arms around my body. "Whoa! I'm not going to die or anything."

"Don't even say that." She stepped back and slapped me on the shoulder. "I don't want to find out if Bessie can do a rescue drop."

I snatched up a comlink and shoved it in my pocket. "Keep the scanner on. I want you to see where people go."

"Any reason?"

"Just in case they say no and we may have to snatch the leaves."

"You'd really do that?"

"If I have to, but I hope it doesn't come to that. Besides, why would one Noorthi deny another in something like this? It's not in their nature." I had a thought. "In fact, if you track down where the garden is, check it out. If they can spare it, take a plant or two and we'll see if we can grow it on Heaven. That means digging it up, Malt, not ripping it out. We need roots and all, and some soil. Understand?"

"I'm not two years old, J. I think I can handle this."

"Good girl." She pursed her lips. "Er... woman... young woman. Oh, you know what I mean. Good job, Malt."

I was wondering if this was payback for not letting her come with us. I turned to leave. "Oh, and don't tell the girls about the plants. Let's get home first so I can run if I have to." I left to Malt's soft laughter.

The Noorthi were milling around outside waiting for my return. Beri was trying to keep Rice occupied, but the child had too many new things to look at to worry about her mother.

"Let me take her," I said. Beri put her down on the ground. Before we both knew it, Rice ran off in a completely different direction straight into the undergrowth. "Wait here. I'll get her." I trotted off after her.

"Just wait till I catch you, you little devil." I heard the giggling, but Rice was well hidden in the bushes.

"Come on, Rice, we don't have time for this." There was a rustle of leaves and I suspected that Rice was on the move again.

"Rice!" I said sternly, hoping that the grown up voice would make her pause. "Come back this instant!" The silence told me what she thought of that idea.

It had now progressed beyond a mere game of hide and seek. "I've got a sugar leaf." Would she come for a sweet? This kid knew how to negotiate. "Damn it, Rice." I reined in my anger and my swearing. It wasn't the sort of thing for little ears.

Now I had to call in Malt. "Malt? Can you find Rice with the heat sensor for me? The little scamp is hiding."

It took a few moments before Malt responded. "She's about twenty feet in front of you, at about thirty degrees to the right."

I stepped carefully through the heavy vegetation and I spotted a dash of color in the mass of green. I moved past her to make her think I didn't see her. After a couple of steps I pounced, reaching out quickly and wrapping my hands around the wriggling body. "Just for that, young lady, no sugar leaf."

She pouted at me and hit my shoulder.

"No!" She blinked a few times, her hand sitting in the air as if she was going to hit me again. "No." She swung down and clipped my arm. "I said no." It seemed I wasn't playing her game and she didn't like it.

"Bad Ra."

"No, bad Rice. You ran away from Mama."

She lifted an index finger and sat the tip in her mouth, presenting a very cute, and manipulative, picture. She looked up at me through her long lashes. The kid was trying to charm me. It was working, but I knew I had to be strong. If Rice didn't learn that it was wrong to run away, she'd be doing it all the time.

I left the scowl on my face as she tried to worm her way out of trouble. "No, Rice. You have to stay with Mama. Okay?"

She looked up at me and I wondered if she understood. "Otay."

The kid said the sweetest things, but that didn't answer my question as to whether she understood what I was saying. I'd just have to take her otay as a yes.

I put Rice down and took her hand. Carrying her back would seem a reward, so I made the hard choice of making Rice walk back herself. "Let's find Mama."

A couple of minutes later we emerged from the bushes. I was surprised that Beri wasn't upset with Rice's escape, and I was about to ask her that question when she tapped her head.

"I thought I told you no peeking in my mind."

"I was worried."

"Okay, I'll let it go this time."

"Otay," Rice piped in. It seemed this was her new word and she was going to use it often. I relinquished my hold on Rice, after I made sure that Beri had hold of her, and I collected my pack. "Let's go while we have light." I wondered how long the light lasted on this planet.

†

It was hard work making our way through the dense forest. The progress was slow, and nearly two hours had passed by the time we reached our goal. We stepped out of the wall of greenery onto a small cleared area of ground. On the other side of the space was a large building, two stories high. A large staircase ascended to the massive opening in the front of the structure.

We stood at the bottom of the steps leading to the foyer of what I assumed to be the Great House. I'm sure that my bottom jaw was touching the ground because, well, it was more than I could handle. Grit stepped up beside me.

"Should it be this... er... pretty?"

"Pretty?" She glared at me then huffed. "Gaudy, more like it. It must be recent."

"Recent as in when you left here, or recent as in yesterday?"

"How do I know what happened while I was not here?" I just knew she thought I was an idiot.

"Well, you seem to make a habit of knowing things no one else does, or am I mistaken? After all, you're four thousand years old." I raised my eyebrow at her. We both knew her real age, but I was playing a game with her.

"Ratha, you may think you are invincible, but you are not."

Oh, yes. I was an idiot, at least in her eyes and at this particular moment. Who could say what would happen tomorrow? Then again, I didn't want to test Grit on that point either.

"Let's get this visit done with. We have some sick people who don't give a craz about social niceties." I took my first step toward the Noorthi headquarters. I'd only seen it from the outside and I already hated it.

Once we had climbed the stairs our footsteps echoed noisily around the foyer. It was like a mausoleum, empty and deathly still. "So much for the welcome," I muttered to no one in particular.

The noise we were making drew out the sisterhood. I wasn't sure what I was expecting, but this wasn't it. Beri and her sisters were healthy-looking individuals. They had an aura about them, sure, that made them more than they were, but they looked normal. Sort of. But these women were tall and pale, shrouded in heavy

35

cassocks of pale brocade. To me it was ostentatious for an order whose faith centered on spiritual matters.

"That makes me feel much better."

"What?" Beri looked at me.

"It makes me feel better about helping you girls. You may be mystical, but at least you don't advertise the fact."

"Raa!" Rice squealed. In such a wide open space the sound was like a lycet wail – it was ear piercing. Her tiny finger pointed and I looked. A procession was coming our way. There was no other word for it. All it needed were acrobats to complete the scene.

Grit dropped to one knee and the rest followed. I stood there stubbornly refusing to bow. Beri tugged on my pants and I knew she wanted me to play along. I had to see the woman who led this group first before I decided whether she was worth bowing to.

They walked as one, their heavy gowns swaying in unison with the motion. Their movement was barely audible and I glanced at their slippered feet. They stopped about ten feet from us, standing silently. I wasn't sure whether we were supposed to do something, or they were waiting for something, but it was an impasse. My Noorthi sisters stared at the highly-polished stone floor while the other Noorthi stood with heads bowed. I just glared because I was good at it.

Rice didn't like the silence and began to wriggle. Just as Beri was about to lose her hold I grabbed her and lifted her into my arms.

"Raa."

"Shhhh. You have to be very quiet, squirt."

"No fun."

"You got that right."

Who is this outsider?

She is our Ratha.

I heard both voices clearly in my head and, by the look on Rice's face, I suspected she could too.

Ratha? She is an uncouth savage.

Please. She is our friend and savior. She is a Noorthi.

The woman who questioned my identity as a human being looked me up and down. *You too, pal,* I thought.

I think not.

"You want proof? Here." I wrestled the wristband off, giving it to Rice to play with. I presented my wrist for her inspection.

She looked at the scar, then looked me in the eye. "Sarka non di parsis." *This is not possible.*

"You are insulting me by not speaking in my language." I was barely holding onto my temper. "I know what you're saying."

"This... woman is our savior?"

"Not yours, Focar-Sa. She saved us from certain death. She can protect us when we cannot."

"Focar-Sa?" I was unfamiliar with that particular position in the hierarchy.

"I am as far as you will go, stranger."

"So you're not number one?"

"I am Ashaltea-Sa's second."

Just as I thought. The ramrod position and the snooty-nosed attitude told me as much. She wasn't a number one but a number two, if you catch my meaning. "And who is this Ashaltea-Sa?"

"She is the leader of our sisterhood."

"I thought you were Ashaltea," I asked Beri.

"I am Ashaltea of the Juno Noorthi."

"Ashaltea-Sa is supreme head of the sisterhood."

"And has this person got a name?"

"Clea."

The new voice was low and a little mesmerizing. The woman was beautiful, sure, with jet-black hair and dark, piercing eyes, but her aura seemed wrong. She was calm and serene but the tell-tale mystic air surrounding the Noorthi seemed a little faded around her. She must have been someone of high position within the Noorthi because she had her own small procession behind her.

"Mistress, I can take care of this matter for you."

"These are our guests, Tikka."

So it seemed that the leader of the Noorthi was gracing us with her presence. She was surprisingly young for such a powerful position. No, not powerful. *Responsible.* At least that's what Fen would say. I said powerful. There was something about this young woman that was setting off my internal alarms something fierce.

"Come," she invited. "And bring the child."

Beri took Rice out of my arms. Rice whimpered and I had to hold myself back from reacting to her distress.

"Where the kid goes, I go." I was not letting Rice out of my sight.

"This is none of your business, outsider," Tikka said.

"This kid is my child, tikka-too."

"Tikka, please. This woman may accompany us. Do you have a name?"

"Jordana, Clea. Your Noorthi sisters call me Ratha."

Her pale eyebrow rose as I said the name. "Really? That may prove difficult as we already have a Ratha. Jute!" Clea's voice wasn't loud but it carried.

From the far end of the corridor came a woman. I couldn't see her clearly at first as she strode toward us. The passing columns threw her body in and out of shadow until she was about fifty feet from us. In one particularly bright spot her skin fairly shone. Was she wearing something metallic?

"As you can see, we are more than adequately protected by Jute."

I heard a tinge of pride on Clea's voice. Was the leader of the Noorthi sisterhood showing a vice?

The woman was closer now, about twenty feet away, and I saw that she was large. She was easily a foot and a half taller than I was. Craz! I was going to get a crick in my neck having to look up so far.

"Jute." Clea announced as her protector stood by her side. "These are some of our sisters from the outer regions." The woman bowed her head in acknowledgement.

Now that she was close I didn't have to strain my eyes to look at her skin.

"Do you wish to ask something, er...."

"Jordana," I supplied.

"Ah, yes, Jordana. You do not need to stare."

I felt a blush coming on. I had been caught. "I was, er, wondering about..." I just couldn't blurt it out, so my finger waved in Jute's direction.

"Her skin? Jute." The woman responded to Clea's command and stepped up to me until my nose was planted firmly between her breasts. While it was not an unpleasant place to be, I took a step back. I looked up at her face and into her eyes. They were black as night and told me a lot about the giant standing in front of me. She had drawn the line and I wasn't allowed to step over it. In fact, she had drawn the line, stepped over it herself and then rubbed my face in the dirt, metaphorically speaking.

My gaze dropped back to her breasts, since they were the closest things to me. I lifted my finger and poked her skin. I looked up again and smiled. There was no point in getting killed because of a little innocent poking. Her skin was strange. I wasn't sure what it was.

"Jute's skin has been embedded with kerinnium mesh."

"That must have hurt," I mumbled and looked up for a reply.

"She cannot speak. She has no voicebox."

"Sorry, sweetheart." I said sympathetically. I'd be half the woman I am without my voice. How could I start a fight, order a drink or insult anyone without my voice? Still, these days I didn't get much of a chance to do any of those things anyway.

I kept prodding her in the chest, testing the skin under my finger. "So, it's pretty flexible. Interesting. A sort of built-in suit of armor." My gaze skimmed over her body and plenty of skin was on show. I suppose with that sort of protection clothes were pretty redundant, especially around a woman who couldn't care less what she looked like.

Jute's hand shot out and grabbed my wrist to stop me poking her. Her furrowed brow and shaking of her head told me in no uncertain terms she'd had enough of my touching. She turned my hand and looked at my wrist. The scar was clearly visible and she studied it for a moment or two. She glanced over her shoulder at Clea.

I had a thought. In turn, I grabbed her wrist and turned it over. I rubbed my thumb over the firm flesh and felt the pock marks of the mesh under her skin. But there was no tattoo. I looked up at her and saw a moment of sadness in her. Was she not considered good enough to be anointed? The sadness washed away and Jute jerked her arm away.

Her large fists grabbed me by my shirt and lifted me off the ground. She pulled me until I was face-to-face with her. At that moment I felt like a rag doll as she shook me. Jute's muscles bunched and flexed as she held my weight off the ground with very little effort. I made a note to myself not to piss her off.

"Jute!" Clea barked. "Put her down!"

Reluctantly, the giant did as she was told, keeping eye contact with me as she let go of my shirt. Oh, yes, I was lying face down in that metaphorical dirt and she was stomping on my back. As far as she was concerned she was *the* Ratha and I was the pretender.

My impression of the situation was slightly different. Jute wasn't a Ratha. She was a predator. A hunter. A killer.

I had killed only once that I knew of, and I'd only come to terms with that in the past year. Despite Vel's heinous crimes I still had remorse for my actions. In my book it was a choice of either the universe or her and at the time that seemed an easy enough decision. I think I had too much time to think about it afterward as I lay recovering from my near fatal laser blast.

Was I like Jute? I was guilty from time to time of aggressive posturing and even an insult or two, but would I impose my will on another I'd barely met? It was a fine line. At that moment I allowed Grit's words to soothe me. She had called me a hero. It wasn't a word that I would use to describe myself, but if Grit believed it then sometimes it was good enough for me. Maybe that's why I had the tattoo and Jute didn't.

Clea jerked her hand in some sort of signal and Jute withdrew to stand behind her. It was obvious that Clea was angry and she was making little effort to hide it. I watched the interaction and wondered. Beri had been angry and Grit had been angry, but this was different. There was subtle hint of malice behind it, or so I thought. Maybe I was imagining it. But one thing was clear. Clea was treating Jute like a pet, scolding her for snapping at a visitor.

Clea turned her attention back to our party. "And why are you here?" Her voice was light and conversational.

"Our community...."

"Not you, Jordana. Ashaltea Beri may speak."

"Ashaltea-Sa, our community is in need of your help. We have been struck down with a Monolial outbreak. Our *Parisah* is in need of the *casidium* for a cure. We ask your indulgence to collect some leaves."

"The Monolial pestilence is the universe's cleansing process. We will not go against nature's decision," Clea said.

"You're going to allow a hundred and thirty people die when you can do something about it?" I couldn't believe it. "That is a load of craz!"

Some of the sisters gasped in horror, but Clea stared me right in the eye. She was seriously going to let her Noorthi brethren die.

Chapter Four

Absence Makes the Heart Grow Fonder

Grit stepped forward and dropped to one knee. "Please, Ashaltea-Sa, most of those people in danger are Noorthi. Are you saying that our sisters are not righteous enough to be saved?" Her head rose and she looked at Clea. She remained there silently awaiting Clea's reply.

Clea looked around the small group. Grit, Carn bless her, had forced Clea's hand. If she said no, she was saying that the Noorthi were not worthy. "Of course. Tikka, please arrange for the collection of the leaves."

"Just show me where they are and I can do it myself," I offered helpfully.

"The Sacred Grove is not for your eyes, outsider." Tikka was beginning to annoy the hell out of me.

"What are you afraid of? Scared someone will find out your secret?" I had no idea what I was saying, but I was getting angry with all this fussing around. If there was one thing that infuriated me about the Noorthi it was their incessant discussion of everything. Why didn't they just *do* instead of talk? "We're working to a deadline here."

Beri frowned and Grit clicked her tongue.

"What? What did I say?"

"*Dead*line."

I can be such a narkimp sometimes. "Sorry, but we are. We need those leaves now."

"Then we will hurry." Tikka said. She gave me a harsh look. I just knew that if she wasn't a Noorthi and had a sharp weapon in her hand, said weapon would be buried in my chest right now.

"Thank you." I didn't say it with a lot of sincerity.

Tikka bowed and backed away, a swift jerk of her finger signaling to two nearby sisters to follow her. The woman strutted down the corridor while her two assistants glided like they were floating on air. In my mind Tikka was everything the Noorthi were not.

"She will return to us shortly. Come." Clea extended her hand in invitation.

I allowed the Noorthi to proceed, encouraging Beri to walk with me. Rice had been way too quiet and I knew she was ready to burst out. "Here, give her to me."

"Why?"

"Because she's about to scream."

"And how do you know that?"

"She's a part of me, isn't she?" I gave Beri my best rascally grin.

"And that's why she needs some isolation from you. How can she learn if you're there enticing her to play?"

"Why? Because kids her age should be playing not praying."

"We are the Noorthi."

"Yes, we are. And every now and then even the Noorthi should have a little fun. Remember?"

"Not now! Can't it wait until we're back home?"

Home. It was such a lovely word, full of warmth and affection. I'd like to say love, but with Beri it was one step at a time. Love? My guess is it would be about twenty years before B says that word to me, if at all. She is stubborn for a holy woman. Nearly as stubborn as I am. Maybe that's what drew me to her.

"We'll have to leave straight away." I was not going to wait around for the infernal Noorthi niceties to finish. Rales was back there and every moment I stood around here while they chatted increased his chances of getting sick. If they thought I would allow that to happen then they didn't know me very well.

"I have arranged for some of our sisters to accompany you."

"We don't need their help—"

"But I insist. Our Juno sisters will stay here and you can take my representatives in their place."

Yeah, right. As if I was going to leave Beri and my kid behind. "That is not acceptable."

"You have no choice in this matter. If you want the *casidium* leaves you will do as I say."

Clea had said *say* and not *ask*. It was an order, not a request.

Beri stepped in between us, Rice restlessly shifting in her arms. "Just go. We'll be here when you get back."

I gently grabbed Beri's upper arm and steered her away for a private conversation. "I don't trust her, B."

"How can you say that? She's our supreme leader."

"I know that, but I have a bad feeling about this. I need to stay. Sasha can take them back."

"She may not let you stay."

"Yeah, I know, and that's what's worrying me. Why does she want me to go?"

"J, you're being paranoid."

"And I thought you didn't want to be here in the first place," I countered.

"True, but I can't change it now. She has asked us—"

"No, she *told* us. There's a big difference." My hand touched her cheek for a moment before moving to Rice. "You take care of Mommy now, you hear?" Her little head bobbed up and down enthusiastically. "That's my girl." I kissed Rice and resisted with Beri, knowing such affection would be frowned upon.

"Have a safe trip."

"And you be careful. All of you stick together." I looked over the top of Beri's head at Clea. Maybe I was imagining it but it nearly looked as if she had a triumphant look on her face. If it was there, it was gone in an instant.

I left Beri, Clea and Rice alone and I went in search of Grit and Fen. I knew both would be annoyed with me if I didn't at least say goodbye.

The small Juno Noorthi group was sitting cross-legged on the floor, much to the amusement of their fellow sisters. Grit took notice of my approach and stood. When the others moved, I held up my hand. "Stay seated, sisters." I made a sign to Grit that I wanted to talk to her. We moved to a quiet corner.

"What's your feeling about this, *memesh*?" The term of affection escaped my lips.

"It is strange indeed. Why have we been asked to stay?"

"You're asking me? I thought you were the one with all the answers as the Hedera of all things past, present and future."

She blushed. It took her a moment to recover before she continued. "My insight did not see this. Most strange."

"I'm not going."

"But—"

"No. I have to stay. Sasha can handle this."

"Your duty is to protect our sisters. That means you must make sure that they have the means for a cure. We will be safe here."

"I—"

"No!" Grit's bark drew the attention of everyone in the room. She dropped her voice to a low murmur. "Do your duty."

I was going to do my duty, all right, just not the one Grit was talking about. "Fine."

I moved to Fen and touched her shoulder. "I'll be back as soon as I can. Be on guard." I waited for Fen to ask the question but she just nodded. Had my expression said it all?

Tikka appeared with a bag, followed by six of her fellow sisters. "Here." She handed me the bag and stepped aside. "You may leave."

"May I?" My sarcasm was rearing its ugly head. I was being booted off the planet with a 'don't come back' message on it. I glanced at Grit and Fen before walking down the corridor to the front foyer. I looked over my shoulder and the sisters were keeping up with me.

I continued down the staircase and crossed the ground quickly to the ship. "Come on, ladies. We've got some people to save." I all but pushed them up the ramp and showed them to their seats. "Buckle up." I knew I was in trouble when they stared at me. "Like this…" I took the lap belt and drew it across a Noorthi sister, touching the tab to the magnetic closer.

As I left I muttered, "Stay seated while we take off. Please pay attention to the no smoking sign. Leave your trays in an upright position." I laughed. Carn, I loved twentieth century Earth.

I found Sasha in the cockpit. "We've got six Noorthi from here. Here's the leaves. Make sure they both reach Heaven. Put them to sleep if you have to." I tossed the packet of leaves onto Sash's lap then reached into the overhead locker and took out one of Floric's cloaking devices, pinning it to my shirt.

"Whoa! Slow down, J. What's going on?"

"The Ashaltea won't release our Noorthi. I'm staying here to see what's going on. They're expecting me to go with you, so make sure these women think I'm on board."

"Er, okay." She shook her head. "Run that by me again?"

"Leaves." I pointed at the packet sitting on her lap. "Noorthi." I pointed toward the back of the ship. "Me." I pointed at myself. "There." I pointed toward the Noorthi stronghold. I didn't give Sasha much of a chance to argue because I was already out of the cockpit by the time I said, "Got it?"

Luckily there was a wall between the Noorthi women and myself as I exited the ship. It was difficult to get to cover without being seen, leaving me no choice but to walk in a line out the front of the ship where only Sasha could see me from the ship. I took cover and waited until it took off, heading to the stratosphere smoothly. "Good luck."

I jogged back toward the Noorthi Great House, taking a more indirect route to my destination. Any approach along the pathway could be easily seen from the top of the staircase so I had to fight my way through the rugged vegetation surrounding the structure.

Could this all be a case of misunderstanding or, even worse, jealousy? That deadly sin was not normally in my repertoire. Then again, I didn't have a steady girlfriend either. Was Clea moving in on Beri? It annoyed the hell out of me that she had B wrapped around her little finger. Do this, say that, sit down, stand up. It really burned me.

I slowed as I came closer to the House, pushing aside the huge plant fronds carefully to advance. From where I was standing the foyer looked deserted. Still, I wasn't going to take any chances. I tapped the small brooch pinned to my shirt. My hand disappeared from my sight. Thank Carn for Floric's camouflage. I gave the old man a fond thought. Just when I was getting used to his crotchety ways he passed away. *Rest in peace, my friend.*

I stepped out of the vegetation and onto bare soil. While the cloaking device was effective, it didn't solve one remaining problem–my footsteps in the soil. I plucked a frond and began to sweep away any evidence of my passing as I slowly moved toward the Great House wall. Making my way along the exterior I looked for an alternate way in. Would they have the proverbial back door?

It took some minutes to skirt one wall. Finally I reached the back of the building and continued my search. Surely there had to be another entrance, or did everything pass through the foyer entry?

I was about to give up on finding anything when I discovered a small recess in the wall at the far end of the back of the building. Half a dozen steps led downward to a door. I smiled. Always keep your exits covered.

I placed my ear against the door to listen for evidence of Noorthi inside. It seemed quiet. Maybe too quiet. My hands ran around the edge of the door looking for the device to open the door, but I couldn't find anything. No infrared beam or magnetic closure. As a last resort, I pushed and it opened. My eyes looked skyward. Oh, brother....

The room contained a number of open fires with huge pots sitting over them. I had discovered the kitchen. My stomach grumbled with the reminder and I poked my finger into the pot. I nearly spat the food out as quickly as I put it in. Now I knew where the Noorthi learned to cook. It was inherited.

The sound of approaching voices sent me into a panic. I threw myself against the wall as several Noorthi sisters entered the kitchen and returned to cooking duties. My heart pounded. It took me several seconds to remember that I was invisible to them. It was then that I realized I really wasn't good at subterfuge. I was more a rush-in-and-bang-some-heads-together type of gal.

The Noorthi nearest to me stopped her work and looked around the room. Her gaze rested momentarily on me before moving on. Could she sense me? While I tried to empty my mind I could just imagine Sasha making some pithy comment about it only taking a second or two. I must have snorted because the Noorthi woman looked back at me, her eyes narrowing in suspicion. I had to get out of the kitchen before I gave myself away.

I waited for the cook to return to her duties and shuffled along the wall to the doorway to the rest of the House. Hugging the walls, I made my way silently down the passageway toward what I thought was the front of the building. There were so many corridors and rooms I was losing my bearings. Finally I must have taken a correct turn somewhere because I saw greenery at the end of the long corridor. It was the foyer leading to the outside.

I found a staircase to the first floor and decided it was a good place to start my search for Clea. She would have a room that was her sanctuary and it was there I would find what I was looking for. Her secret.

One by one I eliminated the rooms off the top floor corridor, until I was left with only one. The entrance faced the length of the corridor, making the room the most important one on that floor. It would be logical that Clea would claim it as her own, imposing her will on those underneath her.

It was then that I realized that I had stopped thinking of Clea as Noorthi. Was I doing her an injustice? What was it about her that annoyed me? As I approached I heard muffled voices behind the door. But that was as far as I could go, at least not without announcing my presence to whoever was inside.

As if fate was on my side, a Noorthi sister arrived carrying a pitcher and two goblets laid out on a finely crafted metal tray. She knocked on the door.

"Who is it?"

"Your refreshment, Ashaltea-Sa."

"Enter."

When the door opened and the woman entered, I slipped in behind her and stood with my back to the wall. While the furnishings were simple they were certainly lavish. A heavy, intricately-woven brocade blanket lay on her bed, topped with a number of over-stuffed pillows. B slept in what would have been called a camp bed in the olden days. She had a blanket that was in reality a furry skin from a hootken, and her pillow was usually whatever clothes were lying around before washing day. Mine was no better. Clea seemed to be suffering from a common malady–too much power.

The Noorthi woman left and I observed the two women present. Tikka poured the drinks and offered one to Clea. Whatever it was, it certainly didn't look like water. Clea sipped her drink and leaned back in her chair. She studied the wall or, more to the point, what was on the wall. I moved to get a better view. The wall had been painted black and covered with splashes of white. If I didn't know better it looked like a star map. There were colored crystals fixed to the wall. I wasn't sure of their significance, but the fact they were there made me study the map more closely. What were they?

The white spots around the edges of the wall seemed familiar. They were star systems nearer my home planet. I watched as Clea handed Tikka two crystals. The woman took a sip of her drink, then put the cup down to drag a chair to the wall. She smeared each crystal in a pasty mixture sitting on the table. Tikka stood on the chair and fixed the two crystals to two white spots near the top of the wall. I knew that map. It was Juno and Rigeus. The blue crystal represented the Noorthi clan and the red crystal was for the mine. Clea had a universal star map and she was collecting the locations of the Noorthi sisterhood and the mines.

A chill went through me. Didn't Fen say to me that no one sister knew everything because the entire truth was just too dangerous to place in one person's hands?

I looked at the star map and there were several red and blue stones already in place. Suddenly the Noorthi warning came into clear focus, and Grit's prediction echoed in my mind. A great upheaval, she had said, and Clea looked like she would be the one responsible for their downfall.

Clea stopped drinking and focused her gaze on where I was standing. My heart was thumping wildly as I waited for her to uncover me. How did they do that? Was my apprehension about her plans sending out some sort of signal to her?

"What?" Tikka asked as she stepped down off the chair.

"There's… something." Clea closed her eyes for a moment.

I willed myself to calm down, trying to think of nothing but a wall blocking out my thoughts. I mentally painted that wall white, and watched as the chaos behind it slowly disappeared under the paint. When the wall began to crumble I painted again, making sure that nothing peeked through to destroy the peace I was trying to create.

My gaze was focused on Clea. Her eyes opened and she tilted her head to one side. There was a knock on the door.

"Enter."

The Noorthi woman who had brought the refreshments appeared again, this time to remove the tray. I made my escape through the door with her. That was a close call.

As I stood against the wall to gather my scattered wits, Tikka exited the room and strode down the corridor to the far end and the staircase to the ground floor. I had to find my sisters and get the hell out of here.

I checked each door as I made my way toward the exit. There was a familiar whimpering behind the second-to-last door. I tested the door slowly, hoping there wasn't some sort of guard on the other side. When it seemed safe, I entered.

"Raaa!" The squeal nearly deafened me.

"No, Rice. Raa isn't here. She's gone back to help our sisters."

"No! Raaa!" Rice pointed directly at me.

"No." Beri looked over her shoulder. "Raa's not there." She looked again then smiled. "I think you're right."

I touched the cloaking device on my shoulder and the veil disappeared. "Hey there, shortie. Have you been good for your mama?"

Little Rice wiggled out of Beri's grasp and ran across the floor to me, her little arms wrapping themselves around one leg like a limpet. I walked across the room with Rice attached to my leg and sat down. She let go and held up her hands imperiously. "Up!"

I didn't even think twice and lifted her up to my chest. She threw her arms around my neck and squeezed.

"Is everything all right?" I asked.

"I was about to ask you the same thing. Aren't you supposed to be heading back home?"

"I was, but something was telling me to stay."

"I'm perfectly safe, as you can see."

I didn't say anything because I didn't want to start an argument. How could I explain my gut feeling to her? "What does Clea want?"

"She doesn't want anything. You've got it all wrong."

There was a knock on the door.

"Shhhh," I whispered. "It's a secret." I handed over Rice to her mother and tapped the cloaking tab. I moved to the wall to observe. Rice followed my movement and Beri had to distract her to avoid revealing my location.

"Come in."

Clea entered smiling. "I hope this room is comfortable."

"Very comfortable, thank you. In fact, I can't remember a bed being so nice before." Rice fussed. Beri shifted her daughter's position so she couldn't see me.

"I have some questions I'd like to ask you about your sisterhood, if I may. You may find it more comfortable in my chambers." Clea had already begun to move toward the door and she fully expected Beri to follow.

"Uh, yeah... sure." Beri stood with Rice in her arms and followed, stopping in the doorway to look over her shoulder at me, but I didn't find her smile reassuring.

I followed Beri into the corridor and watched her walk to Clea's room. I stood there until the door closed. Now that things were quiet it was a good opportunity to look around. I crept down the stairs and stood in the foyer. The huge hallway on the ground floor ran the length of the building, branching off into a T intersection at the far end. There were a number of rooms either side of the hallway and I was going to investigate every one of them.

†

There were sleeping quarters on the two floors, ranging from ornate to basic, and to me that reflected the position the Noorthi was placed in the hierarchy. At least on Heaven everyone slept on the same type of bed. We didn't have the luxury of distinguishing between stations in life. A bed was a bed. Our Noorthi seemed like a poor relative compared to the Alengolan Noorthi, but in my eyes my girls were the more emotionally balanced.

I grabbed a spare robe from one of the rooms. If Clea had sent someone out to search, the cloak may divert their attention away from me.

I finally found Grit and the others in one of the rooms on the bottom floor, which was situated below ground. I felt a shiver as I entered the room. It reminded me a little of the Juno Great House with the dungeon. There were no good memories of that place. Despite my misgivings, I would stay with them for a while in case Clea was looking for someone in general or me in particular. The last thing I wanted was to meet up with Jute because she'd break me in two.

The room, like the rest of the house, was ornate. A large pool occupied the centre of the room, its water glowing and giving light. A number of stone benches surrounded the pool and many of these were already occupied.

It was interesting to watch the two tribes. The Heaven Noorthi chatted animatedly amongst themselves, while the Alengolan Noorthi sat quietly, whispering to one another so as not to disturb the peace of those next to them. It was an almost reserved stance on their part and presented a rather insular way of existence. Was this Clea's doing or was this a Noorthi trait that had been instilled into them since they were born?

There was a young Noorthi seated away from the rest. She looked more like Beri's Noorthi, without the haunted look that surrounded the Alengola Noorthi. Sitting next to her was Fen, talking in muted tones. While Fen carried on the conversation, I observed the young woman. I estimated her to be roughly Fen's height with short-cropped black curls sitting close against her head. But the most striking feature was the dimples etched into her skin. Fen must have said something funny because when the woman smiled her dimples sank even deeper into her cheeks. It was then that I decided I loved dimples. The transformation of the woman's face when she smiled was astounding. The joy in her smile carried all the way to her dark eyes, and I found myself smiling with her. Who was she?

I tried not to stare as the conversation continued. The woman glanced at me a time or two, so she must have felt my gaze on her. Grit sat down beside me and I was grateful for the distraction.

"What are you doing here? You are not performing your duty." Grit's harsh tones told me what she thought of my presence.

"Relax. Sasha has the leaves and is taking the Noorthi back to Heaven."

"*You* are supposed to be taking the Noorthi back to Heaven."

"I felt this was more important."

"Nothing is more important that saving Noorthi lives."

"Even when it's your lives I'm trying to save?" I was getting annoyed.

"That is not important."

"Don't tell me what's important, old woman!" That was it. I'd had enough of Grit telling me how to be Ratha. I regretted the outburst. "I'm sorry, Grit, but I won't apologize for being here. My gut is telling me to stay, and I want to protect those closest to me."

She opened her mouth then shut it again, as if she was going to say something but thought better of it. She leaned across and patted my hand.

"Who is that Noorthi? The one Fen is talking to?"

"She does not look Alengolan," Grit looked at the person I was talking about.

"I was thinking the same thing. From the looks of it, her sisters don't think so either." I was rather disappointed by their treatment of her. "At least we would have made her welcome."

"We?" Grit chuckled. "It is 'we' now, is it?"

"*Memesh*, it was always we. On Heaven, everyone has a say."

"Some more than others, Ratha."

"Are you saying that ignoring her like that would be acceptable on Heaven?"

"Of course not."

"Everyone has some basic rights there. If they didn't, it wouldn't work." It was necessary to have rules for everyone to keep the jealousy and hostilities to a minimum. Malt wasn't treated any differently just because she had four arms, and I'd be the first one to step in if someone did.

Fen stood up and moved to us. She sat down facing away from the woman.

"Who is she?" I asked even before Fen's ass hit the floor.

"Her name is Delphan."

I waited for more information but Fen said nothing. "That's it? There must be more." Fen smiled. The woman was doing this on purpose to annoy me.

"She's an orphan. The ship carrying her family crashed here and she was the only survivor."

"Why didn't they send her back?"

"In what? If you haven't already noticed, there aren't any ships here. They had no choice but to raise her."

"Is she Noorthi?"

"You both share something in common. You are adopted Noorthi."

"So they don't consider her *true* Noorthi. Snobs."

"That may be, young pup, but they have not had the benefit of your influence in such matters." Grit was doing it to me again.

"Are you saying I'm pushy?"

"Pushy, arrogant, aggressive, thoughtful and ours, Ratha. I would not have it any other way."

What could I say to that? I was about to make some pithy remark about the first bit, then Grit had to go and say the rest. No wonder she had such influence in our community. She could sweet talk anyone into anything.

"What were you two talking about?"

"Finding out about Clea, of course."

"Of course." Finally, I came up with that pithy remark. I was wondering where my acerbic tongue had gotten to.

Fen pursed her lips and glared at me. "She said Clea is not a native of the Alengolan Noorthi. She comes from one of the distant sisterhoods."

"And yet they allowed her to be Ashaltea-Sa?"

"Not at first. The previous Ashaltea-Sa, Rexis, was growing old and her child was about to ascend to Ashaltea-Sa."

"What happened?" Despite myself, I was on the edge of my seat.

"The child became ill and died."

"She could have been saved," Grit suggested.

"That's the strange thing. They tried all known Noorthi potions but nothing worked. About six months after the death of the daughter, Rexis died as well, from the same illness."

"How convenient." Even a blind man would question the obvious sudden deaths of the two people who would rule over the Noorthi. "How did Clea get her hands on the job?"

"She said she was the daughter of the Ashaltea on Peralis. Her sisterhood had been wiped out by the Consortium and she was the one remaining survivor. She claimed her right to rule. The Noorthi here had no legitimate heir to call upon, so they passed the duty to Clea."

"How long ago was this?"

"About seven years."

I had to congratulate Clea on her persistence. If she had found the number of Noorthi sisterhoods and ochre locations on her wall in only seven years, then it wouldn't take too much longer to find the rest of them.

"The next time you talk to Delphan please invite her to our circle. We will welcome her with open arms." I said succinctly. It wasn't a big circle but it was friendly. "Come to think of it, we're all outcasts."

The room suddenly shook and showered us with dust. "What the craz was that?" Our Noorthi looked scared, but the Alengolan Noorthi seemed unconcerned.

"Go ask Delphan," I directed Fen. I watched her go and a few moments later she returned.

"She says it's the Great One talking to their Ashaltea-Sa."

"Talking?" That was the most absurd thing I'd ever heard but, then again, we're talking about the Noorthi. "That was no talking. That was a tremor."

"Why do you doubt what you are told?" Grit asked.

"Why? Why would it be necessary for your beloved Great One to talk in such a manner? Why not just talk to her in her head?"

"Maybe it is a sign for those who do not believe her Word."

"Now you're just rationalizing it. The Noorthi are capable of great things without such a cheap trick."

"Cheap trick?" Grit sounded astonished. It was a cheap shot on my part, but despite these women's mystical powers sometimes they were naïve. Unlike me, they believed everyone had good intentions and told the truth. I would have thought that Grit knew by now that wasn't the case. Or maybe it was the fact that it was one of their own who made the claim and that made it true.

"Maybe this is the great upheaval you were talking about."

Grit remained quiet. I had obviously given her something to think about.

"Fen, can you see if you can find out where the ochre mine is?"

"Why? Do you think there is one?"

"Every Noorthi enclave seems to have access to a mine. If this is the Noorthi home world there has to be one close by."

"I'll see what I can find out." I watched Fen walk away.

"And what does the ochre mine have to do with this?" Grit asked.

"Do you honestly think these women would lift a fingernail to mine ochre?" Grit looked at me. "That's what I thought. Maybe the mine can tell us something about this planet and the Noorthi sisterhood."

"You have everything you need to know, Ratha."
"That may be, but I won't be happy until I see it for myself."
"And you're willing to risk your life?"
"If I have to."

Chapter Five

Hi-Ho, Hi-Ho

Half an hour later I was standing on the edge of the clearing looking out over the jungle at the back of the Great House. The Alengolan Noorthi couldn't, or wouldn't, tell Fen where the mine was. Delphan could only tell us of a path behind the Great House. The rest was up to me.

I was not prepared for this little expedition, so I'd have to make a detour to the kitchen. The sisters were finishing up their chores and left me alone. I took a kitchen knife, a flask of water and a jar. If I couldn't find my answers at the site then I'd take a sample for Malt to look at.

My stomach rumbled and I'd realized that it had been quite a few hours since I'd eaten anything. The smell from the cooking pots did little to stir my appetite, so I raided a food bin for a piece of whatever passed for fruit or vegetable. The purple color was a little bit off-putting but I bit into it, pleasantly surprised by the juicy sweetness of it.

Standing outside the kitchen in the small clearing eating my purple food, there was very little sign of a break in the line of undergrowth. The Noorthi hadn't traveled this way in quite a while. I extended my search to cover both sides of the House as well, in case someone had exited closer to the entrance, but there was nothing. I didn't like being stopped before I'd even got started.

I was left with little choice but to strike out in a direct line from the back of the House, praying that I'd come across some sort of path to follow. The foliage was thick and cumbersome, slowing my pace to barely a walk. I tried not to disturb the leaves, at least close to the House, so no one would know of my search. Once the House was out of sight I began to snap the occasional leaf to help me retrace my steps back to my Noorthi.

The search seemed to turn up nothing and I was about to give up when I saw it. A moss-covered path lay undisturbed and half-buried by wild ferns. It seemed odd that the Noorthi sisterhood hadn't visited the mine for such a long time. Maybe they had stores of ochre that I hadn't found as yet.

The ground shook and I stumbled. The Great One talking, my ass. In the stillness of the forest there was a hiss, followed by a plume of steam. It was still quite a distance away but I changed my direction and headed straight for it. Surely, this had to be it.

The path I'd found meandered in and out of sight as I waded through the heavy undergrowth toward the rising steam. Had I found what I was looking for? It certainly looked like it as both my path and the mossy path converged. Tiny wisps of milky cloud emerged from a hole in the ground. As I got closer I saw that the hole had a crude staircase built into the side of it. The rocky slabs also had moss growing on it, although a lot of it had turned brown with the heated air. It certainly didn't look like it had been used for many years. Stranger and stranger.

The stairs disappeared down into darkness. I had no light of my own so if I proceeded it would be by feel alone. The answer lay down there. All it would take was that first step. But was I prepared to step down into the unknown without light? It only took a moment for me to decide.

The heat was palpable the moment I took the first step downward. It was going to be hot, sticky and dark. But I didn't let that deter me. If I was right, here lay the source of the Noorthi. This clay was the trigger for their evolution. I suppose I didn't really need to know, after all it would destroy all the mystery surrounding them, but I had a feeling that the information was at the heart of Clea's grasp for power. If the Rigeus ochre could be converted to a mind drug, what could this ochre do? I didn't need to be Malt to figure out that the environment would play a key part in the ochre's makeup. Air, soil, and water–all would contribute to the many and varied changes the ochre would undertake until it reached its present form.

Each step I took led me closer to an answer I wanted to find. I only hoped that whatever this ochre did, it didn't kill us all.

Funnily enough, the darkness slowly dissipated and became lighter. Why? By the time I reached the bottom of the staircase the mine was lit up. There was no obvious light source, such as a magneto lamp or even the ancient electrical source of my favored twentieth century. No, the mud walls glowed brightly from within. Maybe there was some sort of biological source to it but I didn't have the time to analyze it. That was Malt's job. However, I did want to get a sample of it. I left the walls alone and scooped up mud off the floor. The thought of all those tiny bacteria busily giving off light in the mud stopped me from gouging it out of the wall. I didn't want to commit mass homicide. Out of curiosity I shook the jar and the mud glowed brightly. I must have woken them.

"Sorry, little guys," I muttered.

The mine was extraordinary in itself, even if it wasn't *the* ochre mine. I could see clearly the mining that had gone on. The area had been widely excavated, leaving behind an empty space of about thirty foot square. A small corridor led off at the far end of the cavern, for the present in darkness. There were no usable implements as such, just discarded pieces of what was once mining equipment. I picked a piece up and examined it. The metal looked vaguely like a pick head of some sort, but this type of implement hadn't been used for centuries.

I staggered under the implication. This ochre had been mined thousands of years ago. But why had the mining stopped? Had they discovered the awful secret that burdened the Noorthi for millennia?

I hunkered down and studied the floor. There were a lot of long-forgotten footprints in the mud-covered floor, but there was also a fresh set of footprints planted over the top of them that led from the passageway to the bottom of the staircase. I looked twice and stood, going back to the staircase. No, there didn't seem to be any disturbance of the moss on the stairs. A shiver ran down my spine. How did he, or more probably she, do it?

Maybe I should have left this alone, but I found myself walking along the corridor. The walls suddenly lit up as I passed. Did they react to my presence or the vibration of my footsteps? It was a question for another day.

The passageway went on for quite a way, perhaps fifty or sixty feet, to abruptly end at another hole, this time in the floor. An ancient rope ladder was slung over the side and disappeared into the darkness below.

I don't know why I did it, maybe it was the fresh footprints, but I looked around to see if anyone was watching. It's funny how such ingrained instinctual behaviors could occur at the strangest times. What did I have to lose? There was a ladder right there for me to go up and down on, so there was no real danger unless, of course, I lost my footing and fell. I considered the strength of my luck. Was I going to be stupid enough to get myself into trouble? If Malt were here, she'd say 'yes'. Then again, she'd say 'yes' to just about anything I did. She knew me too well.

I wasn't sure how far the ochre ran down the walls in the well so I looked for something to hold the jar. The little buggers could be of some use yet. I found a piece of discarded rope and spent some time trying to tie knots. It was a lost art and one that I was now wishing I had followed up on. After much swearing I managed to make something of use. I only hoped that the knots stayed together long enough.

I slipped the jar into my makeshift rope basket and slung it around my neck. I lifted the jar and looked inside. "Okay, fellas, do your stuff." I shook it, but not hard enough the give them concussion. Now I was worrying about creatures that I couldn't even see. This Ratha job was seriously denting my sanity.

I sat down on the floor and let my legs hang over the edge. The ochre was wet despite the heat. "Just great." My pants now had ochre stains. And these were my favorite pair. "Craz!" I was just about to get ochre on my new shirt too.

There was nothing to grab onto, leaving me no choice but to roll onto my stomach. I then had to shimmy out over the hole until

I could bend at the waist and grab the loops with my feet. Normally I didn't worry about what ended up on my clothes, but this time I just knew it was going to be messy.

I inched my hands along the rope until I could stand up in the stirrup. My little jar shook violently and the ochre shone brightly. "Sorry guys, it can't be helped."

Maybe I should visit a sertech for some of that twentieth century medicine thiro…, throo…, thrip…, that feel-good stuff that didn't make you so crazy.

"Come on! You always seem to come up with the right word when I need it!" I whispered. Now my vocabulary skills had decided to take a holiday. They only wanted to perform in front of an audience. Since they decided to ignore me I started down the ladder.

The ochre blazed brightly in the hole but petered out about fifty feet down. It was then that my friendly little glowing buddies came to my aid and sent out their light. Not that the walls changed. It was a straight up and down well and, by the looks of it, it didn't end. I looked up and saw that the corridor was still lit. How long did the bacteria glow after being disturbed?

I stopped where I was. Was this ladder going anywhere? My gut was saying yes, otherwise what was the point of the ladder in the first place? Just as I was about to start my way back up again the ladder shook. I was pretty sure it wasn't another tremor. It actually felt more like tension on the rope. I glanced up. "Hello? Anyone there?"

The rope jerked and I had a bad feeling. I started down in the hope of finding ground, and quick. "Oh, craz, Malt. I hope you're not right," I muttered as I struggled to keep my feet on the rope. She'd be saying 'I told you so' right about now.

Suddenly one of the ropes gave way and the ladder collapsed to one side. I had one foot resting precariously on a loop with little chance of finding the next loop down.

"Hang on fellas," I said to my little companions, "it's going to be a bumpy ride." I had barely said ride when the second rope gave way and I fell. My fingernails dug into the wall with little effect, leaving gouges in the soft soil. Frantically I reached for the knife in my belt and dug it into the ochre to try and slow myself down.

I stopped quickly as I hit bottom, literally in both cases. My ass was on fire as it cushioned my fall. Oh, Carn! I didn't think I'd be able to sit down for a week, which would make flying Bessie an interesting prospect. That is, if I got out of the predicament I was in.

The jar let off a muted light as it lay beside me. "You okay, fellas?" I was really in need of some serious psychiatric help here. Gingerly I stood up and rubbed my ass. "Craz!"

The jar flared for a moment. "Sorry boys. I didn't know you were listening." They were Noorthi bacteria all right. I held up the jar and checked my surroundings. There were two paths, one on either side of the hole. I looked at my little companions. "Which way?" In answer to my question one cave lit up.

What else could I say? "Thank you."

I followed the path being illuminated, stepping carefully as it steeply descended farther into the planet. The heat had been steadily increasing from the moment I started down the hole and now I felt the ochre sticking to my slick skin. It was sort of like the mud wrestling whores on Denizon, except for the three breasts of course. Right now I wanted a bath.

By the time I reached the end of the passageway the sweat was flowing freely from my temples down to my chin.

"How do you live in this?" For a moment I thought I heard them say something. "Nah, just my imagination."

The passage opened up to another, even larger hole in the ground. It was more a cavern really, as access to the other side would require a considerable leap from me across the abyss. The space was bathed in a muted red glow coming from below. From my position I couldn't see the bottom, but I could take an educated guess. It led to the heart of Alengola.

I was about to take a closer look when movement on the other side caught my attention. I stepped back into the shadows and observed. Across the chasm appeared someone else. It didn't surprise me who it was, but what they were about to do, did. Jute stood on the precipice for a moment then picked up a small packet of something and threw it into the hole. She stepped back and waited. The earth heaved for a second and settled. Jute smiled, turned around and left. What the craz was that all about?

I could imagine Clea claiming that the Great One had talked to her. Maybe it was all part of the manipulation. The Noorthi were the twentieth century equivalent of sheep and Clea was the lion. They blindly followed wherever she led them, even into her den.

I lifted up the jar to my face. "So, what do you think?" I moved the jar to my ear for a moment then returned it to its place in front of my face. "Yeah, that's what I thought." Whether the little fellas actually talked to me or not depended on my state of mind, but if it helped me make up my mind then a little deception on my part was a small price to pay.

"I've got to get across to the other side, any suggestions?"

This time I was sure I heard a tiny squeak, barely imperceptible above the hissing of steam and the rumbling from below. There was a small ledge running along the wall but it was too risky to take. My feet were just too damned big.

"Hmmm? What did you say?" I lifted the jar again. "Not a bad idea."

My Noorthi bacteria had come up with a solution. I lifted them gently out of the rope basket that cupped the jar and undid the knots. They fell apart as soon as I touched them, so I was glad that I had saved my buddies from certain death. They excitedly moved about in the ochre, creating a handy light source for me to attach the knife to the rope.

"You think this will work?" The light flared. "Okay, if you say so, but if I lose the knife it's your fault." The light blinked a couple of times. "Don't get huffy with me! You were the ones who suggested it." The jar vibrated. "Hey! Calm down! It was a joke." I held up one hand in surrender.

The gap was about fifteen feet, so the target was big enough to hit. I hoped. I threw the knife at one of the packets sitting on the ground. It stuck in deep. I pulled steadily on the rope and removed the knife. When I had the knife back in my hand I sniffed the blade. "Doesn't smell like any sort of explosive that I know of." Tentatively, I tasted it. "It's ochre." I swallowed what was in my mouth and I felt the heat of it steadily flow through me, following the veins and arteries to reach my heart and my head. More was revealed to me, like the second ochre was adding another layer of Noorthi knowledge and understanding over the top of what I already understood. There were fleeting images and long forgotten messages that I couldn't quite grasp.

"Wow!" I looked at my little friends who blinked at me.

I didn't have time to spend studying the effects of the two ochres. "Let's try the other tunnel." I picked up my belongings and walked back up the incline to where the two tunnels met. Maybe this second passage would lead to the far side of the chasm I had just found.

I didn't have to travel far in this one. It came to an abrupt end fifteen feet along and opened up into a small alcove. There was nothing there, just empty walls and silence. "Nothing." As I turned, my jar flared into life again. "Is there something here?" If they said so, I'd look.

The walls were muddy, sticky and intact. Whatever they said, or what I thought they said, had been wrong. The jar flashed on and off and the wall lit up in a small circle in response. "Okay, I get it. Dig here." Who was I to argue? I wasn't driving this train; I was just along for the ride. "I'd tell your buddies there to move out of the way." The glow faded in the wall and I took it as a sign to go ahead.

Just wait until Malt heard about this.

I dug at the area with my knife, piling up the viscous mud to one side. What was I supposed to find? Was it a way out? Why was I even listening to what was obviously a hallucination?

The hole was getting deep and my back was aching because of the angle I had to dig. I leaned back on my knees and looked at the jar by my side.

"Listen, guys, I don't think this is leading anywhere…."

The jar vibrated and the light flashed wildly. "Hey! Hey! Hang on! Don't get excited. I'll give it five more minutes." The bacteria settled down, and the jar returned to a muted glow. "Sheesh. Now I'm getting bossed around by microscopic bugs."

The ochre gave a quick burst of glaringly bright light, as if to say 'you got that right'. I let out a chuckle and went back to work.

Five minutes passed, and then another five. "I've given it my best sho–" The knife hit something with a clunk. "Okay, I take it back." I slid the knife around the edge of what seemed to be a box, carving the outline and working outward. I didn't take too much care about where the mud landed and I was flicking it in all directions in my effort to get to the box.

However, the box was deceptively long and it took many more minutes and a sore back to get farther into the hole to cut away the mud. I'm sure I educated the little bugs with my colorful cussing, but this was getting ridiculous. It was like it was saying 'here I am' then refusing to give it up. "I could use some help here." Not that I expected any.

I gave a final heave and the box came free, landing in my lap as I sat on my sore ass. Cra..." I had cut my cussing short in deference to the bacteria. I could sure use a happy tablet now.

I used the knife to prize open the lid. Inside were a mass of mysterious sheets which, I assumed, were paper. I hadn't seen paper before, although I had seen it in archival material about the twentieth century. It seemed fragile and I had to handle it with care. "What's this?" I lifted a sheet up and held it close to the jar. The characters seemed vaguely familiar and yet not. One or two were reminiscent of Noorthi. Was this a long lost script of the ancient Noorthi? Grit would be excited to see the writings.

"That's it?" I thought there would have been more evidence. The paper was all that was in the box. I was disappointed. Still, whatever was written within these pages might hold the truth to everything.

On the back wall appeared another bright spot. "Are you telling me I have to dig again?" My back was already hurting and now they wanted more? The spot flared. "Geez, my Noorthi aren't as pushy as you are."

I replaced the lid and crawled into the hole. Normally I'm not claustrophobic but the heat and the damp, and the fact that my arms were forced out in front of me, did little to calm me. The hot and stale air had me praying that it didn't take too much longer.

I wasn't able to swing the knife at the wall because of the restriction, leaving me to pick away at the mud. This was taking way too long for my liking. I shimmied out and took a break, taking in deep breaths of the warm air in the alcove. "Are you sure?" I looked at the jar accusingly. "Why me?"

The word Ratha formed in my head. So this was all because of who, or what, I was. This was a discovery meant for only me. It revitalized me knowing that there was something worthwhile awaiting me on the other side of the mud wall.

"Is it a way out?" I certainly hoped so, otherwise all the treasure in the universe was useless to me.

It took another half an hour of sweat, tears and mud flinging before I finally broke through the wall. While I was excited at the discovery, it took another fifteen minutes to make the hole big enough for me to crawl through.

By the time I was standing comfortably in the new room I was covered head to foot in mud–cloying, hardening mud. I stunk, like a ristak stunk. My smell would rot the fruit I had been eating earlier. I glared at my priceless jar. "If Beri catches me like this, so help me..." A few choice words crossed my mind but I held my tongue. What was the point of swearing at mud, except to let off some steam?

The little creatures burst into life and the walls in the cave did the same. The lights flickered on and off as they appeared to be talking to one another. Slowly the darkness faded and revealed its treasures.

I didn't know what to look at first. Here were the remains of the Noorthi culture, expressed in its few precious carvings and canisters. These were from the beginning, I felt it. From a time when the Great One was nothing more than a sole believer.

It was here that I felt the pull of the Noorthi the fiercest. It was like facing the tempest and either bending to its will or be swept away. Oh, craz! Suddenly I felt the full brunt of being the Ratha. Before, I could always blissfully deny that nothing was certain in my future. Now that uncertainty was gone. It called out to me and, willingly or unwillingly, I responded. My future was now set in stone.

"You did this to me," I growled at the jar. "And how do I get out of here?"

The hole I had dug slowly closed on itself. "Wait!" I made a move toward the exit and the hole closed quickly. "What's going on here?"

Another hole opened up on the other side of the room, its ragged edges touched with the ghostly glow of the bacteria.

"And you made me dig that hole? I did all that work and you could have done that?" I accused my little buddies. "I'll remember this."

It took quite a few steps to traverse the thickness of the wall. It would have taken me days to do it myself, that is if I didn't lose heart before reaching the end. On the other side of the wall was a staircase. It didn't lead directly to where I was standing, but passed it by, descending farther into the depths of the planet.

I looked back at the room and its contents. Why was I shown this room? Was it to reinforce my place in the scheme of Noorthi things? Was this property now my responsibility? I stepped back into the room.

You have finally arrived, Ratha.

"Who said that?"

There is nothing to fear.

"Yeah... right." The voice seemed to be coming from the walls.

Your strength will be needed soon.

"And who are you?" This was the final step on my road to insanity. Now I was hearing a voice.

I am Neela.

"Good for you."

And you, Jordana Laren, are my chosen protector for my sisters.

"Sorry, I'm not convinced. Now, if you don't mind, I'm busy." The hole closed suddenly and I was stranded. "Hey!"

You are a non-believer.

"Listen, lady. I don't care what scheme you're pulling here, but I've got things to do." I didn't know where to turn. "Do you mind?"

What will it take for you to believe?

"Why is it important for me to believe? You have my support. Isn't that enough?"

Without belief the actions mean nothing.

"So saving the Noorthi means nothing? I don't think so."

But you believe in yourself to do the things that you do.

"That's belief in me, not in what the Noorthi think I am."

It is not such a large step to believe you are Ratha.

"Ratha means protector. I can protect without having to live up to all the hype of being their savior. I'm nothing more than a pilot who ended up in the wrong place at the wrong time."

You underestimate yourself. I did not choose you on a whim, Jordana. You can achieve so much more if you only believe in your destiny.

"See? There you go again!" I yelled. "All this destiny crap! I don't need it and I don't want it!" I was about ready to explode. "If you push too hard I'll walk away, I swear it!"

Do not make promises you will not keep.

"Who the hell are you?"

I am Neela.

"So you say."

My sisters call me the Great One.

I stood there, a mixture of anger, disbelief and fear running through me. "No, this is all in my mind. You don't exist."

The mud wall moved and formed a face. *Will this help you?* The mud lips moved in synch with the words.

"Carn! Now I'm seeing things!" I really wished I was somewhere else. "You should have left things alone. I would have looked after them because I had made that promise to them. Belief wasn't asked for and wasn't needed. Why is it so important now?"

There will be a great upheaval.

"So Grit said."

Some things will be lost forever. Some things that need saving. Some things that need the commitment of belief to become possible. The ochre eyes stared at me and it was unnerving.

"Fine, I believe." The mud lips pursed. "It's not going to happen, so just let me do my job, okay?"

The face disappeared and became the wall again. The hole re-opened and my access to the staircase was restored. A great upheaval. It seemed to be a common theme and something that I felt I couldn't ignore. I wasn't sure whether this upheaval would happen on Alengola or not, so I would move the treasure from the depths of Alengola up to the surface just in case. It would be my secret for now until I decided who were worthy to be the caretakers of the Noorthi culture. At present, I sided with my Juno Noorthi because I knew their hearts, but I was prepared to give the Alengolans a chance to plead their case. Whichever way I was swayed, I was risking a lot bringing the treasure out of its hiding place. What if something happened to me? Would the artifacts be decimated in the atmosphere of Alengola? I couldn't doubt myself here. I had to believe I was doing the right thing at the right time. Believe. How ironic was that? I argued the validity of belief, and yet here I was moments later using that very excuse for what I was doing.

After a number of cumbersome trips, I stored the goods in the undergrowth near the Great House. If I needed to leave in a hurry I wanted them easily accessible. There were six empty pots left by the time I cleared the room of everything, from statues down to dried seeds.

"Who wants to go for a ride?" I asked out loud, holding the first pot next to the wall. When nothing happened I added, "I'm not going to do all the work here. If you want to go, now is the time to move."

The mud slid down the wall, over the pot lip and into the canister. Once the mud began to move, I had filled the remaining pots in no time. This was as much Noorthi culture as the statues and parchments. I wanted to make sure that no matter what happened, their precious history had a chance to survive. I left my buddies in the jar with the treasure and told them to look after it. As if.

For my own curiosity, I went back to the cave and I followed the steps down to the bottom. As I suspected, this was where Jute had entered the mine. There were many footprints in the mud and I followed them to the other side of the chasm from where I had previously been standing. I examined the packets of mud, wrapped in cloth and stacked high. From what I had seen of just one packet thrown into the hole, there was enough explosive mud here to blow up the whole planet.

As much as my little voice was telling me to get rid of it, I hesitated. However, that didn't stop me from taking a couple for testing. If I dismantled the stockpile they'd know I was here. It could put Beri, Rice and my Noorthi in danger. No, I had to hope that Clea wasn't too nuts to want to destroy everything. Why didn't I believe that?

Chapter Six

Caught Between a Rock, a Hard Place and the Ground

I returned to the Great House and went in search of Beri. We had to get off this planet, and quick. My comlink so far had been unsuccessful in contacting Malt. Where was she? More importantly, was she all right? Had Jute found her and eliminated her? If I found out that she had, nothing would stop me from killing the bitch.

I entered through the kitchen and into the heart of enemy territory. It was probably not the right word to use for this place of worship, but Clea had made it that to me. She was not one to be trusted as far as I was concerned, and somehow I had to convince the others of this.

I started to climb the staircase to the first floor when I saw Beri playing with Rice at the edge of the cleared ground outside. I stopped short when I spotted Jute watching them from a short distance away. Stepping back into the shadows, I observed the trio, envious of Jute's apparent babysitting job. She was spending more time with Beri than I was. I traced my steps back through the building and out into the jungle. One way or another, I needed to talk to Beri.

"What are you doing here?" Beri found me hiding in the bushes a mere foot or two from where she was playing with Rice. "What happened to you?

"If you expect me to leave you alone with that woman, you've got another thing coming." I answered the most obvious question first. "I fell in the mud." It was a simple answer to a convoluted experience.

"What is the matter with you?" she whispered. She glanced over her shoulder and saw Jute standing some distance away observing her.

"Rice, honey!" she yelled. "Don't go too far away!"

"I don't like her giving you so much attention," I muttered grumpily.

"Raaaa!" Rice screamed.

"No honey, Ra isn't here," Beri announced.

"But, Mama—"

"No, Rice. Ra will be back soon."

"It's a game. Shhhh," I whispered to Rice.

She looked at me and giggled. "Ssssssss." She imitated me by putting her finger over her lips.

"I'm not in any danger," Beri continued the conversation.

"Of course you are!" The woman was so damned frustrating.

"You're jealous," Beri said.

"I-am-not!" I cried. I slapped my hand over my mouth and held my breath. I glanced past Beri to see if Jute had moved. "Can't you see she's after you? She's not who she says she is, B, and you're falling right into her trap."

"What trap?"

"I can't see that yet, but—"

"You're accusing her of something you don't even know? Do you know how idiotic that sounds?"

"Mama! No!" Rice slapped Beri's hand. Beri picked up Rice and moved her a few feet to the right. She sat down and allowed Rice to climb into her lap. With Jute watching, it was near impossible to move with Beri.

"B!" I hissed.

"Go away," she mouthed at me.

So it was going to be like that. We'd had fights before, but this was the first one that involved our relationship. I thought we had gotten past those particular trust issues but obviously I was wrong. She wasn't going to trust my judgment on this one and it was going to take more than my opinion to sway her. "Fine."

I backed away slowly, but Rice wasn't happy about it.

"Ra! Come!" she cried out. Rice leapt out of Beri's lap and dashed toward me.

"No, Rice!" I whispered harshly. I started backing away quickly and Rice continued on after me. Jute had moved and would soon be upon us.

"Shortie, go to Mama!" She refused to listen. I shoved her backward and ran like hell in the opposite direction. I reached for a branch and swung up into the tree. I really hated doing this to the kid. What was she going to make of this?

"Ra?" I heard the hurt and confusion in my name.

I was seriously tempted to go and kick Jute's butt and just take back Beri and Rice. They were mine. Craz, what a mess.

"No! Ra!" I heard Rice struggling, her tiny voice grunting and squealing as she was being bodily carried back to her mother. I watched as Jute handed back Rice and saw Beri shake her head in my direction. B took Rice back into the House and back to *her*.

I was about to swing out of the tree when Jute looked back, her black eyes scanning the vegetation for something moving. Did she know it was me, or was it her natural hunter instincts that made her do it? I waited until Jute disappeared inside before letting myself down to the ground.

"Craz!" I growled. What was I going to do? If Beri needed proof then I'd go and find it. I slapped my head. I didn't even get the chance to tell her about the ochre mine.

†

The corridors were empty. There was no one to be seen. Where was everyone? Knowing how much the Noorthi liked to meditate, pray or have a meeting it wouldn't surprise me if they were in a large room somewhere contemplating the lint in their navels. While it made my passing possible, there was a certain uneasiness present in the abandoned passageways.

I returned to the room Beri had been resting in, but neither she nor Rice were anywhere to be seen. I silently checked the other rooms to no avail. That left me one other room on the first floor. Clea's room. I sneaked up to the door and put my ear against it.

There was definitely someone in there talking, but it was impossible to hear the conversation, let alone discern the people doing the talking.

I ground my teeth. Was Clea with Beri again? Since I decided that Clea was capable of deception, was she also capable of lust? I didn't consider the word love because to me that required a certain amount of honesty on her part. Was Clea lusting after Beri or was she insinuating herself into Beri's good graces? Was she after information or satisfaction? As far as I was concerned, Clea wasn't entitled to either. And especially little Rice. No one was going to step into my shoes with my kid.

There was no choice but to withdraw. Beri and Rice were out of my reach for now. I did the next best thing. I went in search of Grit, Fen and my Noorthi.

A good place to start was where I had left them, in what I considered the reflecting pool. In fact, it was where I still found them.

"Ah, you are back." Grit didn't seem too concerned about my departure for an hour or three.

"And you're still here," I replied.

"We were asked to wait here, and wait we will."

I knew I was covered head to toe in mud and Grit did little but raise an eyebrow. "You don't want to know what happened?"

"It seems you were playing in the mud," she replied blithely.

Sometimes these women irritated me. I turned around and stepped into the pool, ducking under the water and shaking myself to dislodge the clumps of mud.

"What are you doing?" Grit asked when I surfaced. Her face was priceless. Her open mouth was so wide it was nearly dragging on the floor.

"Getting rid of the mud."

"But… but that is a sacred pool."

"Now it's a dirty but sacred pool." The blue hue emanating from the pool changed to a burnished gold, lighting up the room even more brightly.

"Oh…oh…." Finally, I had her speechless.

I stepped out of the pool and shook myself like a shaggy hok, scattering muddy droplets everywhere. The Alengolan Noorthi present dropped to one knee and bowed their heads, while the Juno Noorthi stood there their mouths agape.

"How did you do that?" Fen asked.

"It might have something to do with the ochre mine I was crawling around in."

"You found it? The mine?"

"The original mine. The mine of legend. Yes, I found it."

"And?" Grit moved closer.

"And I think we have to get off this planet soon."

"But did you find anything?"

I was so close to telling them the truth, but I decided against it. This particular truth was best told at a later time. "A warning. Your great upheaval has begun, *memesh*."

Grit's lips tightened and she considered my statement. "What do we have to do?"

"Be prepared to leave at a moment's notice," I said in a low voice. "Don't say anything to the Alengolans yet because they won't believe you. We can't let Ashaltea-Sa know just yet. However, if you get the chance, find where the Noorthi artifacts are located. You may need to rescue them if time runs short."

"Time... runs... short?" Grit stared into my eyes.

This planet may be doomed, memesh. I let my mind tell Grit what my mouth wouldn't.

How so, child?

Jute is dropping explosives into a deep pit, causing the tremors we feel. I don't know how much more the planet will take.

Are we in danger?

I weighed my answer and opted for the truth. *Yes.*

"Do you know where Beri is?"

"The last time I saw her she was going for a walk outside," Fen said.

"I found her. She was being followed by Clea's pet."

"Beri wouldn't let Rice out of her sight."

"Good girl." So whoever was in Clea's room, it wasn't Clea or Beri. Despite Beri's reaction to my ravings, I had to find her and get a warning to her somehow.

Before I had a chance to act on that thought Grit stopped me. "Ratha. It is time."

"Time? For what?" I thought that I had more than enough to think about, but apparently Grit didn't think so.

"For you to receive your legacy." An old woman stepped up beside Grit and uttered some words.

"Please, not now."

"No, the time is right."

"For who? You?" I scoffed. "Look, you may not realize it, but you are in deep trouble. I've got to figure a way to get us off Alengola, stop Clea, and try to avoid Jute killing me, and that's just on this planet."

Grit placed her hand on the top of my head while the other elder did the same on the other side of me. My scalp began to itch and I was tempted to scratch it. Grit's lips moved, but I couldn't quite catch what she was saying. The other woman did the same in time with Grit, murmuring a Noorthi incantation. The air overhead came alive with tiny lights, floating around as if riding a current of air. It was like the tattoo ceremony again, except that this took two *hedera*, or so I assumed. The other woman looked as old as Grit and was doing exactly what she did, so I felt it was a fairly safe assumption on my part.

The itch turned to a tingle. I felt every single strand of hair in my scalp, each one sending a tiny signal to my brain. There seemed to be a faint buzzing that was steadily growing louder. As the intensity increased the sound dissolved into a voice. A sweet female voice that seemed to be coming from inside my head.

"Oh, no, no, no, not again. I am not playing someone's home for the next twenty years."

Do not fear me, Ratha.

"Listen, sister, I am not having someone in my head again. I've already been through that once and it was enough for me." I hadn't even realized that I had said it out loud. "You!" Grit stood there with her mouth open in mid-word. "I'm not some vessel you can just drop some spirit into when the mood takes you."

"This is your legacy," the other woman repeated.

"So you keep saying. Grit, you tell her. You tell her what I went through."

"Heed her no mind, Kollura. She had an experience with a spirit a few years ago. She is misguided—"

"Misguided? Did you say misguided?" I stood up and forced them to drop their hands off my head. I was taller than both of them by a good six inches, so I looked down and gave them my very best scowl. "I'm leaving, and I don't know when I'll be back."

I said it in anger and really wasn't thinking straight, but I was sick of them just doing stuff to me without even asking. I was like some doormat that they kept wiping their feet on.

I stomped off, and probably looked like a spoilt child while I did it, but I didn't care. I needed to find somewhere to cool off before I said something I knew I would regret later. Not that I had anywhere to go. I was stuck in the room with the rest of them, so I did the only thing I could. I found a corner and sat there.

I let my head fall back gently until it touched the wall. "Carn! What am I doing here?" This was one of those few times where I wished I had succumbed to the desert on Rigeus.

Your fate was not to die there.

"Stay out of it," I muttered.

I cannot. You and I are destined to be together.

"That's what you think. When I figure a way to get you out, you're on your own."

That is not possible.

"I've been told nothing is impossible, especially as I'm the one and only Ratha."

And hubris does not suit you. You have much to learn.

"Who from? You?" I laughed sarcastically.

Yes, from me. I am the wellspring of Noorthi knowledge.

"And I'm Father Christmas."

Who?

My twentieth century knowledge reared its ugly head. "Never mind." The reference was lost on whoever was residing in my head.

You do not understand—

"No, you don't understand. I don't want you, I don't need you and I certainly don't want to listen to anything you have to say." I slapped the side of my head. "Why don't you scatter yourself to the far reaches of space?"

I cannot do that. I am highly regarded.

"Now look who's talking about hubris." I mentally patted myself on the back for using the word.

Grit came and hunkered down beside me, her aged bones creaking with the effort. "Let me explain—"

"What's to explain? You've dumped me with another one of your Noorthi lost spirits. I want her out, *memesh.*"

"This is your legacy."

"Can you please stop saying that? It means nothing to me."

"What you have inside you now is our Noorthi heritage. It is everything that we were and have become."

"I don't understand."

"It is not a Noorthi sister, but our history."

"You mean like a book?"

"Something like that, but more."

"Is it sort of like a living book?"

"It carries all the Noorthi secrets."

"You mean like *the secret*?" Oh, craz.

"That, and others."

I am the Noorthi. I am here to help you. You, in turn, must protect all that I am.

"And what if I die?"

A Noorthi will carry the burden until you rise again.

"It's a burden now, is it? First it was a legacy, then a gift. Now it's a burden. This just gets better and better." I gently hit the back of my head against the wall.

Stop that!

"Are you going to be talking all the time, because I have to tell you that I hate that. Yakkety-yak. Never stopping. It makes me very cranky."

"The book was carried by myself and Kollura." Grit said.

"And did she talk all the time?"

"I have never heard the voice, Ratha. That is yours alone."

"Just great." I brought my knees up and lay my head in my arms. "Carn must really hate me."

I must have looked lost because Grit moved from a crouch to sit on the ground. "Listen to me. Do not fear this, Jordana."

That got my attention. She had always called me Ratha. My name sounded strange from her lips. "How can I not, *memesh*? I'm scared to death." It was a big admission on my part.

"It will not hurt you. It is there to help you. But, know this…," she paused and waited for my gaze to find her eyes. "You must never reveal it to anyone."

"Not even Beri."

"No one, Jordana. It does not exist to the universe. It is yours and yours alone."

"Except for the Noorthi who will take it on my death."

"Do not invite death so soon, Ratha."

I felt a little better. She had called me Ratha. All was right with the universe. "Did the root make me invincible?"

She laughed gently. "No, but it will make you resistant. You will not give up life so easily."

"I can live with that."

"You made a joke."

I made lots of them. They were just lost on the Noorthi. "Is a Noorthi going to follow me around day and night in case I get killed?" Grit pursed her lips. "I'll take that as a no."

Your spirit guardian has already been chosen.

"And does she know?" The way the Noorthi worked, I seriously doubted it. "Who is she?"

When she smiles, you can see it in her eyes.

"Dimples." *Delphan?* I kept that name to myself.

"Did you say something?"

"No, just thinking out loud."

She is connected to me. She will not know who or why, but when the time is needed she will be ready.

But she is not Noorthi.

And neither are you.

I thought that was strange. *Why?* Why indeed. The most powerful thing in the Noorthi religion had placed its future in human hands.

Even though she is not born of Noorthi, she is passionate about her beliefs, something that is sadly lacking of late in my sisters.

And me?

You were born to be who you were. Nothing would have changed that. Everything you have experienced has led to this point in time and place.

So basically, I couldn't have changed anything in my life even if I wanted to.

Correct.

What could I say? I was so tempted to go out and raise hell for a while just to see if it was true, but I couldn't raise the enthusiasm to do something naughty. My attention returned to where I was.

"Do you accept it now?" Grit asked.

"No!" I said defiantly, but it was a lost cause. I just didn't want Grit to know that.

She laughed quietly. ""Give it time. Can you help this old woman to her feet?"

"Admitting that age has got the better of you?" I earned a pinch for that remark. "Ow! Don't you ever get tired of doing that to me?"

"When you say something worthy of Ratha, I will stop," she said grumpily.

I placed my hands under Grit's armpits and lifted gently. The woman was a little on the plump side and it drew a groan from me to get her onto her feet. She took it as an insult and I received another pinch.

"Stop that!" Suddenly I wasn't worrying so much about what Jute would do to me. Grit was giving me more than enough bruises for this adventure.

I sat down again once Grit had left me. A young Alengolan was nursing her baby.

How does a Noorthi become pregnant? I asked the book.

You already know some of this.

I know about the ceremony. How does it happen?

The ochre is carefully prepared for the ceremony.

Is it some sort of drug? I had imagined something akin to an old twentieth century social drug that relaxed the body and allowed the mind to float free.

Yes, but not for the purpose of dulling the senses. It prepares the way for her gift.

Are you saying that the Noorthi don't become fertile until the ceremony?

That is the purpose of the ceremonial drink.

But that didn't explain how Beri got pregnant.

The chosen's spirit partner offers a part of her spirit for the fertilization.

Okay, so the ochre drink makes it possible for the two spirits to combine to create a new life within the chosen one. That sort of made sense, in a totally unbelievable way.

In essence, yes.

Essence. That was the point, wasn't it? The ochre prepared the way while the spirit created the impossible. *How did Beri get pregnant without the ceremony?*

That was unexpected. Your involvement in the fertilization made it possible.

But—

Ratha, this is a discussion for another time.

The voice was right. But I had already figured that something came from the partner in the ceremony. After all, Rice was a lot like me, probably more than like Beri. At least the tendency for noise and rough play came from me. I felt sorry for Beri. She was going to have her hands full trying to subdue Rice's wild spirit.

Now more than ever she would need me around to help, even if she didn't want it.

How do you know if it's successful?

A baby is born.

But not right away. How do you know after the ceremony?

One does not. We accept her gift if and when she grants it.

Gee, you really cover all the bases, don't you?

Bases? There are no bases.

This was frustrating. *Is there a feeling?*

I do not know. I am knowledge, not emotion. If you want to know, ask the young Noorthi.

She had a point. The best person to ask was the one who had the baby. I stood and made my way to the woman's side. I hunkered down to her level. "Excuse me, sister. May I ask you a question or two?"

She looked at me guardedly then finally nodded. I sat down next to her and watched as she attended to her daughter. "You conceived your daughter in the ceremony?" She nodded again.

"Did you know if anything happened?"

"Know?" Her voice held a soft lilting tone that made me smile.

"Did you feel anything during the ceremony?" Would she answer the question, knowing how the Noorthi felt about their rituals?

She looked at me and I was forced to show her my scar. She pulled away slightly and I tried to allay her fears with a smile. "Please, I want to know."

"Why? Are you…"

"No!" I said too harshly. I said it again more softly. "No. There are not many sisters to ask this. You have just had a child therefore your memory is still fresh. Did you feel anything that made you think you had been successful?"

"I felt a warmth, down here." She touched her tummy.

I think I was asking the questions because I wanted to get a better understanding about what happened between Beri and me. I remembered one occasion when Beri and I sat together. She was pregnant at the time, but I did remember a warmth that traveled down my arm and hand onto Beri's stomach. Was that when Rice left me and entered the fetus?

Is the spirit a new life or an old one renewed?

We all carry parts of our lost sisters, waiting for that moment when we can set that spirit free.

Is that a yes or a no?

What do you think?

You're not going to answer me, are you?

Some things are best left a mystery.

I'll take that as a no.

The book was going to cheat me out of an answer. Maybe it was something that I would have to find out myself.

"Thank you, sister, for your time." If I asked any more questions I might scare her off. I could see that this subject would need more investigation, without getting personally involved of course.

I had wasted enough time procrastinating and stood up. I moved to Grit and hunkered down. "Beri isn't going to budge until I give her proof concerning Clea's duplicity."

Grit's eyebrow rose. Yeah, I'd just shown off with another big word. "Well then, you better find that proof."

"I have one small problem. I haven't been able to contact Malt so we're stuck on this planet."

✝

I stood near the entrance, ensconced in a small niche to look outside. There was no sign of either Beri or Clea. Had they returned or was Clea showing her the wonders of her world? I glanced around and Jute appeared at the other end of the main hallway. I wasn't sure but it seemed like she was looking right at me. She picked up the pace as she moved, coming to a full sprint down the corridor toward me. When faced with an eight foot giant of a woman heading straight toward me, I did the only thing I could. I turned around and ran, taking the staircase to the ground two steps at a time. I heard her behind me, her booted feet sounding loud on the faux marble floor. I stopped and turned

84

around just as she launched herself off the top step, flying through the air like some giant berken. She swooped down on me, her large arms wrapping around my torso with precision. Despite my cloaking device, she found me easily. I was soon discovering the old man's invention was doing me little good on this planet.

Jute hit me like a boulder and I felt every aching inch of her. We both rolled in the dirt until she sat herself on top of me. Her hands grabbed my shoulders, her forefinger brushing the cloaking tab. I became visible and she smiled. But it wasn't a smile of joy. Oh, no, it was a smile of victory.

"Clea sent you." It was a statement, not a question. She had found me and now I was a liability. Suddenly it wasn't about Beri and Rice any more. It was about me, and my death.

I looked up into those black eyes glittering with anticipation. Jute was like one of those hunting beasts standing over its prey ready to consume it.

"I didn't get much of a chance to escape. This is a hollow victory." Would she accept the argument? She snarled at me. As best as I could I rolled my body to one side in the hope she would lose her balance. I scrambled out from underneath her splayed body. Running at this point seemed useless. She could easily catch me within a hundred feet.

I threw myself at her, kicking out with one foot at her midsection. She buckled and I thought I had a chance. But it was only for a moment. From her bent-over position her arm swung up and collected me on the chin, easily sending me plummeting to the ground more than twenty feet away. What just happened? Every muscle in my body ached and my brain was rattled.

She picked me up and held me above her head. She paused as if deciding where to throw me. I was about to offer a suggestion when she walked to the open piece of ground and threw me against a tree.

Okay, I admit it. I groaned. Then for good measure I groaned again, this time loudly.

What is this feeling?
It's called pain, and lots of it.

She strolled over to me with a smile, as if my death was a foregone conclusion. Maybe it was, at least in her eyes. I grabbed a handful of dust and when she reached to grab me, I threw it in her face.

Jute backed away, wiping frantically at her eyes. It took me some moments to get up. Now if the forest just stopped moving in front of my eyes I might have been able to see. My time was running out. Jute was squinting at me, which meant that in another minute she'd have me in perfect focus. I grabbed a branch and just started whacking her. Whether it was doing any good or not I had no idea, but as long as it felt like I was hitting something I kept swinging.

Suddenly what I was hitting disappeared. I stopped to see if Jute was out for the count. Well, she was down but not out. I threw away the branch and took off into the jungle. I ran without thought of direction or retaliation. She had soundly beaten me and I had nothing left to fight with.

A large tree loomed up in the distance and I headed for it. The lowest branch was above my head and I was forced to jump up to grab hold of it. I swung there for a moment, wondering where I was going to get the energy to climb up. The vegetation near me stirred. That was all the incentive I needed.

I ignored the pain and exhaustion that lapped at my body and lifted my leg. It barely caught the branch before I felt my energy lag. The rustling became louder and I was barely hanging on. If I didn't move soon Jute would find me hanging there like a dead mostoon being prepared for dinner.

"Come on, you old bitch!" I growled, willing my body for one last effort to get on top of the branch.

It was funny really. I knew what I had to do but I didn't remember doing it. One moment I was hanging upside down, the next I was near the top of the tree looking down at the ground forty feet below me.

"Okay, this is scary." I should have known better than to question Noorthi mystique, but this was getting ridiculous. It was one more fact pointing me toward becoming a believer.

This is part of you.

What? Doing things I don't even remember doing?

Do not be afraid.

Me? Afraid? Of what? You? I smiled.

I thought I heard a snicker. I don't think the book was convinced either.

My breathing was labored and my heart thumped wildly as I crouched in the shadows. Jute came into view, her gaze darting around the small clearing. She took a few steps and stopped again, her head swiveling from one side to the other. Could she hear me? I tried to calm my breath but my body ached for oxygen.

Jute stopped motionless at the bottom of the tree, as if waiting for a signal from me. A trickle of sweat ran down my temple and cheek, finishing at the point of my chin. I didn't dare move my arm in case she caught the movement, but the drop was about to land on her head if I didn't. Slowly I turned my head and wiped my face on my shirt.

It seemed like forever that Jute stood there at the bottom of the tree. My legs were cramping from the strain of perching on a narrow branch, the myriad of bruises ached and the cuts stung with the sweat on my body.

Just as I was about to decide whether to drop out of the tree on top of her Jute moved on, finally disappearing into the vegetation on the other side of the tree. I dropped my head and let out a huge sigh.

You are Ratha. You fear nothing.

Yeah, only if I'm really stupid. Did you see the size of that woman?

I looked up at the sky and saw that it was getting dark. It seemed whatever this planet called a night was about to descend. I had no idea where I was going in the daylight, so travelling at night was even riskier. The safest place at the moment was where I was. I straddled the branch and leaned against the trunk. My stomach gurgled and I realized that I hadn't eaten for several hours. "Figures." There was nothing I could do about it so I tried to get some rest.

I knew I was in real trouble. Beri, Rice and the others were in the hands of a deranged Noorthi leader and I couldn't get to them.

Worse was the fact that I was the only one who knew she was deranged. The Noorthi were bound by their code to obey, irrespective of what she told them to do. They had no choice. Chaos would rule without order. How many variations of that thought had I heard in the past three years?

Who could I count on? From my perspective, I saw no one. Sasha was on her way back to Heaven, while Malt was sitting in space and I was unable to contact her. Was I imagining the threat? Clea hid her feelings well. It was only my innate suspiciousness that alerted me in the first place. But Jute wasn't part of my imagination. I had the bruises to prove it.

What was Clea up to? The mural on the wall in her private room looked like a star map. Tikka was fixing crystals to two planets, which I recognized as Rigeus and Juno, the locations of the ochre mine and the Juno sisterhood. There were other crystals on that wall. Were they the locations of other ochre mines and Noorthi sisters throughout the cosmos? Didn't the Noorthi believe that it was too dangerous for any one sister to know it all?

My mind ran through various scenarios and none of them were good. To me, it seemed that Clea was intent on knowing the whole truth, but to what end? Universal domination? Again? Hadn't I just got rid of one megalomaniac? Was Vel going to be replaced with someone even more insidious with the full power of the Noorthi behind her?

All these questions swirled around in my head. "Oh, Carn. Malt, I could use your help right about now."

This Malt you speak of. Is she someone I should remember?

Oh, yes, she's a very important someone. She's the one who rescues me when I'm in danger.

But you are a ratha. You have no need of a savior.

You're going to learn very quickly that I need saving... a lot. I can help you.

She helps better. I wasn't going to swap Malt for a book.

You do not know what I am capable of.

But I do know what Malt is capable of.

Then–

Please, not now.

Tiredness swept over me and I put aside my worries for a while as I dozed off.

†

Who is this Great One that everyone seems to revere so much?

She is the founder of our Order. The source of our soul.

Pretty words, Book. You need to explain.

Nyssa was her name. Neela Wyshart. In the beginning she was the Order. She lived alone on this planet, seeking the solace of the plants, the air, the earth and the sun. She gave up everything to find the inner peace of mere existence.

Was it only women from the beginning? That sort of philosophy would attract both men and women.

Yes, it would, and it did attract men at first. But the selfishness of men stopped the progression of the Order. They were not able to put aside the physical excesses that had ruled their lives. They lost sight of the prime directive of those wanting to find that one real truth.

You expelled them?

No, the men were not suited to this life and drifted away, pursuing a more secular lifestyle.

How did you evolve?

Neela and her followers used all parts of nature for their medicines, food, water, cloth and dwellings. There was nothing like this Great House then.

A mental image came into my head of Heaven.

They lived much as you do, as they should do now. Some Noorthi have forgotten the path they had chosen to walk.

So, you're saying that something on this planet helped them to take an evolutionary step that humans haven't taken yet? Was this the secret that the Noorthi were hiding?

Yes, and no. Whether it was the ochre that is found on this planet or the universe aiding our divine purpose, we will never know. Our existence has been rewarded and we will praise its name.

89

Yes, but what is it?

Do you not pray to one God? To Carn as you call it?

I suppose I do.

Do you know who or what is this Carn?

I really didn't want to get into a philosophical debate in my head. Okay, I get the point.

The universe is our deity. We praise it for the joyous wonders it has given us.

Grit was mentioning a great upheaval. What is that?

It has already begun, Ratha.

But what is it? I know I was trying to cheat but I wanted to be prepared.

You cannot, as you say, cheat. You will know what to do when the time comes.

You sound just like them. Tell me everything by telling me nothing.

Some things are meant to be clouded until they are ready to be revealed.

See? You speak in riddles. You must have classes at Noorthi school called Riddles 101.

What is this Riddles 101?

Never mind. All you need to know is that the Noorthi are very good at saying a lot without actually saying anything useful.

We cannot lie. You know that.

Maybe, but you lie by omission. I ask a question and you skirt the issue. If you're not going to answer it then don't talk at all.

I had hoped that it would the end the conversation because I was tired.

✝

I woke and it was dark. It took me a second to realize where I was. There was barely any light, so all I saw were varying shades of darkness, except for the two luminous eyes staring at me. Had I imagined the conversation in my head, or did it really happen? Now the damned thing was trying to teach me while I was asleep.

"Who's there?" I said in a low voice.

A small circle of light appeared in front of me and around its edges I caught a glimpse of something familiar... something metallic... something deadly.

This was so not fair. She kept coming up with some new power that I couldn't counteract. At the moment the score was Jute ten thousand to Jordana one. No, not one. One half. At best, my kick knocked the wind out of her.

"Why can't you leave me alone?"

The two eyes tilted to one side, as if the owner was observing me with some amusement.

"Couldn't you go back and say you killed me without actually doing it?" It was, come to think of it, a really stupid statement since she couldn't talk.

The ball of light moved up to Jute's face, her black-hued eyes glittering in the light. Why did I have the feeling that her expression said no? Her large hand swept around and caught me upside the head, sending me toppling out of the tree. I found every tree branch on the way down and each one left its mark on me.

The two seconds it took me to hit the ground seemed like an eternity. I barely had time to think of those I would leave behind as the hard earth did little to cushion my sudden stop face down.

This was not good. Bones were broken and I was sure that something soft inside was broken too. The pain rolled over me like a wave and I didn't fight it. It was like I was lying on broken glass, with each piece piercing my skin and finding an organ.

My eyes were open when the circle of light came into view. This was it. Jute was coming in for the kill. She lay down beside me so I could see her face. It seemed she had decided to take pleasure in the kill, and I couldn't stop her.

But I was not going to beg. That time was done. "Promise me something," I gasped. "Protect the kid from her, will you?"

Jute's head tilted again. I repeated the request in Noorthi. "Cootha na sica abee Clea."

Jute's eyes closed for a moment. Was that a yes? I wished this woman came with subtitles. She stood and looked down at me, her booted foot rising slowly. I turned my head away. If she was going to stomp me to death, I wasn't going to watch her.

91

A white light appeared all around me, almost blinding in its glaring intensity. Had I passed on and this was heaven? Funny, I didn't remember the kill stroke. I tried to move and the pain welled up. Shouldn't all the pain go away? It did the last time I died. I moved again. Nope, it was still there. I had a sudden thought that maybe I went to the other place where bad girls go. No, not Rigeus, but something very close to it–hell.

I turned my head again and saw Jute standing there looking up at the sky. The ball of light I thought she held in her hand was actually *in* her hand. Carn! This woman cheated with everything.

She turned her attention to me and took a step forward. She now had a better view of my death. Her step was stopped and she was immobile, her foot swaying in mid-air as she tried to put it down.

The air vibrated around and through me, jostling my injuries. I couldn't stop a moan escaping my lips. What was going on? Was Clea saving my death for herself? My body rose from the ground, cradled in the gentle invisible hand of the light surrounding me. I continued to rise and I watched Jute's angry expression as I slipped from her grasp. At this point I didn't care who had me. If it meant I wouldn't become another statistic for Jute then it was fine with me.

Far above the forest, I saw the Noorthi Grand House in the distance, lit by a myriad of gaseous glowing balls of light. Would I ever see my family again? I was not ready to leave this plane of existence just yet. There was still too much to do, and high on that list was to watch little Rice grow up into a young woman. I owed her that much.

I floated above the forest as the beam that held me moved me away from immediate danger. There was a metallic taste in my mouth and my biggest fear was realized. I had internal damage, and if I didn't get help soon I didn't need Jute to finish me off.

We descended some distance away, the beam slowly lowering me to the ground. The craft followed suit and I waited for the pilot to find me. The ground was definitely harder than I remembered it and my pain re-surfaced savagely. I groaned.

"That's no way to greet me, J."

I couldn't help it. I smiled. "Have you become a mind reader?" My voice was harsh and cracking.

"Let's get you to help." Malt put her hand on my arm and I winced.

"Don't!" That one word vibrated through me. "Body broken."

Malt's concerned face came into my view. "What do I do?"

"Something... flat."

Malt disappeared. I was trying to get my mind ready for pain, and lots of it. Any sort of movement was not going to be good, so moving me onto a flat surface was going to be agony in the extreme.

Malt was back with a board. "Now what?"

I couldn't think straight. It was like I was drowning in pain and I was struggling to keep my head above it all. "I... I..." My mouth was dry and nausea swept over me.

I think Malt saw I was struggling and she acted on her own. The board sat next to me and she positioned herself on my other side. She checked my body cursorily for breaks and placed her hands where she thought it was safe to do so. Slowly and evenly she began to roll me onto my back. I had no idea what damage this would do to me, but there was no choice. I had to get onto that board and this was the only way. My only prayer was that I survived until I got medical attention. *If* I got medical attention.

Malt pulled and grunted as she moved the board slowly toward the ramp of the ship. It took several minutes of heavy work on Malt's part to get me to the bottom of the ramp. An alarm went off and Malt disappeared inside the ship.

Moments later she re-appeared with a hand-held device. "Time to go," she said urgently. "Something is approaching fast."

I barely acknowledged the last comment as the board began to move steadily up the ramp to the inside of the ship. As it passed Malt she looked down at me. "It works on reversing magnetic polarization. You have to have metal underneath it for it to work."

If I had the strength I would have said "Good work, kid." The best I could do for now was smile.

"Let's get you strapped in." She looked nervously outside as the ramp retracted into the ship. The sound of the alarm rose to another level. "No time." I was left on the corridor floor. The ship vibrated as we took off.

"Oh, craz!" I heard Malt say. "She's latched onto the underside of the ship!" There was a banging on the outer hull, then a crumpling sound. We rose steadily and the banging stopped. "That is one crazy woman."

I felt a slight shift in air pressure as we left the atmosphere of the planet.

A short while later, Malt appeared with an atomizer in her hand.

"We're on auto pilot for Jarmin. This should help." A moment later the entire scene faded to black.

Chapter Seven

Hitching A Ride

My mind was awash with drugs and I struggled to make sense of the conversation carrying on beside me. I knew both voices; one I had been talking to just before I passed out and the other I hadn't heard for about eighteen months. I opened my eyes slowly and shut them again at the glare in the room. From what little I had glimpsed I knew I wasn't on the ship or back at the Noorthi settlement. Malt had said something about Jarmin. There wasn't a lot on Jarmin that I could remember, except a mining colony and a medical facility.

"Malt, be patient. She'll be up and about soon."

"But, doc, Beri and her kid are in trouble. Time is wasting."

"Listen to me, young lady, if Jordana leaves here before she's ready she'll fall flat on her face at the first swipe from this person you described."

I prized my eyelids open again. On one side of the tank was Malt, her four hands resting on the edge. On my left was Gorin. I hadn't seen him since Floric's death. He'd made a request to attend the burial and we'd obliged.

"What are you... doing... here?" I struggled to say the words.

"I could say the same thing, J. I thought you'd given up dying."

"I wish." I tried to laugh but ended up coughing.

"Settle down."

"Where am I?" I spoke slowly.

"The medical facility on Jarmin."

"And you?"

"Malt contacted me when the fight started. I don't even want to know about that one. I'm here for the fall out of some sort of a tree."

"Malt?" I croaked.

"Sorry, I tagged you." I heard the scuff of her boots on the floor.

"Again?" Gorin laughed out loud. "You are such an easy target, J."

"This time… okay." Without Malt's incessant mothering of me I'd be dead again. I would have to grow another toe to increase the count of her saving my life.

"What… wrong." I felt exhausted and maybe it was a question for another time, but I needed to know how much time I had to recuperate before I could go back.

"As you landed face-first, broken forearms and legs. You also have a couple of broken ribs, one of which shredded your spleen."

"How… long?"

"You should be up and around in a couple of days. The bones have been fused and the spleen replaced. It's now a matter of skin regeneration over the injury sites. We'll have you out of that goo in a couple of hours."

"How did you contact him?" I fixed my gaze on Malt, who had been suspiciously quiet.

"He gave me his ID code at the funeral in case we needed help. I thought we needed help."

Gorin dropped a small tablet into the gelatinous goo I had been laid in. A moment later I felt a sweeping lethargy that quickly pulled me down to sleep.

"You… cheat…"

"See you later, J." The last conscious sound was Gorin's easy chuckling.

You won this round old man.

†

True to his word, I was back in Bessie two days later. I still felt a little woozy, but I knew it would pass. I said goodbye to

Gorin in the hope that I wouldn't need his kind of help in the near future, but I suspected that I would. Jute was still in my way and I had to figure a way around her without getting myself killed.

Malt had made use of the time while I was being patched up. She had located Clea's home and we were heading there now to find out what was going on. I was going to have some harsh words with Clea's mother about the way she raised her child.

I lounged in the copilot's seat while Malt was driving. I never thought I would find myself in this position, but things had changed. She had earned her right to sit in the captain's chair, and besides Bessie had gotten used to her touch. It was then that I realized that my life had changed. In the past, anyone else flying Bessie would do so over my dead body. While Andrissa had stolen her and flew her without my permission, Malt had my approval.

"What did you find out?"

"Not a whole lot. It's on the border of Consortium space."

"How did you know about Peralis?" I knew I hadn't said anything to Malt.

"Because I heard Clea say it."

"For Carn's sake, Malt, make some sense."

"You weren't the only one I tagged."

"I'll talk to you about this later." But I took a bit of pleasure from the fact that I wasn't the only one Malt could fool. "Who?"

"Beri. I knew you'd want to keep an eye on her." Malt said smugly. The kid was nearly as arrogant as I was.

"All right, smart ass. What's going on?"

"Clea told her that you'd gone back to Heaven."

"I think they all know that's not true. I just came from a meeting room in the basement. Grit and the others were there, as well as a group of Alengolans. So that means that they don't know anything about Jute trying to kill me."

"Not that she's telling them." Malt said. She flipped the autopilot on and stood up. She moved to the computer and quickly did the computations for the hyperjump.

"Wait! You're hyper-jumping into Consortium space?"

"Sure. I thought that's what you wanted." She looked over her shoulder at me.

"Well, yeah, but it's not the sort of area you just go barging into. The borders are pretty closely guarded."

"Do you want me to go back to Jarmin and get Gorin?"

"Let's keep him out of this for the moment." I was trying to think of a way in. I brought up the holomap and looked for Peralis. It was on the far side of Consortium space from our present location. "We can't plow through the middle of this." My finger pointed to the large dark space that marked Consortium territory.

"But it's going to take too long to skirt around it."

Malt was right. Could we afford the extra few days it would take with the long route? Peralis could hold the missing piece of information to Clea's plans and motives. "It's a shame we can't hitch a ride."

"Maybe we can," Malt said thoughtfully.

"And do what? Stick our thumbs out and say 'are you going to Peralis?' I don't think so."

Malt continued to tap on the keyboard and the screen changed rapidly. "There's a Consortium freighter passing near Covaris in about twenty hours. We can hitch a ride with them through restricted space to the other side."

"Hitch a ride? Are you listening to yourself? What makes you think they're going to agree to that?"

"Because they won't know we're there."

Now I was confused. "It better be a damned good plan."

"I've fed the coordinates into the ship. If you can fly us to the rendezvous point, I'll make some modifications to the cloaking device to cover the ship. We can attach ourselves to the underside of the freighter, activate the cloaker and hitch a ride."

It might just work. "What's their destination time on the other side?"

"The mining colony on Jaxon's Hopper. We should save at least a day with the shortcut."

Malt was about the leave the cockpit to begin her work when I stopped her. "How's Beri?"

"She's fine."

"And Rice?"

"They're both fine." But Malt's expression told me something else.

"Malt. How are they?"

"They're safe for now."

"Turn Bessie around, Malt. If they're in trouble I need to be there."

"J!" Malt barked. "Get a hold of yourself. Going back now will only put you back in Clea's hands."

She was right. I was working on gut reaction and wasn't thinking straight. "I just can't leave them there."

"We've got no choice. Clea is hiding her true self from her sisters."

"And that's not easy, considering who she's trying to hide her feelings from." I will have to tease Grit about this when it's all over. I thought *when* and not *if* because *if* was not an option to me.

"Let's get moving. I don't want to take any longer than I have to." Even as I spoke I kicked Bessie into high gear, shoving another metaphorical rocket up her ass to increase her speed.

We had just come up to jump speed when the soft noise of being hailed stopped my scrutiny of the holomap.

"Hey, Malt!" Sasha's familiar voice held a hint of urgency. "I need to get in touch with J quickly."

"I'm here. Is that quick enough?"

"What are you…? Never mind. We've got a problem. The Noorthi potion doesn't work. In fact, if anything, it makes the patient worse."

"How worse?"

"Like dead. We lost Karra a few minutes ago."

"What did the Noorthi women say?" This was not good. I had enough to worry about without this.

"Our Noorthi re-checked the ingredients. It seems the leaves you sent were the wrong ones."

"Wrong ones?" I just knew it. Clea gave in way too fast for my liking. What the hell were we going to do? Grit was still on Alengola and without her we were screwed.

"What's up?" Malt asked as she stood in the doorway.

"Have you finished?"

"No, but I heard the conversation. What about Gorin? He's on Jarmin and we just left him."

"What's he doing there?" Sasha asked harshly. She didn't particularly like him because he was a very abrasive person. That was until he got to know you.

"I took J to see him. She was all broken up."

"Broken? What the craz have you been up to?"

"Later. We haven't got time for this chit-chat. We're trying to rendezvous with a Consortium freighter to get across Consortium space."

"They'll never let you—"

"Who said anything about getting permission? We're hitching a ride."

"Then you better hope you can hold your ship down with your fingernails because those guys carry a repelling force field for hitchhikers."

"Just great!" Things were just not going my way.

"Where are you now?"

"We're heading toward the Covaris system. We're meeting up just outside Consortium space."

There was silence for a moment before Sasha answered. "An old buddy of mine on Covaris may have a spare grappler for you. It makes a small hole in the shield to allow you attach you to the ship. You'll need to shut down the ship though, otherwise the feedback could blow everything on board."

"Sounds tricky," Malt said.

"It's either that or take the long way round."

"We don't have time for that. That Noorthi bitch has my kid!" Oh, and Beri of course.

"Ahh, that explains why you're heading in the opposite direction." The next time I saw Sasha I was going to smack her upside the head.

"The answer lies on the woman's home planet. Or I hope it does, otherwise it's going to be a wasted trip."

"You're risking everything on a gut instinct?"

"Wouldn't you?" I replied. I knew it was a long shot, but I was hoping for someone to say you're doing the right thing. It obviously wasn't going to be Sasha

"Time is short. You contact your buddy and I'll contact Gorin."

"I'll come and pick him up."

"No, I want you there, Sash. Keep an eye on those Noorthi women. Secure the leaves for Grit to have a look at when she gets back." *If she gets back....* Now why did I think that? Did I really believe it was all part of some conspiracy to wipe out the Juno Noorthi? I was being paranoid because I was worried about Rice and B. Right? Right. "Send Rales. I'll see if Gorin can meet him half-way to save time. I'll be in touch soon."

I broke the connection and stared out into space.

"What are you going to do?"

"You mean we, don't you?" I glanced over my shoulder at the young woman standing there. "Come here." I waved my hand for her to come. I stood and pulled Malt into a hug, my chin resting on the top of her head. Her four arms wrapped around by torso and she hugged me back hard. "Thanks."

"What's that for?"

"For just being here. Sometimes things…"

"Yeah, I know. It all gets a bit much sometimes."

"You got that right," I mumbled. Praise Carn! "No point in standing around. We've got a lot to do." And boy was that ever an understatement.

✝

We arrived at Covaris with a few hours to spare. I felt a shiver go down my spine as I studied the planet from the ship. This planet was the start of everything. A simple trip to Covaris turned into betrayal and abandonment on Rigeus. And the rest, as they used to say, is history. Rather than sitting in space, we opted to go down to the planet. There was still time to quickly stock up on supplies and get the grappler.

We barely made it back to the intersection point when the freighter appeared. Malt cloaked the ship as the Consortium ship hit the edge of our scanner range.

"Let's hope this works." If Malt had anything to do with it, the odds were good that it would. She was very capable and smart and I had complete faith in her abilities.

"If you want to back out, now is the time."

"No, we can't afford the extra time."

"You can't afford the extra time. I've got all the time in the universe."

I took a swipe at her. "Don't push it, young lady, or I won't take you on my next trip to Valos." Her smile dropped at the threat. Ever since our first trip to Valos, Malt had been begging me for another trip. "Not so funny now, huh?"

She sat down in the co-pilot's chair and sulked.

"Sorry, kid, I've outgrown the pouty mouth." I hadn't really, but I knew I had to be strong otherwise she'd think she could get anything she wanted with one sad look.

Bessie drifted idly while the freighter approached. I nudged her slowly toward the monolith, drawing the ship slowly alongside the vessel then pushing the thrusters, and finally the engines, to bring Bessie up to speed with our ride.

The cloak stayed solid as Bessie touched the hull. Malt activated the claws and they attached to the freighter with a clang. She adjusted the cloaking device for Bessie to blend in with the freighter hull. "All set."

I shut down the ship and the sound settled to a low hum. "Now we wait. How long?"

"About eighteen hours." Malt lifted her tablet from the dash and leaned back to read.

"Don't you like the new books?"

"The bio-implantation ones?" I nodded.

"Nah. I sort of grew up on these." She waved the tablet at me. "The newer ones are for the lazy."

I kept my mouth shut. If I had to read I'd probably go for the books that required little effort on my part. Malt glanced at me and laughed. She figured it out. Okay, so I was lazy.

"You should try it," she continued. "It'll give you some practice."

"And I'll have to tell that pretty young thing on Valos that you've been grounded for a very long time."

Malt sat up. "What pretty young thing?" I had her attention.

"Oh, just some luscious brunette who asked me your name."

"Really? On Valos?" She slumped back in her chair, feigning disinterest. "She's probably not my type anyway."

"Oh, she was definitely your type. She was breathing." Malt launched the tablet at me and I caught it easily. "Tsk tsk. Such a temper."

"There wasn't any brunette."

"You'll never know, Malt."

There was a rumble through Bessie. "It looks like they're getting ready to hyperjump."

This was strange, however, as I nearly left my lunch behind at Covaris. It was heavy and oppressive, and I felt like I was being squashed into the seat. "This is different," I drawled.

"It must be the fact that we're on the outside of the freighter."

"No kidding. I figured that part out myself. It could also be the fact that it's going a hell of a lot faster than Bessie ever could." I was ready to throw up.

"And we've got another eighteen hours of this."

"Just great." I pulled myself out of the chair and staggered down the corridor to the makeshift toilet. My lunch departed me as we crossed into Consortium space.

By the time I returned to my seat, Malt was engrossed in whatever she was reading on the tablet. I looked over her shoulder and was pleasantly surprised to find that it wasn't some research she was doing. When she was aware I was sneaking a peek she tipped the tablet toward herself. The kid was reading a romance.

I couldn't help it. I grinned at her. "That is so sweet. A love story. Is there any sex in it?"

"Why? Do you need a hand?"

I stopped. Did she say what I thought she just said? "Er."

"Sorry, J. That was out of line. No, there's no sex in it, at least not yet." She blushed then buried herself in the book.

"Is it that obvious?" I sat down in the chair and put my boots up on the dashboard.

"I... I was just embarrassed, that's all. I didn't mean anything by it," she stammered. She couldn't look me in the eye.

"Malt, look at me." I waited for her gaze to meet mine. "You know you can ask me anything, right? If you have a question, then ask." I saw that she was deciding whether to ask or not.

"It's none of my business."

I reached across the distance between the two chairs. "You're family. You can ask."

"You and Beri. Are you...?" She left the question hanging.

"No, and it's driving me crazy."

"What are you going to do?"

"I have no idea. At the moment it's too complicated to even try to think of a solution."

"How do you cope with... you know."

You know. I chuckled. The kid just couldn't say it. I studied Malt and realized that I probably shouldn't call her kid anymore. She had grown up and blossomed. Whoever she eventually found a life with was a very lucky woman. That is, if she got past me.

"Sometimes I don't. Sometimes it's necessary to take emergency action."

"You don't sleep with someone else do you?" She nearly looked appalled.

"No, but there are times when you have to take matters into your own hands."

I saw Malt trying to figure that out. Her furrowed brow gave way to a blush when she realized what I was talking about.

"But it's not the same thing," I continued. "I want love, damn it!"

"Beri loves you."

"She hasn't said it."

"But you can see that she does."

"That unspoken love doesn't keep me warm at night. It doesn't snuggle up and wrap its arms around me." My foot lashed out against Bessie. "Sorry." I patted the armrest. "I just wish she'd show some sign of affection besides an occasional chaste kiss."

"That's not the Noorthi way."

"I keep telling myself that, but it's hard. Her needs are being met, but what about mine? I'm sick and tired of being the one who has to give. I want to receive from time to time."

"Have you talked to Beri about this?"

"And what is she going to say, huh? Sorry, J, but that's the way it is? I know that."

I lifted my hands and rubbed them on my face. I was tired and cranky. No sex can do that to a person. "How many people know about this?"

"Everyone," she whispered.

"Everyone?" Oh, craz. "So our love life is the talk of the village?"

"For the past year or so."

I moved my feet to the floor and stood. "You tell those busybodies that what I do with my life is nothing of their freaking business!" I paced. "Who the hell do they think they are?"

"Settle down, J."

"Settle down?" I yelled.

"Shhhh. They'll hear us."

"What the....." I stopped and lowered my voice. Unspeakable words were about to pour out of me and I didn't want Malt to hear them. I stomped back to the hatch, grabbed my helmet and stuck it on my head. I let fly with the most colorful swear words I could think of, and then some. When I had run out of them I prayed that my new vocabulary skills could come up with a few more.

What are those words you said?

You don't want to know.

Maybe two minutes had passed and I was exhausted. I had put a lot of energy into my expletive-ridden tantrum. Sheepishly, I returned to the captain's seat.

"Feel better?"

"A little. It still doesn't solve my problem though."

"Don't ask me. I don't even know about half the stuff you talk about."

The last thing I wanted at any time was to be discussing sex with Malt and, in particular, my sex life. "Believe me, none of that's going to happen ever again."

"Why not talk to Sasha? She's probably done all that and more."

Okay, that was too much, saying that she was better at sex than I was. It was like saying she could pilot Bessie better than I could, and I knew that was impossible. "No, she hasn't." I said no more. End of discussion.

Malt shrugged her shoulders and went back to reading. It seemed that the only one worried about my love life was me.

I went into the corridor to the replicator and got myself a coffee synth. Maybe Malt had another tablet for me to read. This was going to be a long trip.

†

Finally we came out of hyperspace on the far side of Consortium space. Malt took a reading and plotted it on the holomap. We still had about another hour before we passed the Consortium frontier. It was too early to detach so I took the opportunity to eat. I sorted through the food stuffs we picked up on Covaris and returned to my seat munching on a prouda, its ripe flesh tantalizing my taste buds. I offered the fruit to Malt. "Want some?"

She looked at the fruit in my hand and then my face. "No, thanks." She put the tablet down and disappeared out the cockpit doorway. Moments later she returned with her own piece of fruit.

"I offered you some."

"Yeah, with your germs all over it." She bit into her own fruit, sat down and picked up the tablet to continue reading.

"There's just no pleasing some people."

"If you've forgotten, we have Monolial on Heaven. Do you want me to get sick?"

"I'm going to make you sick?" I didn't know whether I should be insulted or not.

"You never know. You've got Noorthi protection. I don't."

She did have a point, but it was a point made with little regard to my delicate sensibilities. Okay, maybe not delicate, but I did have feelings. "That's the last time I offer you my food."

"And I thank you for that." She took another bite out of the prouda.

"You've become awfully cocky around me, kid."

She looked over her tablet and raised an eyebrow.

"Feeling safe, are we?" I added.

She just grinned. Was it only three years ago since I found Malt and she was a frightened fourteen year-old who was so scared of strangers that she kept silent for quite a while? Now look at her. She was so at ease around me that she constantly took verbal swipes at me with her sharp tongue. We'd both come a long way, her and me, and it made me smile. "Just as well I like you."

"Or I could call in a favor or two for all those times I saved you."

"You're putting a price tag on that?"

"Of course not." She looked sheepishly at me.

"Just kidding." I reached across and waited for her to take a bite of her fruit. I pushed it into her face, covering her in sticky juice.

"Hey!"

"Shh, they might hear," I whispered. "That killed about five minutes."

Malt stood and went in search of something to clean up with, and her look of displeasure told me what she thought of my joke.

There is so much conflict within you.

So? What's it to you?

How am I supposed to work with you?

Oh no, no, no. You work for me, not with me.

You have so much to learn.

I picked up the discarded tablet and looked at it. I had tried to read it, I really did, but I had the attention span of Rice. Unless there was a fight, a sex scene or at least a decent wound I became bored easily. What I really needed was a tablet with pictures. Better still, the bio-implantation ones then I wouldn't have to waste my time by reading. No, I take that back. I'd read anything about twentieth century earth. Anything after that time was not worth the bio chip it was saved on.

I tossed the tablet a few feet across the cabin and it landed on Malt's seat a second before she re-appeared in the cockpit. I sighed deeply.

"It's fifty-seven minutes, J. Can't you keep yourself occupied for fifty-seven minutes?"

"No. I'm bored." I sighed again and Malt rolled her eyes. "Wake me up when we're ready to detach."

I stood up and went to find a quiet place to curl up for a nap. Not that I would sleep. I was too wired up to sleep.

✝

"J. Time to go."

"Are we there yet, Dad?"

"Yes, honey, we'll be there in a few minutes."

"Wha....? Where am I?" I said with a slur. I yawned. "I must have been more tired than I thought."

"Probably had something to do with all those extra parts the doc put in your body."

Maybe the injuries had taken their toll on me and I hadn't realized it. "Where are we?"

"We'll be detaching in about two minutes." Malt extended two of her hands to help me up. I was tempted to bat them away, but I saw Malt's concern in her eyes.

"Thanks, kid." Despite her offer, I did most of the work when she teetered forward with my weight. "Let's go find this Peralis." We couldn't waste any more time on this expedition than we already had.

"From what I've found out, Peralis is undergoing restoration. Something happened about seven years ago."

"I think I can guess what, or who, was responsible," I said as we moved into our seats. "A black hole called Clea."

"You think so?" Malt tightened her harness.

"The coincidence is too much to ignore. I'm hoping to find out what the woman has in store for the Noorthi, and if she is a Noorthi at all."

"Does she have the tattoo?"

"I didn't see it clearly, but it appears so."

"Then why would she do these things you think she's done? I thought it was impossible for the Noorthi to do wrong."

"You mean like it's hard-wired into their psyche?" I asked. "I can't say I've thought of it like that. She's got that giant of hers on a leash, that's for sure. That's very un-Noorthi-like."

Malt chuckled. "Un-Noorthi-like. Is there such a word?"

"I just invented it. It's a bit unwieldy though."

Malt reached out to the side and a moment later the ship fell away from the freighter. We floated aimlessly while we watched the massive ship continue on its journey.

"Do you think they know we're here?"

"No. The cloak is still firmly in place."

We waited a few more minutes to allow the vessel to sail out of scanner range before we started Bessie's engines. "Let's head that-a-way!" I cried, pointing at the direction out the front window. Malt shook her head and turned the ship around. "Like I said, that-a-way!" While I was still pointing out the window we had rotated one hundred and eighty degrees.

"The woman thinks she's a holocomic," Malt muttered.

"Things are going to get very serious soon enough, my child. Laugh while you can."

"I will when there's something funny to laugh about."

I sank down into my chair. "Everyone's a critic."

†

Luckily for us, Peralis was close and didn't require a jump. We arrived in orbit an hour later. The scanner didn't show a whole lot there. The only signs of life appeared to be a small sector of about a mile square. The landscape surrounding it was bare, so landing wasn't going to be an issue.

Malt put Bessie down gently and I silently applauded her skill. If nothing else, she was one person I was proud to have been involved with. I had changed her life and she had changed mine.

"Let's go see what's going on." I didn't think being armed was necessary so I didn't reach for a weapon. The air was breathable, if a little dry, and the natives didn't appear to be hostile. We walked down the ramp to step onto the dusty landscape. "What is it about me and deserts?"

"Sorry? Did you say something?"

"Nope, just making a social comment."

Our appearance hadn't caused much of a stir and we had to go in search of someone to talk to. We found a man scratching in the dirt, looking weary and downtrodden. Obviously living on Peralis wasn't easy.

"Excuse me, sir," I asked politely. "Have you heard of someone called Clea?"

He stood up from his planting and stared at me like I had insulted him. "Why do you ask?"

I glanced at Malt before addressing him again. "We've met a woman claiming to be a Noorthi named Clea. We wanted to make sure she was who she claimed to be."

"Noorthi? There are no Noorthi here. Never have been."

"Oh, thank you."

We were about to return to the ship when he spoke again. "We know of the demon Clea though."

"Demon?" My eyebrows rose.

"She was born here. Her mother couldn't handle her and took her to the Noorthi."

"And they accepted her?" I was surprised. From my dealings with them, they didn't accept outsiders lightly.

"Had no choice. The mother disappeared."

"And she's a demon?" Malt asked.

"Not for that. It's what she did after."

Black hole Clea was beginning to form and she was intent on sucking everything into the void. "What did she do?"

"You see this?" He indicated the barren landscape.

"She did that? I thought Noorthi were peace loving."

"Not this Noorthi. Her and her giant pet swept through our settlement, leveling it."

"Did she give any reason?"

"Said something about a quest to cleanse the universe of those not worthy of redemption," he said angrily. "I think it was more revenge."

"Sounds like someone we know. So there's no Noorthi around here?"

"Try Exeter." He went back to his planting.

"Thank you. You've been most helpful." He didn't look up.

Malt and I walked back toward Bessie. "Now what?" Malt asked.

"We try Exeter."

Chapter Eight

Hide And Seek

Exeter was in the same system as Peralis so it was only a twenty minute flight. Its landscape was similar to the planet we had just left. Had black hole Clea struck here as well? Was she so angry at the universe that she was destroying it piece by piece? Sooner or later she was going to run out of places to live.

The main city was located on the far side of the planet from where we were looking. The Noorthi compound, however, was strangely quiet. From our view in Bessie it appeared intact. There was a bare strip of land a little north of the encampment and I put Bessie down softly. While I wasn't expecting trouble, this time I took a weapon.

"What's the matter with this woman?" Malt asked.

"She's pissed off at the universe. That's her problem."

"You think so?"

"I'm hoping that's it, otherwise she's nuts and is intent on cleansing the universe of those not worthy of redemption." I paraphrased the old man from Peralis.

"Is she going to kill the Noorthi?"

"I hope to Carn not, but I may have to go on that assumption." I looked at Malt's concerned face. "Don't worry about it. I won't let her harm our girls."

But Malt didn't look convinced. To achieve that I had to get past Jute, and so far I hadn't succeeded. "That thing of hers is tough."

"And are you saying I'm not?" I gave her a shocked look. "I won't let Jute harm the Noorthi." I also silently promised myself that, although I refrained from making the promise verbally.

"Uh huh, and what with? A fusion bomb? Because that's about as close as I'm going to let you get. I've picked up the pieces once already, and I won't do it again."

"She got the jump on me," I explained. "Stop worrying." But worry she did. My constant disregard for my own safety was wearing on Malt. But I had to do this. How would it look if the Ratha backed away from a fight? I know I had to pick my fights, but at some point in the future I had to go through Jute to get to Clea. That was the way it was. "If I can end this without violence then I'll take it, okay?" Yeah, right. I couldn't solve anything peacefully. It was physically impossible.

We stepped up to the Noorthi Great House and found it had doors on it like Juno. "You knock," I told Malt, "you've got more hands."

While she did a rolling knock that went on and on I looked around. The vegetation was almost non-existent and blackened, like a fire had destroyed it. Clea was one angry woman.

When I felt that Malt had been knocking long enough I stopped her. I tested the door and it opened. We stepped inside and called out, "Hello? Anyone home?" My voice echoed around the large foyer. "This is not good."

"Malt, you take the right, I'll take the left. Comlink me if you find something." I watched Malt walk away. I don't know exactly what I was expecting to happen. Would a Noorthi or two ambush her and wrestle her to the floor? It was hardly likely, unless they'd given up their Noorthi ways. After all, when I first met Epi she threw rocks at me.

I left her checking each room along the corridor, while I investigated my side of the house. Where was everyone? "Hello? Anyone here?" Maybe it was the words. "Harki! Soona ish?"

I opened the first door and found it was sleeping quarters. It looked like it had been used recently, so someone had to be nearby. They were hiding. Were they fearful that Clea had returned?

The decor of the House was interesting. It had neither the ostentation of Alengola nor the Spartan decor of Heaven, instead being somewhere in the middle of the two extremes.

As I looked around further, I found artifacts and signs of habitation. The sisters were somewhere. They wouldn't abandon their religious heritage, Grit had taught me that.

"Malt," I murmured on the comlink, "Any luck yet?"

"There doesn't seem to be anyone around, but it doesn't look abandoned either."

"My thoughts exactly. On Alengola the sisters took refuge in a below-ground room for reflection. I might check it out to see if these sisters have one, as well. Keep checking this floor."

"Right."

I half expected Malt to argue, but she didn't. It took me several minutes to find the stairs leading down to the basement. As I descended, the light faded until it was pitch black. I reached for my torch and lit a path in front of me. It was completely dark. Where had they gone? I switched off my torch in frustration and tried to think in the dark. Yeah, I know, me thinking. It wasn't the best option in the light, and it didn't work well in the dark either.

I found a wall in the blackness and leaned against it. I slid down to the dirt floor and contemplated what to do next. We needed to talk to the Noorthi to find out what Clea was like, because it would determine how I would approach her. If I chose the wrong way I could end up killing us all.

I was about to give up trying to think at all when I saw a sliver of light at the base of one of the stone blocks. Now why didn't I think of that? Oh, that's right, I couldn't think in the dark. Or daylight for that matter. Or awake. Or asleep. Well, you get the point. I was more a woman of action than a thinker. That's what Malt kept complaining about. I was usually in danger before I even thought whether there was danger to worry about. Hey, I was that kind of gal.

I contemplated whether to announce myself or not, but doing so might make them run for it. I stood and inched my way along the wall, not using the light in case they caught a glimpse of it under the door. My hands ran around the edges of the rock to search for anything that would trigger the opening, but there was nothing obvious. I put my shoulder to the wall and pushed. There was a slight creak. As the noise had effectively announced me, I shoved hard to get inside the hidden room before they had a chance to do anything.

The rock pivoted on a central hinge and I nearly fell in.

"Ladies," I said, right before they started screaming at me. I held up my hands to try and calm them down but it only seemed to inflame the situation.

"Malt!" I yelled into the comlink, "Downstairs, now!" I didn't wait for a reply before I replaced the communicator in my pocket.

"Sha ni turkashik na!" I spoke firmly and quietly.

The noise slowly abated, the Noorthi sisters standing there staring at me. "Yeah, I speak Noorthi. I won't hurt you."

"Who... are... you?" one young woman asked haltingly.

"Jordana Laren, young lady. My Noorthi are from Juno and I am their Ratha."

"Ratha?" That word she and the others knew.

I took off my wristband and held up my wrist to the light. "Ooohhh." I was like a child's convention. I had shown them a trick and they were suitably impressed. The young woman tentatively reached out and ran her finger across the scar.

"Ratha-nishki!" she announced. They all dropped to one knee and bowed their heads. That was when Malt stepped into the room.

"Showing off again?"

"Very funny. They saw the scar and did this. The same thing happened on Alengola."

"It must mean something."

"Maybe," I said. I knew what it meant but I wasn't going to tell Malt just yet. I was still trying to get my own head around what it meant. "Can anyone speak?"

"I can." A young woman, barely a teenager really, stepped forward.

"And who are you?"

"Canthi." She glanced at Malt then back at me.

"Hello, Canthi. Do you know of a Noorthi named Clea?" There was a collective gasp. "I'll take that as a yes."

"Why do you ask?"

"Presently she is on the Noorthi home planet of Alengola. She is claiming to be Ashaltea-Sa, but I doubt her claim. What can you tell me?"

"Only a true-born Noorthi can claim that title. The daughter of an Ashaltea."

"That's why I'm here. Is she the daughter of an Ashaltea?" I already knew the answer to this one, but I started with something easy for them to talk about.

"No. She is *wurabi*, an outsider."

"I thought you didn't take outsiders."

"We do not." An older woman stepped out of the crowd. "Her mother pleaded with us to take her."

"Why?"

"She felt her daughter was in need of some order in her life. She was willful and wild and very resistant to our ways."

"Why didn't you just return her to her mother?"

"The woman died not long after Clea was admitted. She had nowhere else to go."

"So what did you do?" Malt asked. When she finally came forward the Noorthi stared at her, four arms and all.

"What could we do? Turning her away in her time of need was against our Way."

"She did things we would never do," Canthi said.

I was afraid to ask. "Like what?"

"She lied. She stole." The young woman spat out the words like they were poison.

"And we think she killed. Our Ashaltea mysteriously became ill, as did her daughter, leaving us without a leader."

It seemed that Clea was a creature of habit. Eliminate the leadership then move in. "Let me guess. She offered to take over."

"Not long after that she nominated a Ratha."

"A metal woman about eight feet tall?" I responded

"How do you know?" Canthi inched closer.

"Because that same woman is at Clea's side on Alengola."

"She cannot be stopped," the older woman said.

"She cannot be stopped… yet. I will do my best to end this." I was making another promise that I might not be able to keep. What was I doing? "Did Clea say why she was doing this? Was it revenge for being abandoned or was it something else?"

"She kept those thoughts very much to herself. She could not easily be read."

"Did anyone catch a thought?" I looked around the sea of faces hopefully. "An idea, a flickering image, a single thought? Anything?" It looked like the trip was not going to be wholly successful. We had part of the information but not the important piece.

None of the sisters offered, but I saw that Canthi had an internal conflict. I stepped up next to her. "Did you hear something?"

"I… I don't know." She looked around at her sisters. "I think I imagined it."

"Tell me what you know. It may help."

"Those who are not worthy will perish," she said.

Canthi didn't imagine it. The Noorthi would have no concept of retribution, but I knew Clea did. I patted her arm. "Thank you."

"What does it mean?" I saw the confusion on her face.

"It's something that you didn't imagine, child."

"I am not a child!" she said. "I will be accepted soon." My eyes glanced at her wrist and saw it was unadorned.

"Congratulations. The sisters will be blessed with a true believer." She beamed at me. I had said the right thing. "Now you can return to your duties. We are here alone." They looked at one another uncertainly. "I'll protect you."

Those three words were enough. The sisters filed out of the hidden room, up the stairs and out into the sunlight. Outside, I got a good look at them. They were slightly different again from their sisters, and yet still held that unknown mystique that marked them as Noorthi.

"Something wrong?" Malt had obviously been observing me as I was observing the Noorthi.

"I was just thinking about how the Noorthi look different wherever we go. They're the same, but different at the same time."

Malt glanced at the women standing around waiting for some sort of direction.

"Yeah. I suppose where and how they live has a lot of influence on them."

"I bet none of these women even knew there was a home world. They've been separated from one another for so long they knew little of the sisterhood's existence outside their own world."

"And what are you going to do?" Malt asked, "Bring them all together?"

"Now that would be just plain cruel."

"So what do we do now?"

"Now we go and get our girls."

"And Clea?"

"Well, she's about the most dangerous thing out there right now."

"Yeah?"

"Yeah. She's a pissed off crazy woman who thinks that every living thing is not worthy to exist. I've yet to decide whether she thinks that includes herself or not."

"And is that important?"

"It tells me whether she's planning to sacrifice herself in this mission of hers or she has an escape plan."

"And?"

"And, my dear Malt, that, in turn, gives me an answer as to whether I have any leverage with her life or not. If she's prepared to die, there's nothing I can bargain with. We've found out all we can do in the time we've got. Let's get going."

I addressed the sisters. "Thank you for your help. You don't need to fear her return."

"How can you say that?" the older woman asked.

"Because I am Ratha and it is my duty." There. I admitted it out loud.

I turned to leave. "Wait! Can I come with you?" The young Noorthi named Canthi asked.

"Why?" I had a sudden flashback to a young girl named Rice. Her curiosity signed her death warrant.

"I feel that my calling is elsewhere. I cannot explain it."

I smiled. I knew that feeling. "And what do your sisters say?"

"I...," she hesitated. "I have not asked them."

"So it was a spur of the moment thing, huh?" She blinked at me confused. "You only made the decision now."

"I did." I saw the quick glance at Malt. "There is so much to learn, so much to discover."

"My sisters. Canthi wishes to accompany me. Do you have any objection?"

They glanced at one another.

"Her destiny may lie elsewhere, in the service of the Noorthi."

"She is not anointed."

"I will see to it personally."

They stared at Canthi in awe. I didn't see what the fuss was about, but it seemed I had given the girl a special honor. Little did they know that Grit would be doing the ceremony and not me. If I tried to tattoo someone I'd probably end up with a twisted flower and wilted stamens. No, leave the tattooing to the professionals was always my motto.

"Go, Canthi. Collect your things." I gave the girl a gentle push. We were in a hurry and there wasn't time for niceties. While she was gone I asked another question. "Did Clea hurt anyone here, or asked for something strange to be done?"

The Noorthi woman who had spoken before replied, "We had a tremor or two while she was our Ashaltea. She claimed it was the Great One speaking to her."

"Where is your ochre mine?"

The woman pointed to her right. "About two miles that way. We haven't been there in a while though."

"You have stores of ochre?"

"No," she answered, "We have had no need of it after Clea left."

"Why not?"

"Clea claimed the ochre was useless. That it was nothing more than mud."

"That way, you said?" I pointed to my left.

"About two miles."

"Malt, go get the ship and bring a large canister and a video comlink. We should document this." I was already on the move. "Tell Canthi to wait for our return. Malt, meet me at the mine."

My journey started as a walk, slowly building up to a trot, and finally ending in a jog. My stamina was in serious doubt as I breathed heavily. I wasn't even half-way there and I was gasping for air. When I got home I needed to get into shape. The three year holiday I had just taken had eroded away my strength and resilience. No wonder Jute beat the crap out of me.

By the time I reached the two mile mark, Malt had already landed and was leaning against the ramp with her arms crossed. "What took you so long?" I bit my tongue because I knew she would say that. The kid couldn't help herself.

"I... took... <wheeze> ... the scenic.... <puff>..... route."

"Maybe if you took the direct route you wouldn't be blowing so hard." I decided next time Malt could do the running and I'd take the easy route.

I didn't stop walking and moved to the mine. I wanted samples collected quickly so we could get on the ship and I could have a sleep. "Have you got the video on?"

"Yes, J." I heard the disdain in her voice.

I turned on the torch attached to my shoulder patch and waited for it to illuminate my way. The mine was similar in setup to the Alengolan site, but without the glowing walls. There was a familiar smell about it and I scooped up a handful. I brought up to my nose and breathed deep. Where had I smelled it before? Before Malt cringed I dipped my finger into the mud and tasted it. That was it.

"Spread out, Malt. We have to find the cavern that leads down toward the core of the planet. We'll need rope, hover pads, laser, weapons, light generator and a videotag for cataloguing."

"We've run out of rope and we don't carry the hover pads any more. Expecting trouble?"

"I hope not, kid, I have a feeling that Clea has left a present behind and I want to intercept it before anything can possibly happen."

We worked in the mine filling the storage canisters with the stuff and marking it Exeter. It had the distinctive taste of the ochre in the bags that were being thrown into the chasm on Alengola.

We pushed on farther into the mine and found the stairs leading down. It was steep and slick with the oily ochre. We held on tight to the railing as it wound its way downward, the staircase wrapping around a central pivot point that was used as a pulley system to bring up and lower ochre parcels.

"Anyone home?" I called out.

"What did you do that for?"

"Just seeing if anyone was down there." No, it was to see if the little shining bacteria on Alengola inhabited the ochre here, as well. The walls remained dark all the way down. I began to wonder when we would reach bottom when I ran out of steps. Unaware that I had stopped, Malt slammed into the back of me.

"About freakin' time," I muttered. I didn't want to insult any ghosts, demons, spirits or sprites that might he hanging around in the depths of the planet, but it was a long way down

"What exactly are we looking for?"

"Something that doesn't look right."

"And if everything doesn't look right?" Malt persisted

"Something that looks like it might explode."

"Oh." Malt went silent.

I began move away from the stairs but Malt seemed content to loiter around them. "Come on."

"But the explosion...."

"Honey, if it explodes it's not going to matter where you stand." Now I had her worried. "Let's find this thing and get out of here." Clea's obvious history of using explosives was making me nervous.

I followed a passageway that headed downward. Based on Alengola, Clea placed the ochre as close to the core of the planet as she could.

"And ochre does this?" Malt asked.

"From what I saw Jute do, the ochre reacts with the heat of the core of the planet and bam!" I smacked my hands together and Malt jumped. I laughed.

"Don't do that!" she said nervously.

"From what I've seen so far, each ochre mine has its own distinctive properties. The mine in Rigeus that Grimm was interested in could be modified to be a mind control drug. Luckily he never discovered the additive to make it that. The ochre mine here has explosive properties."

"And the Alengolan ochre?"

"I'm not sure yet, but it has a bacterial component that makes it glow in the dark."

"Really?" I heard the scientific curiosity in Malt's voice.

"I have a job for you when we get back to Alengola. I've got some relics and jars of ochre that I want you to recover while I get Beri and the others out of the Great House. Maybe Canthi can help you with the plants."

"Sure thing. Where's the hole?"

"I've already brought them out. They're buried at the base of a few trees in line with the front of the Great House entrance." I stopped and turned to face her, grasping her shoulders with my hands. "This is very important, Malt."

"All right." She looked at me strangely.

"No, this is Noorthi history. If we don't take care, it could be lost forever."

"I understand. What's the problem?"

"The problem is, Malt, is that it's more important than me. You have to protect it with your life."

"It's that important."

"To you, Malt, it's the most important thing in the universe. But first we have to save this planet."

"Are you sure it's in danger?"

"No, but there's only one way to find out." I shone my light around the cavern and found a passageway in the far corner. "Are you coming?"

"Do I have to?"

"Well, no, but if I get into trouble...." I left the comment hanging because I knew she couldn't resist.

"Let's get this over with." She brushed by me and stomped off down the path.

"That's my girl." I followed Malt down the passage and I saw her displeasure in every angry line of her body. Oh, yeah, she was not happy.

The tunnel went on forever, or so it seemed. The path tilted slightly downward and became a little steeper. Surely, we must've been close because the heat was increasing with every step.

There was a familiar faint red glow up ahead. As expected, we came out on a small ledge overlooking a chasm. On the far side was a platform laden with sacks of ochre, however this particular platform was about to give way. I saw that a few of the support beams had been dislodged while a few more were on the verge of breaking.

"Now what?" I heard the edge in Malt's voice.

"We've got to get across that."

"We?' Her voice rose to a squeak.

"All right, me."

Malt looked at our supplies and then studied the layout of the cavern. "Give me your belt."

"My belt? Why not yours?"

She answered me by removing her own belt. Sighing, I did as she asked. To my surprise my pants stayed up. It was then that I realized that living on Heaven wasn't good for my health. I had developed a few bad habits and put on a couple of extra pounds in recent years. Without a word I handed her the belt.

Malt pulled one of her tools out of her pocket and fiddled with the clasps on the belts. She somehow managed to get them connected together like a long rope. "Do you think you can snag the rock outcrop up there?" She pointed to a small overhang above the chasm.

"That?" I said in disbelief. The outcrop was fine. It was the roof of the cavern that worried me. There must have been a gap of about two feet between the outcrop and the roof. Getting the belts into that small spot would be no mean feat. "Sure, no problem."

Malt clicked her tongue and gave me a look. She obviously didn't appreciate my devil-may-care attitude at such a tense time. Someone had to keep our spirits up.

I stood at the edge of the ledge and Malt handed me the belts. I felt the weight of them in my hands and eased out a small length. I let it swing back and forth, trying to find some sort of rhythm in the action. When I felt the time was right I let one end go, aiming for the small target given me. I didn't even realize that I was holding my breath as I let go, and it was only when the belt buckle banged against the stone that I noticed the pain in my chest.

"That's one."

"You're keeping count?"

"You said, sure no problem. I'm just wondering how long it's going to take."

"Do you want to try?" I pulled in the belts and offered them to Malt.

"No! No, you're doing fine." She held up all four hands and backed away.

"Then stop counting!" I was getting irritated.

While she didn't count aloud I knew she was doing it in her head. By the time I reached nineteen, I was about to write the exercise off as impossible.

Nothing is impossible.

I don't see you helping.

You need to focus.

Focus. Smocus. It's impossible.

And that is why you fail.

You think you can do better? I could nearly feel an air of smugness in my head. Your hubris is showing.

Try once more.

Okay, it's your dime.

What?

Never mind.

To appease it I tried one more time. As I let go, I growled, "Come on!"

With bated breath I watched the belt sail through the air, clunk against stone, skitter off and fall through. "Craz!" I did it. Except that the buckle was dangling in mid air instead of winding around the rock to secure itself. "Now what?"

Malt stood there with an open mouth. It took her a second or two to realize that I'd asked her a question. It all looked rather comical with her mouth still open and her absently reaching into her pocket to take out her gizmo tool. She tore her gaze away from the hanging buckle and fiddled with her tool, finally aiming it at the buckle and switching it on.

In slow motion the buckle moved, attaching itself to a metal piece farther along the belt.

"And you expect me to trust that, do you?" I seriously doubted that it would take my weight.

"You got a better idea?"

"I could try floating across."

"Be my guest."

She had me. I tugged on the belts and they held the pressure. But pulling was completely different to putting my entire weight on it. Ahead of me was fifteen feet of empty space. "Could that thing of yours levitate the bags over here?" Hell, I was up for anything at this point.

"Yeah, right."

"Really?"

"No," she said emphatically. So much for that idea. "Are you going to cross, or can we go?"

"I can't leave it like that."

"Then cross."

I had put the swing off as long as I could without admitting defeat. It was time to be Ratha or back away. I pulled on the belt hard and it held firm. Before I had a chance to think any more about it I jumped off. Either exhilaration or sheer terror carried me across that chasm, because when I reached the other side my heart was beating wildly out of control. "Whoo!" I yelled. I barely stopped myself from swinging back. There was no point in risking my life again. I'd save that for when I had to leave.

Malt shook her head.

"What?"

"I finally realize that you can't help yourself. Putting your life in danger is like a drug to you."

Maybe it was, and that was a dangerous state to be in. Sooner or later my luck would run out.

Listen to the girl.

Don't start. It's going to take time to break that habit.

A habit that could kill you.

I know that. I do... I think.

"Let's dismantle this thing and get going. I have an itch to see what Rice is up to." That was true, but more importantly I wanted to be off this planet.

"Then *you'd* better get to it." She secured the makeshift rope under a rock.

I looked around the tiny ledge I was standing on and grinned wickedly at Malt.

"What?"

I picked up a packet of ochre and threw it hard at Malt. "Catch!"

"What the craz are you trying to do? Blow us up?" She jiggled the cloth bag in her arms.

"Did you just cuss, young lady?"

Malt glared at me. "I'm serious here. You could have killed us both."

"It's one packet, Malt."

"And it may only take one packet to blow this planet up." She was really nervous about this.

"Okay. There's nowhere to put the packets here. We'll have to carry them out."

"All of them?"

"Yep. The whole lot. Put that down in the corridor, then come back and get ready to catch." Malt slouched and carried the packet like it weighed fifty pounds. Not a happy at all.

You are too wasteful with life.

Look, Book, I bore easily so don't distract me.

Yet how do you learn?

Usually by making mistakes.

But this mistake could kill you.

Then I'll remember it well.

I kept the packets moving at a steady pace, throwing them gently into Malt's waiting arms. That was until the last few pieces, which sat precariously near the edge of the platform. "Any suggestions?" I asked Malt.

She had seen me try to get them earlier, but when the platform dipped, I backed away.

"You could always use your pants."

"My… pants." Sometimes I wished Malt made sense.

"Take them off and tag the packets with them."

"Can't we use something else like, say, your pants? I am not taking off my pants."

"Fine. I'll begin moving the ochre up the path." She turned to walk away.

"Hey! Are you going to leave me here? You could at least give me the rope."

"Use your pants," she called over her shoulder.

"Malt! You get back here right now!" I was using my grown up mommy voice on her but she was ignoring it. "You are in so much trouble."

"Get the packets and we can both leave." I had to strain to hear her as she walked away from me.

So it was going to be like that. Malt wasn't backing down, which left me with no recourse. I undid my pants and dropped them. I wasn't too stubborn to stand there for hours on end to win a point. Now Malt would say the direct opposite—that I would be *that* stubborn to sit around for days waiting for her to give in. I'm not like that. Really. Am I? Maybe. No. Unless someone pissed me off. I wouldn't be so childish at a moment like this where our lives were at stake. At least I don't think so. No, definitely not. Then again… Do I have to answer this question right away?

I managed to get the crotch of my pants around a few more packets of ochre and I slowly pulled them toward me. There were two left sitting right at the far edge of the slowly disintegrating platform.

I tested the boards with my foot and they creaked ominously. This was not a good sign. The packets were out of range from the ledge and the only way to get them was to go out on the platform

127

and get them myself. My only solution was to spread my weight over a wide area.

That was how Malt found me when she finally came back. I was spread out on the platform, slowly inching my way out over the chasm. I just couldn't help it. I looked down. Below me rose a red hot heat from a bubbling mass of molten rock that fed it.

"J!" Malt barked, and I jumped.

"Don't do that!" My heartbeat thumped loudly in my ears.

"Are you crazy?" she hissed loudly.

I tried to lasso the final packet with my pants but to no avail. "I... can't... reach... it."

"Then leave it."

I looked across at her and she was fidgeting. "What if it falls in?"

"Like you said, it'll probably just set off a tremor."

"That's not what you said–"

"J, please! Get off that before you fall in!" Malt was frantic.

"Okay, kid." She was terrified that I was going to die. Was she like this every time I did something stupid? I admit I'd never given any thought to consequences before. There was something to be done, so I did it.

Trying to crawl backward on the platform wasn't as easy as it was forward. Every time I tried to shift my weight to my forearms to push backward the wood creaked. "Er. I'm stuck."

"What?"

"If I lean forward it's going to break." Just as I said 'break it' did just that. The wood lurched forward and I watched helplessly as the last packet slid off the platform. My gaze followed it down to its final destination and a second later the cavern shook. Bits of wood began to fall away underneath me, the platform's lean increasing with each support beam crumbling. "Oh, craz." This was going to be my last uttered word.

Now's the time to leave.

It is not your destiny to die here.

Fine, but I don't want you complaining in the afterlife.

Something grabbed my ankles tightly. I glanced over my shoulder to see Malt hanging on for grim death. She was vainly trying to pull me but my weight was too much. One of her hands let go and grabbed the belt rope. "Here, grab onto this!"

She let it go and it swung back across the chasm. Blindly, I stuck out my arm and snagged it as it passed by. As my last lifeline, I hung onto it with both hands. Malt let go of my feet and I felt the drag as the rope carried me out over the open hole. This particular adrenaline rush shot through my body like fire. It was all too much, and I was glad to find the other side. I sent the rope back to Malt and dropped to kiss the ground. My tongue touched the ochre and I felt a tingle through my body. It was like another piece of a jigsaw puzzle was slid into place, but I couldn't see the complete picture just yet.

Moments later Malt was at my side and handed me my pants and belt. I looked up to see the rope gone. The kid was quick to dismantle the thing. Obviously, she didn't want to hang around any longer than necessary.

"Let's get the ochre to safety." Once my pants and belt were back in place, I felt like my old self again.

We spent the next hour moving the ochre to higher ground, storing it away in the upper cavern where the staircase was. We took a couple of sacks as samples and made our way to the surface. We had one more stop to pick up our passenger before heading back to Alengola.

Why had I so readily said yes to Canthi coming along? On second thought, she should have stayed here where she belonged. Did I see a little bit of me in her? I honestly didn't know why I agreed.

She should stay here.

Even Book was agreeing with me.

She should be given the chance to see the universe. Everyone should have at least one chance to do that.

Her path does not lie with yours.

My gut feeling then and there was telling me to listen to Book, but I didn't. Was I going to rue my decision, or was it a matter of worrying about Rice's death again?

Chapter Nine

When Is A Plan Not A Plan?

We were on our way back to Alengola when Sasha hailed me.

"Why aren't you on Heaven?" That was my first question.

"Gorin wanted me to find you."

"Why?" I interrupted. "What's wrong?"

"Nothing's wrong. Things are fine. He wanted the sisters to be immunized before they came home, to stop the disease from re-infecting the colony."

"Oh, I suppose we can do that." It sounded reasonable to me. "Who's looking after the sisters?"

"Dad is."

"Right." I could just see Rales trying to control a hundred women who would ignore his every word. Sasha would be lucky to see her dad again with hair still on his head because he would have ripped it out long before then. "Where are you?"

"I'm heading toward Stereng."

"We're about two hours out from Exeter."

"How about I meet you at Jola? That's another two hours for you on a heading of 173982.001."

"But you're well on your way—"

"Never mind that. I can take a short cut."

"That takes you close to the Consortium border."

"Do you want the serum or not?"

"Why not...." I was about to suggest that we just meet up at Stereng when I had a thought. "Okay in two hours then. In the meantime, do you have a buddy in the Stereng system that you can call in a favor from?"

"Maybe. Why?"

"I'm looking for a freighter to transport a hundred passengers."

"Why?"

"Just in case I have to get everyone off the planet in a hurry."

"Why?"

"Look, just… just… just do it, okay?" If she said why again I would scream.

"Why?"

"Aarrgghhhh," I bellowed over the comlink.

"I'll take that as a 'no'." The comlink went silent and Malt stared at me.

"I'm thinking it all in my mind."

And I can hear it.

"Change course for Jola."

"Why?" When she heard my teeth grind Malt fell silent and changed the heading.

Malt remained quiet for the two hours. I'm not sure what the expression on my face was, but she kept sneaking a look at me. Maybe I should go and talk to the girl.

I stopped at the replicator and requested two drinks, a synth coffee for me and water for Canthi. The girl was sitting in her chair, her fingers grasping the armrest firmly.

"Hey," I said gently.

Her head shot up and she looked terrified.

"Don't worry. Malt is an expert pilot." I handed her the cup and her shaking hand took it. "Are you okay?" It was a stupid question because I saw she was anything but. "Do you want to go home?"

"This is my first flight."

"No kidding? I couldn't have guessed."

Do not insult her intelligence.

But the girl smiled. "That's better."

I do not understand. You said something condescending and yet she smiled. Why?

Arrgghhh.

Perhaps it is a question for another time.

"This is new to you, but everything is fine. We'll be on the Noorthi home planet soon. We are making a small detour to pick something up."

"Detour?"

"Going somewhere else first before the Noorthi. If you wish, you can go with a friend of mine straight back to my home planet."

"And not see the... what did you say... the home planet?"

I smiled. The girl was curious about her heritage. "Fine. You can come with us."

She took a sip from her cup, then another. The cool water acted like a sedative. Each sip made her calmer. I sat with her for a while, sipping my own coffee synth. I was happy that she decided to come with us because her testimony would help dethrone Clea. We had an ochre sample and the video evidence but the word of a native Noorthi would be irrefutable.

As the time approached for the rendezvous I left Canthi meditating, her quiet murmuring fading away as I moved forward. Now all that was left to do was the rendezvous with Sasha, make the swap and head for Alengola.

✝

"Hey J, you out there?" Sasha's call came on time. We had just arrived near Jola and were scanning nearby space for her.

"Yeah, just arrived."

"Be there in ten." I watched as Sasha's ship came into the edge of our scanner range. She was quickly upon us and a few minutes later her ship was docking with Bessie.

I opened the hatch and Sasha stood there in the doorway. "Howdy stranger," I said.

"Er... howdy." I knew I already had Sasha confused.

"Can I come aboard?"

"Sure." She stepped aside and allowed me to enter her ship. I wandered into the cockpit and sat down in the copilot's chair.

"How was the trip?"

"Fine. Why?"

I took a deep breath and let it out slowly. "No reason. You know this area pretty well. Is there a shortcut to Stereng?"

"I'll send the route directly to Malt. Is there something else you're here for?"

"Do you have the serum?"

"Let me get it for you."

"Great." I nestled back into the seat and Sasha left me with a quizzical look on her face. There really wasn't a need to see Sasha personally, but I was glad for a break from Malt's company just for a little while. What I think I really wanted was to be sitting on the plateau on Heaven. I was looking for a place where I could find some peace. Unfortunately, Sasha's ship wasn't it either. I was homesick.

Sasha stood in the doorway. "Great. Where is it?"

"Malt met me at the hatch. I gave it to her."

"Then that's it."

"Looks like it." Sasha stood there expectantly. "Is there something else?"

"No, nothing else. I think I just wanted a change of scene."

"Rrrigghhtt. A change of scene."

"Okay, I was getting grumpy in there. If I didn't get out I was going to explode."

"And I'm sure Malt didn't want to clean up the mess."

"She's trying to be my mother, Sash. I don't need a mother."

"That's not what I heard."

"What sort of crack is that?"

"An honest one? If Malt doesn't look after you, I'm sure you'd already be dead."

"Many times over. She's already saved me once on Alengola." I didn't dare mention Exeter.

"Already? I didn't hear about that one."

"No-one's seen you recently."

"She means well, J."

"I know that! But it doesn't stop the constant watching from being annoying."

The alarm went off and I looked up to see a tiny speck in space approaching rapidly. The screen brought up the source of the speck. "Consortium cruiser!"

"How far?"

"Twenty thousand clicks and closing fast. Craz!" I hit the comlink. "Malt! Get the hell out of here! It can't follow both of us." Sasha was already on the run back to the hatch. "Ten seconds, Malt. We'll meet up at Fornia." I felt the slight rumble as the hatch closed. "Get going!"

I gunned the engines and took off in the direction of the cruiser. Sasha's agonized cry told me my acceleration wasn't smooth. I didn't have a choice here. I needed to attract the cruiser's attention away from an escaping Malt. When the vessel's shape was discernible I changed direction, heading off at a right angle from the cruiser's trajectory.

"Come on, come on," I muttered. Would it follow? The tiny blip of Malt's ship disappeared off the screen and I held my breath. The Consortium ship stayed on course for Bessie and I felt the pounding of my heart. *Please, change direction.*

As if it heard my thought, the cruiser changed direction for us. "Oh oh."

"Oh oh? What oh oh?" Sasha staggered into the cockpit, rubbing her elbow. "Did you have to take off like that?"

"Strap yourself in."

"What are...?" Sasha took one look out the cockpit window and saw our problem. "Oh oh."

"My thoughts exactly. Can your bucket of bolts outrun that?"

"No."

"Just great." My mind scrambled for an idea. Any idea. "Any suggestions?"

Sasha brought up the holomap while I flew the ship. "How about here?"

There seemed to be a hint of humor in her voice so I looked at her. I followed her finger to where she was pointing on the map. "You're a bit hopeful, aren't you?"

"Don't think you can do it?" she taunted.

"Can you?"

"Sure." The woman was lying. Bravado. That's what she was spouting to me.

"Well, what are you waiting for?" Funny, I was doing the same thing. Bravado. What an insanely stupid human trait.

Once she had made the calculations Sasha took the controls and I backed away, leaning back in the chair while she moved her ship into hyperdrive. "Here goes nothing," she said. The air became heavy and alive with energy. Sometimes I really hated hyperdrive, but unfortunately it was a necessary evil.

Three minutes later we arrived at our destination, knowing very well that the Consortium ship was close on our tail. It would have tracked our trip and shot ahead of us on an intersection course.

Sasha brought her ship into real space near an asteroid belt. While the cruiser had superior speed and firepower, we had maneuverability. This was our only weapon in this fight so Sasha decided to even up the odds.

"Let's play tag." Sasha pushed the ship into the field as the cruiser's weapons opened fire. Her tiny ship rocked as it was hit from behind.

"Will she hold up?"

"Let's hope so. Shields are already at eighty percent."

I said no more and let Sasha concentrate on flying. Some of the turns were tight and she had to anticipate the paths of the asteroids to avoid getting hit. I brought up the ship's sensors.

"Are they following?" she asked, her voice tight with tension.

"They're sitting on the edge of the field."

"We'll have to encourage them to follow."

"And how are we going to do that?" My own voice was getting edgy. "Invite them in?"

"Exactly." She grinned as she turned the ship around, bobbing and weaving around space debris. When we were nearly out of the field, Sasha opened fire, strafing the cruiser across its bow. It didn't do a lot of damage, but in my mind it was equal to the old twentieth century ritual of mooning your enemy. Sasha was effectively showing her ass to them and saying 'up yours, pal'. Carn, I loved my colloquialisms.

The cruiser returned fire but made no attempt to follow.

"So much for that idea." I was being sarcastic, I knew that, but we were not in a good situation and it wasn't going to improve any time soon.

"I'm not finished yet." Her ship sped up and headed directly for the cruiser.

"Are you nuts?" I unconsciously held onto the chair. Sasha was going to run headlong into it. "This is not what I had in mind."

"Don't you trust me, J?"

"On some things, yeah. This… I'm not so sure about."

At the last second, she pulled back and skimmed over the shell of the cruiser, her lasers leaving a blackened stream of hits along the outer hull. The cruiser's guns came to bear on us and Sasha had to duck and weave like she had in the asteroid field. She turned her ship toward the field and slowed down as she passed the first piece of rock.

"What are you doing? They'll catch us." I realized what I had said. Sasha let her ship lazily drift into the field, as if her ship had lost power.

"Come and get us, you cretins," she muttered.

"An old pirate trick?"

"I've used it once or twice."

"Did it work?"

"I'm still here, aren't I?" Sasha was about to give up waiting and try again when the cruiser edged toward the field. She nudged her tiny ship a little farther into the field, forcing the cruiser deeper into danger so it could use its tractor beam on us. "See? What did I tell you?"

The Consortium had been so intent on catching us that they lost sight of the fact that they were entering an asteroid field. A large chuck of rock came out of nowhere and crashed into it, exploding the ship and splintering it into hundreds of pieces.

"Great work, Sash!" I was happily slapping her on the back when I noticed a slight problem. "Oh, craz!"

"What?" Sasha turned her head and saw what I was talking about, a second before our own chunk of rock hit us. We had fallen for the same trick. We were too busy watching the cruiser to notice an asteroid heading in our direction. Sasha turned the ship at the last second and the rock gouged out the side of the ship. Suddenly all power was gone.

"This is not good."

A pithy remark was sitting on my tongue and I bit down hard to keep it there.

Another piece of rock clipped the back of the ship and nudged us out of the field and into open space. At least it saved us from being pummeled to death.

Sasha left her seat and disappeared into the hold. I could have followed her but she needed her total concentration to make a full inspection of the damage. I had a bad feeling about this.

Five or so minutes later she returned and she wasn't smiling.

"So?"

"The first asteroid has completely cut power to the ship. I can't fix it. It's all been ripped away. Good news. The hull isn't breached."

"Yeah great, except we're going to suffocate to death." Maybe it would have been better to go out quickly and not know about it. "Do you have an emergency beacon?"

"Yeah, but it's—"

"Connected to the ship's power. Great." I was saying great a lot even though there was nothing great about it.

"Let's take a look at it and see if we can launch it somehow."

I debated with myself whether to launch it or not. I didn't have any friends in this sector. In fact, I probably had more enemies. I feared Sasha was probably in the same situation. It was not a nice piece of the universe. "Is that a good idea?"

"You'd rather die than ask for help?" She looked at me incredulously.

She was right. Even if someone we hated rescued us, at least we had a chance of surviving. "You're right. Let's take a look."

†

It had taken a great deal of time and effort to manually release the beacon, but we finally succeeded. We had no idea where it was heading because we had no sensors. Not that it mattered. One way was as good as the other as far as we were concerned. Friend or foe, we'd take rescue where we could get it.

We sat slumped against the wall in the corridor. We were just too tired to make it to the cockpit.

"Do you have any regrets?" Sasha asked.

"Regrets? One or two." I actually had one or two hundred, but just the time it would take to even think of them all we'd both be dead. "And you?"

"If I knew then what I know now, I'd probably have passed on a few things."

"Like the whole space pirate thing?" I smiled gently, trying to use as little energy as possible.

"Yeah," Sasha chuckled softly. "Do you think Dad knows?"

I thought about that for a moment. "Nah." If I was being realistic he probably did, but a little white lie at this point was neither here nor there.

"Liar," Sasha murmured. "I'm sure I disappointed him."

My hand moved to rest on hers. "He still loves you, no matter what."

"Yeah?"

"Yeah. It's in the father's manual. Didn't you know that?"

"That's stupid."

"Yeah." I looked her in the eye. "Love is deaf, dumb, blind, stupid and incredibly complicated." I felt her hand squeeze mine.

"How many people have you killed?"

Sasha's question came out of nowhere and I gasped. "Is it important?"

"Right now? Yeah, yeah it is." She looked at me seriously.

"Including Vel—"

"You did the right thing, by the way."

"The right thing?"

"Killing Vel. You did the right thing."

"But it doesn't make it any easier to live with."

"Oh." Sasha dropped her gaze.

That answered something for me. Sasha had killed, and not just the once like I had.

"How many?" I asked Sasha the same question she was asking me.

"It's not important."

"I think it is. Let me help you carry it. How many, Sash?"

"Eight," she said.

"Hey." I lifted my fingers to her chin and turned her head. "It's in the past. You've turned your life around."

"You killed someone we all know should be dead. How do you feel? How do you think I feel about eight who shouldn't be?"

"Calm down. You're getting too excited."

"Excited? Damn it J! I don't want to die with this on my conscience!"

"Then I absolve you," I said quietly. Absolve? It seemed my speech skills had decided to come out and play.

"Absolve?" Sasha laughed. "You?"

"Sure. That's what you're looking for, aren't you? Someone to tell you that everything is okay? Everything is okay. You are punishing yourself more than any jury could. Lay it to rest."

"Speaking of laying to rest...." Sasha struggled to stand and went to the cockpit. "We've probably got another half an hour before we begin breathing stale air." She came back out and stood next to me, looking down at my relaxed body.

"Sit down. You're using all the oxygen up."

Sasha flopped to the floor and propped herself against the wall. "I don't want Dad to find out."

"He won't find out from me."

"You're a good friend, J."

"You too, Sash." Her fingers twined with mine and she lifted them to her lips. I must have had a dumb look on my face because she laughed.

"What was that for?"

"Remember those regrets? As it looks like we're going to die...." Sasha wrapped her hand around the back of my neck and pulled my head toward hers. Her lips touched mine, tentative at first, then with more pressure. It was a long, lingering kiss that was sweet and innocent, yet held a hint of wistfulness about it. It was a kiss from someone who wished things were different.

I pulled back and stared. "Well..."

"Surprised?"

Was she kidding? Surprise didn't begin to describe what I was feeling. "Sure. I didn't see that coming."

"Oh, come on, J. Don't tell me you didn't suspect something?"

"I always thought that was anger because of Rales." That deaf, dumb and blind love was sticking its nose into my business again. The next time I saw that thing I was going to blast it to pieces.

"I'm sorry if I embarrassed you." She pulled away.

My hand grabbed the back of my neck, and her hand, before she had a chance to move. "One minute to let my brain catch up. How long, Sash? Why didn't you talk to me about this before?"

"As you know, I haven't been around much."

"Because of me?" Had I unknowingly pushed Sasha into the pirate business?

"Partially. I wasn't ready to stay still on one planet."

"But—"

"J, you've got a family now. Someone you love. A kid."

"True. But that's the infinitely complicated part." I pulled Sasha back in and placed a soft kiss on her lips before letting go. "I lo... lo..." I just couldn't say it.

"Everyone knows you love Beri, stupid, even if you can't say it. That's why I didn't say anything."

"And it's driving me nuts."

"What? That I didn't say anything?"

"No, dummy. I want to be with her and the only way I'm going to be able to do that without going insane is to become celibate."

"I thought—"

"Well, you thought wrong. It's taken three years to get her to kiss me, and I'm talking about a kiss like we just shared. I don't know if it's going to go any further."

"That's it? No, er..."

"No, no er. Not unless you count my right hand as an er."

"No wonder you're cranky."

"Thank you very much, Miss I-Get-It-Every-Day." To prove her point I was getting cranky.

"We're a pair, aren't we? You barely have a love life and I have no love life at all."

I couldn't argue with that. "So what are we going to do? Go to Loveless Anonymous?"

Sasha rolled her head to one side to look at me. "We?"

"Oh no, no, no, no, no." I shook my head but the idea was stuck in there. "I couldn't do that to B."

"No one is expecting you to. I just wanted to you to know before we died."

"Died?" I'd forgotten about that. "I've already died once, remember? That didn't stop me."

"Okay, so I die and you live."

"And you leave me in this predicament?"

"There's a predicament?" Sasha's eyebrows rose. I'm sure she didn't even know she was smiling.

"No! You're going to die and leave me with the knowledge that you had a thing for me?"

"A thing? How romantic." Sasha's flippant tone was shifting my crankiness to downright temper tantrum. "Especially since you're so sure I'm going to die and you'll live on."

"Sasha!" I used my stern tone and all she did was laugh. She was raising my blood pressure and she didn't even seem to care. I looked at my chronometer. Considering we had twenty minutes left before we slowly suffocated, she seemed awfully happy.

"What's the problem, J? In...," she looked at her own chronometer. "Twenty minutes it won't matter one way or the other."

"And if, by some miracle, we survive?"

"We'll worry about it if it happens."

It was then that I realized that Sasha was more like me than I had previously thought. Well, more like me when my life was my own. I had been reckless, I admit that. If I was in this situation I would leave it in the hands of Almighty Carn. If it was my time to die, then so be it.

"If Beri wasn't involved, would I have stood a chance?"

It was a question loaded with lots of pitfalls. How should I answer? Should I answer it at all? My head rolled to one side and I studied Sasha. Here was a woman whom I had considered as a sister of sorts. But she wasn't my sister, at least not biologically. So what did I do? "But I didn't even know—"

"Can't you say it?"

"All right! Yes, you would have." I said that on a gut reaction and not from a considered opinion. Sasha was a great woman— emotionally strong, pretty, petite and, above all, feisty. Being Rales' daughter had always stopped me from pursuing her, but I suppose she had always been on my list.

"Now I find out." She breathed deeply and then coughed.

"Let's get into the suits and use the oxygen." We had held back from climbing into the space suits until the last possible moment to make use of what oxygen was left in the cabin. The time was fast approaching where if we didn't get up off the floor we never would.

I struggled to stand, finally settling for rolling onto my hands and knees and walking my hands up the wall. I was feeling light-headed after the effort and I swayed gently. "Carn!" I ground out.

Sasha was still on the floor. I extended my hand and waited for her to take it. "Come on, you bitch, get your ass moving." She looked at me with glassy eyes. "I'll give you a kiss if you get into your suit." Now why did I say that? Sasha moved like her ass was on fire. She stood and staggered down the short corridor to the bay, scratching at the wall as she tried to lift off the suit.

I followed her, my hands splayed out before me in case she collapsed into my arms. I was seeing double and my breathing was labored. I helped Sasha into the suit and made sure her helmet was securely sealed. My arms felt heavy as I lifted off my own suit. It took a few attempts before I could thread my legs into the pants and it took all the energy I had to get that far.

"J?" Sasha came up to me and lifted my chin. "Focus, J!" It seemed the oxygen had done her some good. She pulled the suit up over my hips and back, helping me to put my arms into the sleeves. Quickly she connected the magnetic strips and closed the suit, following in quick succession with the helmet. Immediately I felt the gentle ripple of fresh air over my face. The life-giving oxygen pumped through my suit, and I took one or two deep breaths. I again felt dizzy, but this time it was from oxygen-rich air.

"Are you okay?" Sasha's voice came from the comlink.

"Yeah" I croaked. I took a few unsteady steps back toward the front of the ship and found a chair. I had to sit down before I fell down. "That was close." I hadn't realized how quickly we would go from stale air to nearly dead.

Sasha followed and stood in front of me. "Now, where's my kiss?"

"I owe you."

"Like I believe that one. Come on, pay up, Laren."

"Give me a minute to get some air." Why was I even encouraging the conversation?

"Beri is not interested in sex?"

"Why do you want to know? Not that it's any of your business."

"It could be…," she said enigmatically.

What was going on in that brain of hers? "What the Carn are you talking about?"

"Well, if Beri doesn't want you, how about me?"

"How about… Are you nuts?" I stared at her, trying to see if it was some sort of joke. "Your brain is dead, isn't it? The lack of oxygen has killed all those little gray cells, because nothing else makes any sense."

"It would solve all our problems."

I slumped back into the chair, shaking my head. "I must be dead," I muttered to myself. "You're ready to kick Beri out of bed and climb in yourself. That has got to be the stupidest idea you have ever come up with."

"Is Beri going to come around to your way of thinking any time soon?"

"I don't believe it…"

"Well, is she?" Sasha persisted.

Reluctantly, I answered. "No."

"And she won't. That's not how the Noorthi work, and we both know that. So what are you going to do about your little problem?"

"I don't know."

"You either look close to home or you go off-world."

"Or I do nothing and become celibate."

Sasha smiled at me. Yeah, it was a big fat lie. I may as well stop breathing. "Or get a mind wipe. Get rid of all those juicy little fantasies of yours."

"That's an idea…"

"Of course, you'll forget how to fly Bessie. In fact, you won't even remember you have Bessie. Malt will be happy."

"Oh, great. I'll lose my mind and you're already carving up my assets."

"Assets? J, honey, you have one beat up old ship. That's it." Sasha took a seat next to me. "Stop changing the subject. This idea could work."

"What I don't understand is why you would want this sort of arrangement in the first place."

"Why?" She studied her gloved hands. "I suppose I have the same problem as you. I compromise or I walk away. I don't know if I can do that." One hand reached out to me, silently seeking my own hand to join hers. "I've always had a thing for you, you big lug. Why do you think I jumped at the chance to join the cause when you approached Dad?"

"And what's going to stop this physical relationship developing into something more?"

"Do you think it will?"

"I don't know, Sash, but there's a real possibility. Do you want to run the risk of losing everything over this?"

"What alternative have we got? Looking outside Heaven has its own risks."

"Don't remind me." I was still feeling guilty about that stupid mistake.

"It's either me, your trusty right hand or dozens of dolbeds."

I thought myself better than using artificial stimulation devices to satisfy myself. Dolbeds were the last resort of a desperate woman. Now that Sasha had put the idea in my head, I was already thinking about where I could pick up the little ball vibrators. "I'll think about it."

Chapter Ten

Colder Than Hell

We had been drifting for an hour now and there seemed to be no sign of rescue. It was probably time to think about rescuing ourselves if we could before the air ran out.

I moved into the cockpit and looked out the window. Looming up large in front of us was a planet, and it looked like we were on a collision course with it. "Sasha!" I yelled at the top of my voice.

She appeared in the doorway banging her helmet. "Did you have to yell so l–, oh, craz!"

"Now, what do we do?"

"Hey, you're the hero. You come up with the idea."

"Me?" My heart was racing, just like my mind. How do you stop a ship from crashing into a planet when you have no power? You don't, and that was the problem. "If you get us out of this one I'll give you another kiss."

"You'll what?"

"It worked once. I'm just seeing if it'll work a second time."

"You still owe me a kiss."

"I'll pay if we get out of this." Suddenly, I was making promises I knew I couldn't keep. "I may have survived before, but I'm not going to survive this one."

"Shut up and let me think." Sash's head bowed as she gave the matter her attention.

Meanwhile I just stared at the huge chunk of rock heading our way. "Is there any way we can change the angle of entry?"

"We've got no power—"

"I know that!" I snapped. "Is there anything that has an explosive head that we may be able to set off to tip the ship?"

"There are a four shot bolts for jettisoning the hatch in an emergency."

"I think this counts as an emergency."

"But we'll lose pressure."

"Hell-o! We've got no air anyway. We have," I looked at my chronometer. "About an hour's worth of air left in our suits. We either go out in a blaze of glory trying to save ourselves or we won't have to wait an hour to suffocate. At this point it's a risk we have to take."

"Will it be enough?"

"How the hell do I know? I didn't design the thing, Sash!"

"Calm down."

"I don't want to calm down! I've had about all the excitement I can handle right now."

Sasha's gloved hand patted my arm. "We both have. Besides, I have a bet to win."

"Sorry, Sash. Forget about the bet. It was cheap and nasty."

"You don't mean it?"

"Yeah, I'll give you the kiss, but it's not dependent on whether you succeed or not. No, I take that back. It will." I grinned at her through my visor.

"Does that mean you've changed your mind?"

Had I? "I meant what I said."

"That's not an answer." She saw through my delaying tactic.

"It's all the answer you're going to get for now. If this doesn't work whether I kiss you or not is going to be a moot point."

Sasha made her way aft toward the cargo hold. "How are we going to time this?"

I was right behind her. "We'll just have to make an educated guess. It's all we've got."

She turned to face me. "We're going to die, aren't we?"

"Yeah," I said seriously, "I think we are."

"Just as long as we both know that, so don't you cheat." She waved her finger at me.

"No cheating." I looked at the hatch. "How do we get to it?"

Sasha studied the door. "I have absolutely no idea."

"Then we have to improvise quickly." I ran my hand over the seal. "Have you got a light?"

Sasha grabbed a torch off the wall and shone it at the door.

"Thanks. See the small bulges?" There were tiny bumps in the door, but they were not large enough to stop the hatch from retracting into the wall. "I think that's them. They seem about right."

"And if they're not?"

"Then I suppose we get a second or two to kiss our asses goodbye." I saw Sasha wince. "Sorry."

"So now what?"

"Now this is the tricky part. We have to set off all the charges at the one time, and without power."

Sasha turned, and I assumed she was searching the hold for something to use. The torch light swept the interior in an orderly fashion, starting on one side and systematically covering the area until it reached the other side. The only objects of use were a number of metal bars and a length of tensile rope. "Maybe." She stuck the torch to her suit and moved to the pile, grabbing two bars in her hands. "How about these?"

"What am I supposed to do with those?"

"Hit the bolts."

"And what if it blows up in my face?"

"Hey! You're the one who wanted to set off the bolts."

"Fine! Just give me the pipes." It was a foolish plan in the extreme. If it worked then we had a plan, and if it didn't... we wouldn't have to wait around to become fricasseed halmet. "This isn't going to be easy."

"I know that, but it's all I can think of in the few seconds we've got."

I put the pipes down, held my breath and removed my helmet.

"What the craz are you doing?"

I reached for Sasha's helmet and removed it. I quickly planted a kiss on her lips before replacing her helmet. I sealed my own helmet and took a deep breath. "I didn't want to die without paying my dues."

Sasha just blinked. "That was unexpected." I'm sure she thought I had finally lost it.

"Let's get to work." I tied the metallic rope to the door and secured the other end to the ship's hull. I then lined up the two bars over each of the two upper bolts, while Sasha did the same for the two lower bolts. "On my mark. Three. Two. One. Go!"

The bars clunked loudly against the metal door, but nothing happened. "Again. This time harder." This was either going to save us or kill us. "Three. Two. One. Go!" Again, nothing happened except the noise was deafening. "Ow!" There was ringing in my ears. "One more time, Sash."

"It's getting hot in here."

"I know. One more time." I threw what strength I had left into my last effort. It looked like we had failed. Suddenly, a small stream of gas emerged from the edge of the hatch door, first in one spot, then another, until all four locations were leaking gas. "Stand back."

We had barely moved when the gas escaped in a massive cloud and the door broke free.

Sasha had been standing in front of me when the hatch gave way and the shudder sent her into my arms. I grabbed her as her suit hit mine and I pulled her away from the door. The heat hit us like a wall, already hot but growing in intensity by the second. The ship tilted slowly. But was it enough?

I moved Sasha out of my way and reached for the cord, pulling the hatch back toward us as fast as I could. Sasha joined my efforts and we brought the door back to the ship in a matter of moments. We tied the door back in place as best we could and ran to the cockpit to strap ourselves in.

"Now we find out if this worked."

Sasha grabbed the controls out of instinct.

"They're not going to work." I suppose it was stating the obvious, but I was nervous enough as it was.

"Habit," she muttered. If it had been Bessie I would have done the same. I was thankful the old girl wasn't in this position. I'd hate to see her burned to a crisp.

The temperature rose, and despite the cooling of the suits, I felt the heat. The view out the window was hazy, tinged with transparent red flames licking the outer hull. I reached out for Sasha's hand and she grabbed it. I looked at her through my visor and nodded gently. I closed my eyes and turned my thoughts to Beri and Rice. This was it.

Suddenly the heat was gone. I opened my eyes and looked out. The red had been replaced by white landscape, and it was approaching rapidly. Sasha was madly trying to pull the nose up, but it didn't budge. "This is going to be nasty," she said.

We didn't really have any time to respond to the new situation. All we could do was pray to Carn and hold on.

There must have been a massive gust of wind or something because the ship heaved and changed direction. The bottom of the ship caught the wind and rode it like an old fashioned glider. I smiled and sent my thanks to Carn, then sent my thanks to the Noorthi as well, just in case. Someone was definitely keeping an eye on me.

The descent was, by no means, smooth. The ship rose and fell hundreds of feet every few seconds, depending on the wind conditions underneath it. If it could get us to the planet alive, I'd take whatever it would give us. We hit the ground hard, bouncing along the snow-covered landscape for a few hundred feet before coming to an abrupt halt. Ignoring the sharp pain in my side, I looked at Sasha and laughed.

"You are the luckiest bitch in the universe," Sasha said. She let out a whoop over the comlink, but I didn't join in the celebration. Each breath was agony. "Are you all right?"

"Yeah, sure. Why wouldn't I be?" My damned ego pushed my common sense aside.

"Because you're an idiot." Sasha snapped her restraint open and stood up. She moved around my chair and crouched down next to me. I had tried to hide the pain, but I didn't fool her. "Craz!" She prodded gently until she heard my hiss. "Sore?"

"Hell, yeah," I ground out.

"There doesn't seem to be a hole in you suit. You may have popped something inside."

"Me, or the suit?"

"Without looking, I don't know. You'd be the one to tell me that."

"Help me up." Slowly I removed the restraint and tried to stand up. As my muscles shifted the pain became excruciating. "Oh, Carn."

"Can you straighten up?"

"This is not my fault."

"I didn't say anything."

"You didn't have to because I can see the grin."

Sasha chuckled.

"Yeah, yeah, very funny," I said wearily. I was getting sick and tired of getting hurt. The past three years had been a welcome respite from that, with only the occasional accident slowing me down. This current adventure, however, seemed to have me in a state of constant disability. I stood slowly and straightened even slower. The pain eased as my body stretched out.

"There's your problem." Sasha reached down to where I had been sitting and grabbed a small metallic canister. She popped it back into the overhead compartment. "It must have fallen out when we hit the ground and wedged between you and the seat."

I prodded gently where the pain was. "Let's hope that's all it was." The sharpness was gone, replaced with a nagging ache. "I've probably got a bruise the size of Grit's ass." Sasha's suit jiggled as she laughed. "And don't you tell her I said that!"

"Then you shouldn't have said it."

I slowly rotated my body, testing out the damage done by the canister. "I think I'll live."

"Good, because I think we're in trouble."

I finally looked outside the window. Snow and ice were piled up against the front of the ship. "Maybe we should take a look at the damage to the hull while we can."

"We can't re-attach the hatch."

"No, but we might be able to restore power to the ship."

"She's not going to fly again." I heard the wistfulness in Sasha's voice. If it were me, I'd be a blubbering mess by now. The death of Bessie would be hard for me to take.

"I doubt it, but we may be able to get the comlink up and maybe generate some heat." I looked at my chronometer. Had it only been twenty minutes since we were up in space, blissfully unaware of the impending disaster awaiting us? I touched the tiny screen and the information changed. The air was still not breathable in the ship, but now it was time to check outside.

I walked a little stiffly down the short corridor to the small cargo hold and untied the rope holding the hatch in place. It had partially melted on entry but luckily it had still managed to do its job. As soon as the rope slackened, the hatch fell outwards and landed with a thud. A blast of snow and ice blew in and coated the hold in white. I checked my chronometer and there seemed to be enough oxygen in the atmosphere to support us. However, in exchange for oxygen we'd have to battle the cold.

"This day is just getting better and better," I muttered.

We stepped outside and looked at the outer skin of the ship. There was a massive gouge along her side where the rock from the asteroid field had opened her up. Some of the connections were damaged beyond what we considered repair. Maybe Rales could do something with it, but neither of us were anywhere near Rales' level of expertise. Between us, we took turns to cut and splice threads. It required us to remove our gloves for the fine work, but the intense cold made it impossible to work more than ten minutes at a time without protection.

Finally, we both decided that we had connected as many cables as we were able to and took a guess or two on a few more. It was getting too cold for even our suits to withstand. With one last check we covered both the gouge and the hatch with filitex sheeting to protect it, and us, from the ice.

Once inside, I removed my helmet.

"What are you doing?"

"The vacuum is gone, Sash, or hadn't you noticed that the hatch door fell off." I reached down the outside of my suit and deactivated the air supply. "Might as well save it for when I need it." I breathed deeply and coughed. The ice cold air burned the lining of my throat. "That is wicked," I croaked.

Sasha stood there with her arms crossed.

"What?" I spread my hands outward.

"You just don't care, do you?"

"Care about what?"

"Dying. Or has that Noorthi stuff in your veins made you stupid."

"You haven't been around me long, have you?" I sauntered up the corridor to the cockpit. Now it was time to see what would work. "This is normal for me."

"Then I'm surprised you've survived this long."

I had expected Sasha to be a kindred spirit. It seemed I was wrong. "Haven't you ever taken a chance or two?"

"Occasionally, yes, but hanging around you I seem to be taking a chance every five seconds. Next time I see Malt I'll be giving her a pat on the back for a job well done. She must be exhausted keeping you out of trouble." Sasha rolled her eyes at me. "Wait! I think I hear something!"

"What?" I listened carefully but I heard nothing.

"Nothing. I thought I heard Malt pull up in Bessie to rescue you. She seems to do a lot of that lately."

"Ha ha." I extended my arm with a flourish. "After you. It's your ship." I watched Sasha sit down and I crossed my fingers.

Nothing happened.

Had everything we done been for nothing? Were we going to freeze to death on this lonely piece of rock? Had I become Ratha to finish my life in this meaningless way? Of course, if I had said 'no' to any of those questions then I would have to believe in my destiny. "Try it again." Sasha flipped a couple of switches and tried to kick her ship into life again. There was a slight flutter and the power flickered. I pounded the panel beside me with my fist.

"Hey!" Sasha protested. She was about to say more but stopped when the flickering turned to a solid stream of light.

"Something I learned from Rales." I didn't really, but someone really wise had told me that once.

Sasha tried for liftoff but there wasn't enough power to shift us from underneath the snow. "Craz!" My sentiments exactly.

"Try the heat." There was nothing but cold air.

"How about the comlink?"

"I'm trying, damn it!"

"Sash, relax."

"Relax? This was our only chance."

"A wise old woman once said—it ain't over till it's over."

"Which old woman?"

"Hell if I know. It just sounded good."

Sasha smiled.

"There you go," I said. I left the cockpit and found the replicator. As I had nothing to lose, I punched in a request for coffee synth. To my surprise it gave me what I asked for. "Hey!"

"What?"

"I just got a synth. Want one?"

"You what?" Sasha emerged from the cockpit and stood in the doorway. "It works?"

"At least we can have hot food. How do you take your synth?"

"Black with four sucarine tablets."

"Four?"

"I like it sweet."

"You like it liquid sweet." However, I did as she asked, waiting for the machine to drop the tablets into the hot beverage. "Here." I handed it to her while I took a sip of my own plain synth.

"Oh, Carn, that is good."

I watched Sasha's serious face disappear and she sipped her own brand of synth. Where did all that sweetness go? Her figure was lean and mean, so it had to go somewhere. It certainly didn't go to her temperament.

Sasha leaned against the wall. "What do we do now?"

I didn't answer her straight away because I had the cup to my mouth. What would we do? "We try each and every thingamajig on this ship."

She shook her head at me. "I have no idea what you're talking about."

"I've got to lend you some reading material on twentieth century colloquial English, then you'll know what I mean. Thingamajig? It means all the little things the ship needs power for."

"They are not called that."

"Just… just… look, believe me. It's a word that covers a whole multitude of things that you can't think of the name of. Okay? Take my word for it."

"I'll take your word for it when you talk normally."

I continued to drink my synth. "You are no fun at all," I said finally.

"And you are crazy."

I grinned at her. "I thought you already knew that." I put out my hand for her cup. "Come on, let's go see what this ship of yours can and can't do."

†

Half an hour later we had pushed, pulled and prodded everything in the ship. By my reckoning, we had food and liquid, light and a weak signal on the comlink. Everything else was dead. No, not like I was dead. It was dead, as in 'Vel is never coming back type of dead'. We set the comlink's emergency signal on open and let it spray out into space in the hope someone would hear it. As to how long it would last, we had no idea.

"So what do we do now?"

"You owe me a kiss."

I had no one to blame but myself for that one. "True. Is there something to snuggle into?"

While Sasha went to look for something, I ducked outside and began fiddling with the connections, trying different combinations in the hope of adding something new to our meager supply of options. That was where Sasha found me.

"If I didn't know better, I'd think you're trying to get out of kissing me."

"Would I do that?"

She glared at me through her rapidly frosting helmet. "Yes, you would."

"I was just making use of the time while you found a blanket." She held up the item in question. "Right. Now we're ready."

155

She stepped aside and let me lead the way. I had a feeling that she didn't trust me and was half-expecting me to make a run for it.

We stepped inside and re-attached the filitex tightly to keep out the cold. Not that it was much better inside. "If you don't want to…" She left the sentence hanging, waiting for me to either refute or agree with it.

"Don't want to? What are you talking about?" Right. We both knew what we were talking about.

"J, please no more games. If you don't want to go through with all this, just say so." Sasha closed her eyes as if waiting for the bad news.

"Yes, I do. I just need a bit of time. But a kiss I can do." I waited for her to open her eyes before smiling at her. I removed my helmet and put it away. "It would probably be easier without the helmet."

After she removed her own helmet Sasha looked at me nervously. "So where are we going to do this?"

"Do this?" I was teasing her, I know, but we were surprisingly nervous about this. It could be the first step along a path neither of us had ever contemplated. "Come on." I led her to the corridor where we sat earlier and where we would sit again. "It seems appropriate."

My suit whispered as I crouched down. Sasha handed me the metallic blanket and I lay it out on the floor. I shimmied myself onto it because I didn't want to end up with a cold ass.

Sasha stood there. I'm not sure exactly what she was expecting, but I extended my hand up for her to take. The two of us sat there looking at one another. Maybe one was waiting for the other to make the first move, I don't know, but it seemed slightly ridiculous. We had both had many lovers in our past and yet here we were acting like two love-sick teenagers out on a first date.

"How about a hug?" I suggested. "That's a good place to start."

"I can do that."

"I'm sure you can." I pulled off my gloves and watched as she did the same. Tentatively, I reached for her and allowed her to meld into my arms, or as well as you can meld with two suits on. I felt Sasha's breath on my neck and it sent a shiver through me.

"Are you cold?" she asked.

"No. I haven't had a hug since… well, since my dad died."

"That's pretty sad."

"Tell me about it."

"Are you afraid of someone getting close?" Sasha whispered.

I drew back. "And you're my mind technician now?"

"I don't need a certificate for that." She drew me in again and hugged tighter. "I won't bite."

"That's not what I heard." I felt her silent laughter rumble through her.

Her face was so close to mine I felt that she could see inside me. My gaze slid across the skin of her cheek up to her eyes. The normal blue of her irises had darkened with the muted light, but there was a fire burning within them. Now I could see the attraction that she had for me. Why hadn't I seen it before? "Wow," I breathed.

"What?"

"You really do have a thing for me."

"You didn't believe me?"

"Well, yeah, but now I can see it in your eyes."

Sasha slowly closed the distance between our lips. It was a mere touch at first, as if she was testing the waters. "That's one," I said.

She sniggered then moved in again. This time the kiss was more, building slowly from a gentle entreaty to acceptance to finally a demand for a response.

All my pent up frustration finally found an outlet. I didn't want to overwhelm her with my need and I was hard pressed to take it slow. Maybe Sasha could sense my urgency. Not that it would have been hard to do. I had been celibate for three years and at my wit's end. Sasha's smell alone would be enough to set me off.

"The rest is up to you," she said. If I made a move then I was condoning Sasha's plan.

But I hesitated. "I don't want to be sneaking around behind Beri's back."

Sasha backed away and rested against the wall. "I see."

"I wish I did." I sighed and leaned back next to her. "I don't know why I've got this block, Sash. You're a great gal and it solves my problem beautifully, so why am I hesitating?"

"Must be all those ancient books you read."

"While they frowned on multiple relationships, it wasn't illegal, unless you married more than one at the same time, but surely that wouldn't be the reason."

"Your dad probably wouldn't be happy with the arrangement."

Sasha was right. Dad wouldn't have been happy, not that he would say anything. I would get the disapproving stare, but not a word. He expected that I knew better, and he would be right. I did know better. So maybe that was my problem. I was torn between satisfying my baser instincts and doing what was right. Unfortunately, it didn't get me any closer to a decision.

"Look…"

"And what if this is the only chance we have?"

"Huh?"

"I mean, if we don't get rescued we're going to die here."

Sasha was right, but was that any reason to jump right into this? "True, but is that a good reason to make love?" What was I saying?

"What are you saying?"

"We should do this for the right reason not the wrong one."

"I think dying before we get home is a pretty good reason."

"What is the problem here, Sash? Are you afraid that I'll change my mind when we get home? Are you afraid of missing your chance with me?"

"Why is everything about you, huh?" She shoved me hard. "You can be such a bitch sometimes, you know that? I'm not that desperate."

"I didn't say you were." I reached for her.

"Get away from me!" She batted away my hands, but I persisted.

"No! Stop it!" I grabbed her hands in mine. "You've got it all wrong. Or maybe I've said it all wrong. Whatever—"

"J, I don't want to hear any more, okay? I get the point."

"But you don't. Sash, I'm really considering this... seriously. I don't know how it's going to work, or if it'll work, but I feel I have to talk to Beri first. I want there to be no secrets. I know you want to be first in my life but you can't. Beri is the mother of my child. I have been with her for three years and contemplated giving up sex for her. But I don't want you to think of yourself as being second."

"But I will be second. Whichever way you look at it, I'll always be second."

"And yet you were prepared to be just that when you suggested this."

"True, but is second good enough, J?"

"Do you want me to say yes? Then, yes it is. I respect you a lot, Sasha, and it's because of it that I'm even considering this. In the universe outside the Noorthi you're the closest I have to a partner. Rales is family. Malt is family. But you are of my own heart, Sash. You understand me better than the rest of them. You understand what drives me. You understand my true nature. Only you, Sash.

"I know you said it was only casual, but it's not cheap. This is a big thing you're offering me, Sash, and it's something I can't make a decision on just like that."

"So where does that leave us?"

"For the moment, it leaves us in limbo. I know I have to make a decision, but I have to at least talk to Beri first."

"And if you don't get that chance?"

"Then I suppose I'll die knowing I didn't cheat on her."

Sasha leaned her head back against the wall and looked at the ceiling. She kept quiet for a while and I was scared to break the silence.

"Is it cheating if she's not interested in sleeping with you?"

"No, Sash, I have to talk to—"

"Wait a minute. I'm not asking about that. I was just curious. In this instance, is it cheating?"

I thought about it for a moment. "It depends on the morals of the person you are asking." I took the wristband off. "Before this," I held up my wrist, "I would have said no problem. This damned ochre gave me scruples. Now it is a problem."

"Ah, but what about thinking about it? Wouldn't that be cheating in a way?"

"You really want me to suffer, don't you?" I rolled my head to the side to glare at her.

"Welcome to my world," she said. "What do we do now?"

"Like I said—"

"Not that, stupid. How do we get ourselves off this ice block?"

"If your heap of junk would fly then we'd be on our way."

"My poor ship."

"We'll get you another one."

"But I liked this one, J. She was, you know—"

"Yeah, I know." I reached out and patted her arm. This was one time I was glad Bessie was somewhere else.

Sasha sat up, her gaze sweeping the corridor. "Did you hear that?"

"I didn't hear a thing."

"You need your ears checked."

"And you have a case of wishful thinking."

Then I heard it. It sounded like a quiet metallic whing. In fact, it was the sound of the filitex being peeled back.

"I just heard your wishful thinking." A small metallic clang followed. "Get out of here," I whispered to Sasha, right before I gave her a shove. I leaned back against the wall and waited for whoever was on the ship. Sasha moved into the cockpit as I sat there. I just hoped that she had a weapon or two stashed somewhere in case of an emergency.

"Well, well," a deep masculine voice said silkily. "This is a bonus."

"I see you got the message."

"Indeed I did, sweetie."

I stood up and leaned against the wall. "I'm not your sweetie. Are you here to rescue me?" He gave me his answer by bringing his pistol to bear.

"It's going to be like that, is it?" I asked.

"I'm here for the salvage, not to rescue you."

"Sorry, but this ship is already spoken for."

"It certainly is… by me." He grinned and I caught a glimpse of his yellow teeth. "Are you going to make this hard for me?"

"What do you think?"

He pointed toward the hold with his pistol. "Move it."

I pushed off from the wall and walked toward the rear of the ship. He followed a few steps behind me, leaving enough space that I couldn't swing around and knock the weapon from his hand.

"Take the suit off," he said.

"I hardly know you." But I still did as he asked. He had the upper hand, for now. I felt his heated gaze as I peeled the suit down my body. "That's going to cost you."

"How much?"

I continued the tease, stepping slowly out of the suit and leaving it in a pile on the floor. "Your ship," I breathed in my deepest voice.

"My what?" He laughed out loud. "I don't think so."

"It's a good deal. I'll take your ship and you can have mine."

"I have a better plan," he said. "I'll keep my ship and take yours as well while you sit out in the snow and freeze to death."

"Well, I'm sorry to hear that," I inched closer as I spoke. "Because that means I have to do something I don't want to do."

He tightened his grip on his weapon, but it wasn't tight enough. My leg swung out and knocked it out of his hand. His advantage gone, he rushed at me and wrapped his arms around my torso. The impetus drove me back against the wall and I hit it with a painful thud. I laced my fingers together and brought my two hands down on the back of his neck. It took several blows before he finally let go and fell to his knees. I lashed out with one foot, hitting him in the temple knocking him out. He collapsed, out cold.

I reached for my back and rubbed it briskly. There would be a bruise soon from the slam against the wall. Sasha stood by relaxed while I fought. She had a pistol in her hand.

"You could have stepped in any time," I said, slightly out of breath.

"You were after a good fight, and we both know it."

"And if I got hurt?"

"You had some steam to let off so I wasn't going to stop you."

"And the pistol?"

"In case he won. Luckily, it wasn't needed. Not that I doubted you for a minute."

"Get your things and let's get out of here before he wakes up." I didn't have anything to collect since I'd left Bessie in a hurry, but I was sure that Sasha had a thing or two and a sad goodbye before we left.

"Can you hurry up?"

"Give me a minute!" Sasha's muffled voice could barely be heard.

I put the suit back on, snatched the pistols off the wall and collected our helmets. "What are you doing? Dismantling the ship?"

"J, please!"

"You take any longer and I'll have to knock him out again." So far he hadn't stirred, but every second longer Sasha took moved me one second closer to just that. "Come on!"

Sasha appeared in the hold with a bag full of stuff. I didn't want to know what she considered worth collecting, but I did catch a peek at a thing or two. Her favorite pistol I could understand, but the holographic dancing image of Corath Blane was a little too much. "What's this?" I snatched a piece of metallic mesh out of her bag and held it up.

"I thought you said we didn't have time." She snatched it back and shoved it in her pack.

"I've always got time for this."

Sasha batted away my hands as I tried to grab it. "It's none of your damned business!"

I laughed. Sometimes she was just too easy to rile. "Come on." The guy on the floor stirred and I struck out with my foot. "We have a ship to find."

One step outside in the cold reminded me why we were inside. It could freeze the nuts off a gennite. Luckily, the guy parked his ship a couple of hundred feet away and the trudge through the snow was short lived. When the hatch closed I breathed a sigh of relief. It was a damned sight warmer inside this ship than it was in Sasha's.

"Can you can fly this tub?"

"A tub? What's a tub?" She held up her hand. "No, I don't want to know."

I saw that I would have to leave my library of twentieth century slang around for her to find, especially now that she could possibly be my lover. I shook my head, I'm not sure why. Was I trying to express my dismay or get the image out of my head? It was probably a bit of both. "Just get us out of here before he comes knocking on the door."

Sasha disappeared forward. "Are you going to strap yourself in or do you want me to practice lift off with you bouncing around the hold?"

I snickered to myself and moved to the cockpit.

The liftoff wasn't smooth but, then again, I didn't think it would be. It took time to get the feel of a new ship. Jerks and bumps were part of the initiation process and this time was no different.

"Smooth liftoff, Sash," I said shakily as the ship shuddered.

"Oh, shut up!" She looked cursorily at the setup of the cockpit, her hands smoothly slipping over the controls.

"Looks like you've got yourself a new ship."

"I liked the old one."

"Yeah, but she's busted."

"I know." She let out a big sigh and pouted. "I want my ship back."

I unbuckled my harness and stood up. I reached into her bag and pulled out the hologram plate, sitting it on the console. I switched it on and watched the image jiggle around. "There. Now it's home."

It looked so ridiculous just sitting there that Sasha laughed out loud. Sometimes life could be full of weird bits of shit.

"What's so funny?" the hologram asked.

"You," I said. "Shaking your ass."

"It's what I'm supposed to do."

"I prefer the stripper thanks." The hologram image changed to a barely clad woman with three breasts doing a seductive dance. "That's probably more to your liking."

"Hi there, girls," the image cooed.

"And I'll run straight into the next piece of space debris." Sasha reached out and switched it off. "You are a troublemaker."

"I know. Let's go find Malt so I can tell her how I got out of this one on my own."

"Hey!"

"All right, I can tell her how I got both of us out of this one."

Chapter Eleven

Out Of The Frying Pan

The flight wasn't without mishap. The ship was unfamiliar to Sasha and it took a small detour or two for her to learn the idiosyncrasies of the vessel. It was a Bik ship and it was designed for a more robust individual.

"It's not my fault."

"You need to grow a few more inches, my girl." I laughed as she fell out of the seat reaching for the side console.

"I hate this ship!"

"And I love it, just for the entertainment of seeing you fly it."

"Then you take it." Sasha sat back, forcing me to take the controls.

"I can't do that. I already have a ship and I know Bessie would be heartbroken if I was wooing another ship."

"Wooing? Ha!" Sasha clicked her tongue in disgust. "You are one hundred per cent certifiable."

"And you love me for it." I puckered up my lips and kissed the air.

"Yeah, I do," Sasha said sadly.

"Sorry. I didn't mean to tease you." Damn! Why couldn't I just shut up?

"It's my own fault." Sasha stood and made a show of checking out the compartments around the cockpit. She was busily rummaging around in a small recess on the side when she bellowed, "Oh, craz!"

"What?" I suddenly jumped and scanned the area for trouble. "What's wrong?" The woman made me nervous. "You should know not to yell like that. I'm likely to hit you."

"I think you better hit yourself because this was *not* the ship to steal."

"Why?" Sasha was breathing heavily like she was gasping for breath. "For Carn's sake, Sash, what's the problem?"

"This ship belongs to one of Wallco's boys."

"And?"

"You've never heard of Wallco?"

"Would I be asking if I did?"

Sasha shook her head. "You need to get out more. He just happens to be the overlord of the Genera Sector."

"Overlord?" I chuckled. "They still use that term?"

"Overlord, boss, owner, call him what you want. He considers this sector his territory and he jealously guards it." She held up a small insignia on what seemed to be a communicator. "We had a run in with him a while back, and he nearly wiped out our organization. That's why I ended up on Heaven."

"And here I thought it was because of me." I nearly sounded disappointed.

"You were, otherwise I'd be laying low somewhere else."

"You were lying to me."

"About what?" Sasha moved back to the pilot's seat and sat down.

"I said you came home because of me."

"Stop pouting. Not everything is about you." I think Sasha enjoyed my uncertainty. "You just gave me extra incentive to stay put for a while."

"Yeah, now you tell me," I grumbled.

"Hey, Pork! Answer your freakin' com!" The deep bass voice growled over the comlink.

"Craz!"

"Will you stop cussing!" We were both working ourselves up into bundles of nervous energy.

"I'll stop cussing when you stop getting us into trouble."

"This is not my fault!"

"You took the ship!"

"And we would have died on that ice hole if I hadn't!"

The argument was useless, really, however it did seem that we were being bombarded by one mishap after another. Who did I insult in a previous life?

"Now we're going to get blasted to pieces instead!"

"Well?" I asked. "Any more pirate tricks up your sleeve?"

"Pork? Get your ass on the link, or so help me I'll take your balls and shove them up your nose!" the guy said.

"Oooh, that's a colorful one. I'll have to remember it."

Sasha glared at me. "You really do have a weird sense of humor."

"It's the only thing holding me together right now." I wasn't going to add 'otherwise I'd be crying'. I certainly felt like crying, but heroes don't cry. When I find the person who wrote the hero handbook I was going to stick my boot up his ass or, as the guy on the comlink so eloquently put it, I'd take his balls and shove them up his nose.

"What are we going to do?" I asked.

"Why do I have to come up with the ideas?"

"Because I came up with the last one."

"And look where that got us."

"Your last chance, Pork." The guy on the comlink said.

"Er, yeah. Keep your shirt on." I growled at him.

"Pork? What happened to your voice?"

"I got a sore throat." I had that right. Talking like a man hurt.

"What are you doing out here?"

"Thought I saw a downed ship," I said. "Checking it out."

"You? You wouldn't go find your own father. Who the craz are you?"

"It's Pork." And, as the saying goes, the jig was up. I brought up the holomap and set the scan for a wide sweep. My mind was racing for a plan and I had no idea what I was looking for.

"There." I pointed and hoped Sasha was paying attention.

"You're kidding, right?"

"Calculate a jump for there."

"You're craz… just forget it. I think we both know that already." Sasha shook her head. "I hope there's a plan attached to this."

"A plan? I hope so. Set the jump for the other side of it."

"That means if we don't time it right we're going to end up right in the middle of it."

"Exactly." I smiled devilishly at her.

"Oh."

"Hey, we've already been almost dead a couple of times. What's one more?"

"And if your phenomenal luck quits just as we come out of hyperjump?"

"Then we won't know what hit us."

"Oh, yes we will. We know what we're jumping into."

Sasha was being a real pain in the neck. "You are just the eternal pessimist, aren't you?"

"I'll never be disappointed."

"And you miss out on all the fun. Get to it. He's nudging his ship toward us." We'd talked long enough to give the guy hailing us the chance to move closer and take a look.

"Hurry, Sash," I said urgently. He was getting too close. "Hurry."

"I am hurrying," she replied.

"I've got to go. He's getting too close for us to make a clean jump."

"Don't push me!"

I made a decision and shifted the vessel into gear. "Do it on the run."

"What the craz are you doing, Pork?"

"I'm sorry, but the gentlemen you requested is no longer present," I announced on the comlink. "You may leave a message if you like."

"You're gonna die, bitch!"

His ship immediately sped forward to intercept our escape, but I was already on the move. "You've got to be quicker than that." I laughed at him.

He cursed me in very graphic and provocative language, all the while his lasers were blasting in a wide arc. He didn't hit a thing.

"See you later, pal." I swept the ship around for the jump and set off at speed. "I need those coordinates now, Sash!" A second later the numbers appeared on the screen in front of me. Sasha jumped into the co-pilot's seat and reached for her safety harness as the hyperjump began. Streaks of laser fire passed either side of our ship as our speed increased and were finally left behind when the hyperdrive made the leap.

"Did you have to do that?"

"What?"

"Tease him like that. If he catches up with us he's going to be mighty pissed."

"That's the point. We want to piss him off so he'll follow."

"But he's one of Wallco's boys."

"Will you drop it about Wallco and his boys?" I snarled. "In exactly...," I looked at my chronometer, "... three and a half minutes he'll be a pile of dust."

"That's assuming he'll follow." She stopped when I glared at her. "What?"

"You do realize that I haven't decided about the arrangement yet."

"So?"

"So, you keep depressing me and I might not be able to make the right decision. Got me?"

"Are you threatening me?"

"I wouldn't do that Sash, but your constant harping on about Wallco, and our impending doom, is not helping the situation." At that precise moment I had an urge for a drink. It was a momentary lapse and the urge was gone before I'd even had the chance to stand. I settled for a coffee synth instead.

"You're pretty relaxed," Sasha said as I sat down with a mug in one hand.

"Nothing we can do now."

Sasha glanced at her chronometer.

"Yeah, two minutes left. Stop checking." I took a sip of the boiling hot beverage.

Sasha began drumming her fingers. I tried to ignore it. After all, Malt used to do the same thing and she had four hands. Sasha's two hands were a mere inconvenience. I positioned my chronometer so I could see the time and continued to drink. There was no way I was going to finish it so I took the mug back to the replicator and got rid of it. Now it was time for the fun.

"Thirty seconds," Sasha said nervously.

"I know." I reached for my harness and buckled up.

"Twenty seconds."

"Sash, I don't need a countdown." The ship vibrated as we started to come out of hyperdrive, the rubble and dust beating heavily on the hull. "Hang on."

The star field in front of us finally came into focus as we re-entered normal space. "Get us out of here!" Sasha yelled.

"I'm on it." As soon as the controls would respond I hit the throttle. We were in the path of a comet and it was bearing down quicker than I had anticipated. Its close proximity made the ship rumble and I was beginning to wonder about the sanity of the plan.

"Hurry, J."

"I'm doing the best I can." I felt the heat of it even through the hull of the ship. "Can you see him?"

"Not yet." Sasha activated the scanner and did a sweep. "Where the craz is he?"

"Well, if nothing else, we escaped." I maneuvered the ship out of the way and turned it round for a view of the comet's passing.

"But he knows who we are."

"Sash, he didn't see us, okay? Stop worrying about this." I quickly glanced at her. "You got a new ship out of this. Be happy about that."

"Oh, no, no, no. I can't keep this. I may as well hang a sign over my head. We've got to get rid of it."

"What? It's practically a new ship—"

"There he is," Sasha interrupted, her finger pointing out the window. I only caught a glimpse of it before the comet swept it away. As expected, there was nothing left behind but a trail of debris.

"Sorry, buddy, but it was you or me," I muttered.

"Don't start questioning yourself, J. It was necessary."

"No, it wasn't. We could have jumped a couple of times and lost him."

"It doesn't work like that, and you know it. Besides, Wallco tags his ships. That guy knew where we were going even before we got here."

"Still—"

"J, listen to me. If you didn't stop him, he would have reported back to Wallco, and we would have been chased until we were both dead. At the least the Noorthi would have lost their Ratha, but more probably he would have killed them too. He's that sort of creature."

I knew she was trying to rationalize my decision, but it was another death that I had to carry. Was this going to be the story of my life from now on? How many more lives would be lost in the name of Ratha? It was a situation that I couldn't see a way out of. I was in too deep to just walk away. "Let's go find Malt."

†

We met up with Malt at Fornia a day later. We had lost so much time. I had hoped that we would be back at Alengola with answers and a plan. Leaving Beri and Rice in the hands of Clea was not my idea of safe, and every moment away from them gave Clea one moment more to steal her away from me.

"Where did you go to?" I heard the concern in Malt's voice.

"It wasn't my fault!" I cried before Sasha had a chance to point the finger.

"It certainly wasn't mine," Sasha added.

"Figures. It was neither your fault that you got into trouble. Is that how the story goes?"

"Yeah, that's the one."

"We jumped and the cruiser followed. We took cover in an asteroid field."

"And you got hit," Malt answered.

"Yeah."

"She didn't look." I suppose I was being petty, but for once I'd like to not be responsible for an accident. Sasha glared at me. "Well, you didn't. It was your idea—"

"I didn't hear you complaining at the time!" Sasha countered.

"Then what happened?"

"We crash landed on an ice planet," Sasha continued "We managed to get the radio going, sort of, and a pirate answered the call."

"We knocked him out," I said. "Then we stole his ship."

"I see."

"We need to get rid of this vessel." Sasha insisted.

"Why?"

"It's one of Wallco's ships."

I could tell by Malt's silence that she thought like I did. Wallco who?

"Oh, for crying out lo–. He's a sector warlord who would blast us to pieces if he found the ship." Sasha was disappointed with our lack of knowledge concerning universal affairs.

"She thinks the ship is tagged."

"I can check that." I heard Malt on the other end working, even though she didn't speak. A few moments later she responded. "Look in the hold. There's a small locker high on the back wall. It should be in there."

Since I was taller, I went and checked it out. As Malt had said, there was a small flap in the top corner of the hold. It took a bit of effort to get into it but when it popped a tiny box fell out.

"Found it." I held up the tag between my fingers and showed Sasha as I entered the cockpit.

"Get rid of it, for Carn's sake."

"Not here. We'll have to find somewhere well away from our side of the cosmos."

"I won't relax until that thing is off the ship."

"Catch." I tossed it at Sasha and laughed as she caught it. She juggled it like it was explosive and, in her opinion, it was.

"Don't do that!"

"When you two have finished playing around, what's next?" Sometimes Malt had no sense of fun.

"I want to get back to Alengola and get our girls out of there."

"And if they don't want to come?" Sasha asked.

"I'll take them by force if necessary."

"That's a bit extreme, don't you think?"

"We got what we came for and I don't want them hanging around that Clea woman. She's no good."

"Them, or her?" Damn Sasha.

"Them... or her... both. I want them back so we can go home."

"Uh huh."

"Sash, don't be like that. I'll talk to her... honest."

"It's amazing what a life or death situation can do to you. You were just tagging me along."

"No, I wasn't. I said I'll talk to her, and I will."

"What's going on?" Malt asked.

"Nothing," we both said at once.

"When do you want to get going?"

I knew very well that Malt's interest was piqued. If I'd heard the conversation we were having I'd be asking questions. "Immediately."

"What about the ship?" Sasha asked me with concern.

"Malt? Any suggestions?"

There was a moment's silence before she answered. "It looks like there's another freighter heading into Consortium space."

"Perfect. This Wallco guy will think his ship has been taken by the Consortium. He's not that stupid to go and get it back."

"I don't know. He's pretty crazy." I saw that Sasha was still a little nervous about keeping the ship.

"We need both vessels."

"You have a plan," Sasha asked.

"No, but just in case things go wrong I want a backup."

"As if...." Sasha grinned at me.

"Are you ready to go, Malt?"

"Sure thing. I reckon we should be back in about ten hours."

"That's about ten hours too long, but I'll take it." So much time had been lost. I just wished it was all over. "Dock with us and we'll give you the tag. We'll go on ahead. Contact me when you arrive at Alengola."

The docking and changeover didn't take long. Sasha and I sat there and watched Bessie head off in the opposite direction before we brought the Bik ship onto a course for Alengola.

"Why aren't we delivering the tag? This ship is a hell of a lot faster than that heap of yours."

It was a valid question, and I had a valid answer. "Bessie has a cloaking device. You don't. Malt isn't exactly going to knock on their door and give them a present. Besides, this ship will get me to Alengola sooner."

Sasha opened her mouth then closed it. What could she say? She knew I was right.

✝

Ten hours later we arrived in orbit around Alengola. This particular trip had luckily been uneventful, and for that I was grateful. No firestorms. No rogue asteroids on a collision course. No Consortium ambush. There was nothing but negotiating the normal course to the planet of Alengola. I was bored.

Was that why I was always in trouble? Was life too boring to live it normally? If that was the case then I agreed with Sasha. It was certainly irresponsible and I was certifiable.

What you are shaped who you are.

So being a little bit crazy is pre-requisite for this job?

You are not crazy. You are prepared to do what is necessary to achieve your goal.

That sounds like crazy to me.

As you wish.

Ah, Book. You give up too easily.

I am here to advise not to argue.

Discuss. The Noorthi discuss not argue.

There was silence in my head. I smiled. It was nice to win an argum… discussion once in a while.

Sasha maneuvered the Bik ship to the ground. I stood up and prepared to leave.

"Be careful, okay?"

"I'll try not to get banged up. After all, it looks like we have a date."

"I mean it, J. I have a bad feeling."

"That's why you're here, as a backup for my own bad feeling." I grabbed Wallco's communicator. "I'll contact you on this if I need you."

"And what do I do in the meantime?"

"Check with your buddy and have him on standby in orbit."

"Are you expecting something to happen that soon?"

"I'm going to start pushing her, and I don't know what she'll do. I'm preparing for the worst."

"The worst?"

"Yeah, that eight foot moanix she calls her Ratha may decide it's time to finish me once and for all."

Sasha reached out and grabbed my hand.

"Nothing stupid, J."

"Don't I always?" She pursed her lips at me. "Check with Malt that she's picked up the artifacts and collected the plants."

"What artifacts?"

"Geez, Sash, I don't have time for this. You check for her. It's at the base of a couple of trees near the front of the building. Noorthi artifacts. I also told Malt to... liberate... some of the herbal plants in their garden."

"Liberate?" Sash laughed loudly. "Tsk, tsk, tsk, shame on you, Ratha."

I agree with the woman. You should not be setting such an example.

And do what? Ask Clea nicely for some plants? Last time I did that she sent poison. Now its time for me to act.

But to steal?

Steal, buy or beg. I'll do what I have to do to ensure these women survive. I won't be sorry for that.

"I'm not coming back here anytime soon."

"Get going, you rascal." Sasha released my hand.

I jogged down the ramp and onto Alengolan soil once more. I had missed my family and didn't waste any time getting to the Great House. I took the front steps two at a time and headed up the staircase to the first floor. Beri and Clea were standing in the hallway. "There you are." I didn't even bother hiding myself. But the look on Beri's face told me something bad had happened while I was away. "What's wrong?"

"Rice is missing."

"I thought she was with you."

"I… I…"

"I looked after the child while Beri talked to her sisters," Clea responded.

I looked at B and she looked back guiltily. "Don't worry, we'll find her."

"She's not in the house."

"Then she's outside." That was an awful lot of territory to cover.

"But it's my fault—"

"No, B. It's not your fault. It's hers!" I stared directly at Clea to let her know in no uncertain terms who I held personally responsible for Rice's disappearance.

Chapter Twelve

A Deadly Game

"If you think I'm going to sit around here while my kid is out there lost, you're sadly mistaken. And if I have to go through Jute to do it, then she'd better get out of my way."

"You do not understand—"

"No, *you* don't understand," I interrupted, "Rice is out there. She could be in trouble or she might be playing a game. There is no way in your version of hell that she's going to allow Jute to approach her."

"She is two years old," Clea announced.

I turned around and walked away. "Two years, going on twenty," I muttered.

"I'm going with you." Beri wasn't going to be left behind, not that I would stop her.

"Oh, no, you are my guest."

"Listen, Ashaltea-poop, she's coming with me to find our kid. End of story." I glared at her and she stood there. "Come on, B."

I extended my hand and waited for her to take it. We started for the door and I looked over my shoulder at my adversary, giving her a triumphant smile. "Oh, since it's late in the day we may not be back until morning."

Ratha, I do not understand.

Book, you will learn never to stand between a mother and her child.

"Ratha?" Clea said politely.

"Yes?" I pushed Beri on ahead. "Collect some things for a cold night, and some food. I'll meet you at the entrance." I waited for Beri to leave and be out of hearing range. I so dearly wanted Beri to hear this conversation, but I knew it was for my benefit and Clea would not say it in front of her followers.

"I wish to remind you that your fellow sisters are in my care. I will do my best to see to their welfare but, as you know, I cannot be everywhere at once. I would hate for something to happen to one of the Juno Noorthi."

I knew a threat when I heard one. "I hear what you're saying, but understand this. If something does befall one of the sisters there won't be anywhere you can hide from me. Do I make myself clear?"

"Surely, but you might find it difficult once Jute is finished with you."

"Jute? Hah!" I laughed heartily. "You still don't get it. I am *the* Ratha, the one and only destined to be the Noorthi protector. Do you think someone like Jute is strong enough to stop me?"

I was probably about half-way to believing that, but a little white lie was needed to put the fear of Carn into her. It worked. I saw the troubled look in her eyes before I turned and strode away.

You may not be able to defeat the giant. What did that achieve?

Doubt.

†

I had to wait a few minutes for Beri to arrive. She had found a blanket and was using it as a carryall. It was bulging with stuff that only she knew might be useful. I, on the other hand, doubted that much of it would help.

"Forget something?" I said teasingly.

"I don't think so." She glanced over her shoulder at the blanket.

"I'm kidding. Let's go." I didn't want to waste time. Rice could be anywhere and possibly getting farther away by the minute.

We trotted down the staircase and stood on the cleared ground. "Which way?"

I knelt and looked closely at the soil where I saw a line of tiny footprints heading away from us. "This way," I said as I stood up, trotting off after the trail left behind by Rice. "How did she get away?"

"I needed to talk to our sisters and Clea offered to mind Rice."

That action, in itself, made me nervous. "Why didn't you take Rice with you?"

"I was going to, but Clea insisted that she was quite capable of looking after a child for a short while."

"I'm sure she did," I said sarcastically.

"What does that mean?"

"B, when are you going to open your eyes and see that this woman is a fraud and, more importantly, a danger to the Noorthi?"

"She is our Ashaltea-Sa, J."

"From what I've been told, she obtained it in rather suspicious circumstances."

"It's your nature to be suspicious."

"And it's your nature to ignore the obvious warning," I countered. "What has she been asking you?"

"She wanted to know about our sisterhood. Things like how we lived, where our home is."

"I hope you didn't tell her."

"I haven't... yet."

"Then don't." I had to look carefully for Rice's trail. The kid was small and she left very little evidence behind. Still, I picked up an occasional broken stalk or muddy imprint to keep me on track.

"I had mentioned Juno and Rigeus though."

"I know. I saw it on her wall."

"Saw what? I didn't see anything."

"The mural on the wall is a star map. The colored stones represent Noorthi enclaves and mines. Clea is trying to find all the locations of the sisterhood."

"Maybe she wants to re-unite them."

"They were split up for a reason, so that no one sister knew it all. Clea is piecing together the Noorthi mystery. Even I know that's not the mission of the Ashaltea-Sa."

You seem to know a lot about us.

It's only logical. Why bring together something you took so much energy to separate?

Beri remained silent for a while as I continued to track Rice. "Hey, Rice!" I called out. "Do you want to play?" I strained to hear an answer, but there was only silence.

"Why did she run?"

"You're asking me?" I don't know why Beri thought I had the answer. I had a theory, but she probably wouldn't like to hear it.

"Yes, I'm asking you. I know you have a suggestion."

"I think Clea is trying to get rid of Rice."

"And she succeeded, but for what purpose?"

I breathed heavily as I pushed my way through the Alengolan jungle. "To take over the Juno Noorthi."

"I think you're being paranoid."

"I prefer to be paranoid than blissfully ignorant until it's too late."

Beri's hand grabbed my arm and swung me around. "Too late for what?"

"Too late to save both you and Rice." Beri stared at me. I think she was trying to decide whether I was crazy or not. "Do you know Clea came from the Exeter Noorthi? You know what I found there? The Ashaltea and her successor are both dead. They'd died of a mysterious illness within a few months of one another."

"So? It happens."

"The same thing happened here on Alengola. The Ashaltea-Sa and her daughter both died of a mysterious illness that struck only them. The healers were unable to save them. In both instances, Clea graciously stepped into the role of Ashaltea and then Ashaltea-Sa."

I felt light-headed from all the talking, but Beri needed to hear it. "And those tremors? She's causing them. Jute is throwing a sack of ochre into a pit deep underground. The heat from the planet's core mixes with the mud and an explosion results. We found a similar set-up on Exeter, left behind to eventually drop a huge load of ochre into a pit that would set off a massive explosion which would destroy the planet. She's not planning to leave any Noorthi alive, B."

Beri shook her head in disbelief. I could understand that. What I had told her seemed stranger than fiction. "She's not true Noorthi. She's like me, adopted into the sisterhood. She doesn't have the ingrained traits that you all hold dear." I stopped suddenly. "Hang on a minute. You did lie!"

"I did not!"

"Yes, you did!"

"When?"

"You have to ask? How many times have you lied?"

Beri pursed her lips.

"Fine. I'm talking about back on Rigeus. You lied to Vel."

Beri ducked her head. "I'm right, aren't I? Otherwise Vel would have been looking for a mine on Juno. Juno Noorthi, Juno mine."

A nice deduction, Ratha.

Thank you.

"She found the other mine on Rigeus and thought it was the mine she was looking for. She was killing us, J. She asked a question, so we gave her an answer."

"Even with the ochre, they wouldn't be able to make the mind control drug work."

"We don't know. We had been unaware of the mine until word of Vel's search had reached us. Maybe it could, maybe not."

"You had no idea what it was capable of," I surmised.

"Exactly."

"So, were you all on it or only a few of you carried on the charade?"

"We are so ashamed. We had never lied before, but our lives were at stake. At the first sign of being tested we failed."

I pulled her close and lifted her chin. "Never feel guilty about saving lives, B. It's a natural instinct to protect those you love."

"But—"

"Look at it this way..." I had to convince her of her innocence, "...if you hadn't lied, you'd all be dead. I'd be on Rigeus alone and dead from lack of food, water, and cover. Vel would have taken over Grimm's organization and she'd now be in charge of the universe."

"When you look at it that way…"

"When I look at it this way, what you did was a good thing." My lips brushed her cheek. "But there are good lies and bad lies. Clea knows only bad lies, B. At least keep on open mind on this. Please… for me."

The Noorthi do not lie.

Sometimes a lie is needed.

I pushed on a little farther and the partial trail ran out. "Rice! Where are you?" I made my search area a little wider in the hope of finding a clue, but she seemed to have disappeared. "Hey, shortie!" She didn't even answer to that. A spike of fear shot through me. Rice always called out when I called her 'shortie'.

"I'm worried," Beri said.

"Me too. She normally responds to me."

"She always responds to you. You represent the chaos in her life."

"Please, don't start this now."

"This is why we were reluctant to have you involved in her training. She loses focus."

"B, the kid's two years old. She doesn't care about focus or lessons. She just wants to have fun and play."

"No, that is not our way."

"Then maybe it should be. There are so many good things out there that wouldn't conflict with your quest for order. Remember when I said that the Noorthi needed to have more fun in their lives?"

Beri smiled, "Yes, I remember. That seems like a lifetime ago, doesn't it?"

"It sure does." I brought up our linked hands and kissed B's skin "Let's find Rice."

I pushed on a little farther, but the trail had gone cold. "Rice? Would you like a sugar leaf?"

"We haven't got any sugar leaf," B whispered.

"It comes in handy that I can lie."

"Why lie to Rice about that? She's going to expect a treat."

"Then I'll owe her one." I raised my voice. "Come on now, Rice, enough hiding. It's time for dinner." I looked over my shoulder at B. "Now you can start worrying." I could see by B's face that she had been worrying for some time. "See if you can hear her thoughts."

Beri stopped in her tracks and closed her eyes. Not that it would do any good, but I did the same. Maybe two heads were better than one in this case. "Come on, kid. Where are you?" I muttered.

I sense nothing.

Then try harder. Even the book was trying to find her.

She means that much to you?

She means everything to me.

"I sense pain," Beri said urgently.

"Where?" My heart rate picked up. "Is it Rice?"

"I don't know. I think so."

"Which way?" I looked around for some sign of the kid.

"This way." I stepped aside and let Beri lead the way. She had the answer this time and I wasn't above handing leadership of the expedition to her.

"How far ahead?"

"I'm not sure. I've never done this before."

"You're doing great. Keep moving." I wanted to tear the jungle apart, but it would be a useless and frustrating exercise.

Beri pushed forward. At times I had to intercede and clear a path for her because the undergrowth was just too thick. She closed her eyes and concentrated, her brow furrowing for a moment before her eyes opened again.

"Any luck?"

"I think she's a few feet ahead."

I looked hard, but I just couldn't see her. "Rice, honey?"

"Raa." Rice's voice was faint and raspy.

That was when I tore the jungle apart. Rice was in trouble and I needed to find her... and quick. It took several minutes to clear a portion of undergrowth away and I was shocked to see Rice curled up in a ball, her tiny body shaking and sweaty. "Oh, Carn!"

Beri pushed me aside with such force that I was nearly splayed out on the nearby ground.

"Excuse me," I muttered. I didn't bother getting up again, instead crawling across the ground to get to Rice. Beri picked her up and cradled her against her body.

"J, do something!" I'd never seen Beri so lost as she was now. Even when she thought she had been assaulted by Vel she was angry and upset, but this… this was sheer helplessness against something she had no idea how to tackle.

"Give her to me." Beri handed Rice to me. "Let's go." I set a steady pace back toward the Great House. We needed Grit for this. When Rice moaned I broke into a run, using my body strength to push a path through the jungle. Beri was right behind me, her ragged breathing suppressed by the swish of vegetation against our clothing.

Finally the tall spire came into sight and moments later we stood at the base of the entrance stairs.

"Get Grit," I said.

Beri took the stairs two at a time and disappeared inside. I sat in the bottom step and cradled Rice against me.

"Hey, squirt," I whispered. Rice's eyes opened slowly and a smile appeared on her fevered face. "What trouble have you got yourself into?"

"Ouch."

"Where, honey?" Rice slowly lifted her hand and patted her stomach. "Grit'll be here soon and make you all better."

"Sugar leaf?"

I chuckled as tears welled in my eyes. "I'll have to owe you one. You've got to get better for a sugar leaf, eh?"

"Mmmm." Rice closed her eyes and remained still.

I lowered my head and kissed Rice on the forehead, right before I heard the sound of running feet on the marble floor. Before I had taken another breath Beri was next to me, followed a moment later by Grit.

"Let me see." Grit extended her arms and expected me to hand her Rice. She took her inside and I was about to follow when Beri's hand gripped my arm.

"Let her be. You'll only get in the way."

"How can you sit there like that?"

"Because it's out of my hands. Grit is our only hope now."

She was right, but it still annoyed me that I couldn't do something.

Clea appeared at the top of the stairs and I knew what my next move was. "You!" It took me all of two seconds to climb up the stairs and stand inches from her face. "You did this!"

"I did nothing," she said calmly.

"No, you did plenty. You poisoned my kid and I'm holding you personally responsible. If she dies I'm coming after you," I growled.

"The child ran away and probably got bitten by something out there. I would not harm her."

"Yeah right, and I have a black hole I'd like to sell you.…"

"I do not understand."

"You understand plenty, Clea. You may have them fooled, but you don't fool me." Jute appeared, taking up her position behind Clea's left shoulder. "And you don't scare me! Just stay out of my way!"

Grit appeared in the company of an Alengolan. "We are going to the herb garden."

"Do you want any help?" I just couldn't stand around.

"To do what? Abuse the leaves?" I saw that Grit was worried.

"If you keep standing here I might do that to the healers instead," I snapped.

Grit passed me by, giving me a pinch for my trouble. But I was worried enough not to make a comment. She glanced at me and our gazes met. Yes, we were both worried.

Why do you say such things to Ashaltea-Sa? There is no purpose to—

Shut up.

"Come on." I grabbed Beri's hand and we went inside to find where they had taken Rice. I was pleased to see that they had settled her in the room upstairs and not down in the basement. Two of our healers and an Alengolan hovered around her tiny form, sponging her down with a wet cloth. On a nearby table was a mortar and pestle, similar to Grit's one on Heaven. The top of it was covered in ochre, so they had started the process.

Beri rushed to Rice and knelt on the ground next to her bed. I stood back and observed the tableau.

Can you do anything for her? I asked the book.

It is out of my realm. Her destiny has been set and what will happen—

I don't need a Noorthi lecture from you, okay? I'm going to do whatever it takes to make sure that Rice is here tomorrow, and the next day, and the next, with or without your help.

I was getting cranky. I hadn't eaten for hours and I was sure that Beri hadn't either. It took a lot to leave the room, but I wasn't able to remain there. Not being able to make this all go away was disheartening to me, and staying in the room was making it worse. Maybe food would restore my mood.

I wandered down to the kitchen, this time not even bothering to sneak around. Clea and Jute knew I was here so there was no point. The smell from the cooking pots remained the same, so I detoured to the food bins to find something to eat. I passed the purple fruit and grabbed a couple of small loaves instead. I took a bite. It tasted a little doughy, but it was edible. The Noorthi diet on Alengola was not much better than that on Rigeus, and I struggled to find something to add to the menu. There didn't seem to be any evidence of meat, only the same bland staple that the Noorthi ate. There had to be something else.

I searched pots, baskets and bowls, finally coming upon a handful of leaves. I bit a tiny piece off and tasted it, hoping that I hadn't just poisoned myself. The leaf had a rich, slightly bitter flavor. I grabbed a purple fruit and sliced it up, placing the slices between a split loaf. I lay the leaf on top of the fruit and I took a bite. Somehow the combination worked. The sweetness of the fruit was offset by the bitter taste of the leaf. I made up a second loaf for Beri and padded back to the upstairs room.

Beri was exactly where I had left her, kneeling next to Rice's bed and gently stroking her daughter's head.

"Here." I offered her the loaf. Beri shook her head. "You've got to eat."

"I'm not hungry."

"B, eat. You don't want to pass out, do you?" I appealed to her mothering instincts. She'd kick herself for not being present while Rice was being looked after. Reluctantly she took the food and ate it slowly. She gazed at me after the first bite.

"Like it?"

"Mmmmm," she hummed.

"You have time to eat?" Grit said as she stood in the doorway with a variety of herbs in her hand. She handed them to one of the Juno sisters and watched as she took them to the table to sort them out. "Jama, the *casidium* first. Here is the vial." Grit reluctantly handed her the precious oil.

I tore a piece off the loaf and handed it to Grit. She remained silent and stuffed the piece in her mouth, chewing thoughtfully.

"What about that root thing you gave me?" I asked.

"The gulacca root. I have never seen the plant that it comes from."

I turned to the Algengolan healer. "Have you heard of it?"

"We do not know of this root."

"The root I carried was very old and very rare. I used what I had to save you."

"Craz!" I hadn't meant to swear and I heard the collective gasp. "Sorry."

"Do not give up. We will try all the plants we have gathered." Grit patted my arm and left my side. She walked to the table and the healers moved into a huddle, chattering as they tore at the leaves and added them to the mortar. Their incessant chattering grated on my nerves so I left.

I prowled the hallways looking for something to distract me. This was the one time that Rice was in trouble and I couldn't help. Now I knew how Beri felt.

Continue your quest.

What quest? I don't have a quest. I have the evidence that I need.

Do you?

What more do you want?

A quest of faith.

For what? Get to the point. I understood where the Noorthi got their annoying penchant for not answering a question.

What are you in need of?

A miracle? Just tell me.

Seek what you need.

"Fine." I had no idea what the book was saying, but I gave up on the conversation. It would go around in circles for another minute before I lost my temper. Unfortunately, this particular voice I couldn't walk away from. I had to get out of the house before I kicked a wall.

I stood at the top of the stairs and breathed deeply, allowing the Alengolan air to fill my lungs. Grit had walked to the left to find the garden, so I followed her path. It was a surprising distance away, maybe five minutes or so, and it opened up onto a field. Row upon row of carefully tended plants sat there, blossoming and growing in an age-old tradition.

I reached into my pocket for the comlink. "Malt? Can you hear me?" There was nothing but silence. "Where are you, kid?" Wherever she was, she was out of comlink contact.

You do not dare.

Why not? They won't miss a plant or two. I can assure you that I won't be coming back here anytime soon.

You are going to steal.

Didn't the sisters tell you? I lie, steal and cheat, and do a whole lot of other things that would make you squirm. Glad you're with me now?

You are Ratha—

Whoa! Hang on there. You chose me. That meant taking everything that went along with it. You've already taken away my drinking. Now it looks like I'm losing the girl, as well. I think I'm due for something to go my way.

And the point is—

The point is, Book, if we can transplant the herbs from here to our own planet, then maybe the other sisters can do the same. You want the sisterhood to grow, don't you?

You have not been paying attention.

What are you talking about? Thoughts and ideas flooded my mind. It was like a tidal wave of information.

There are tens of thousands of us, through a number of universes. You think too small, Ratha.

Did they know where they were going or did you just say go and propagate?

For their safety, their destination was their own choice.

Then how did they know where the ochre mine was? A thought came to me. They didn't. They made it.

Each Ashaltea took a small piece from the ochre mine here.

Those little guys? They built it? I was impressed. My buddies in the mine were special indeed. And that's the secret? Those glowing bacteria can adapt to anything you want it to be?

Not exactly, but close.

What? You just ask the universe, please can I have this?

I had a warm feeling within me. *Something like that.*

"Aaarrggghhh. Carn I hate that phrase!" I screamed. *Then why didn't it work for Grimm?*

Because he is not one of us.

Who you are determines whether the little bugs will do you a favor?

Something li—

Don't say it!!

We Noorthi are highly evolved. We are at one with the universe. We feel it as it feels us.

So, what exactly are you? The peacekeepers of the universe?

I heard a clearing of a throat before an answer. *Peacekeepers* for *the universe. We speak in its name.*

Being pacifists sort of make it tough to enforce. That explains what I'm here for. I hope you're not expecting me to run off every five minutes to break up a fight.

That is not your destiny, Ratha.

Even though I do enjoy a good fight, I'd like to have some sort of life in between catastrophes. The gulacca root. You are from the beginning of the sisterhood. Where is it?

It is no more. You must look elsewhere.

Then that's it. If Grit can't find a cure, Rice is dead.

Your quest of faith.

You keep saying that. Carn, I hate it when you talk around in circles! Say what you mean!

Your quest of faith.

"My quest of faith," I muttered. "If you think I'm going to worry about faith at this time, you're sadly mistaken. Rice's life hangs in the balance and you're talking about my beliefs."

Her life is out of your hands.

Screw you.

I left the garden and headed back to the Great House. This was one of those times where I was out of ideas and I didn't like it, not with Rice's life at stake. Carn, I'd even consider anything that was offered by Clea. Why did that stupid ochre help me but couldn't help my kid? The ochre...

I detoured to the clump of trees nearby. The stack of treasure was thankfully still where I had left it.

"Okay, guys," I said as I picked up the jar. "I need your help here. My kid is very sick and needs your special magic. I'm begging you...." I stumbled over the words. It was really happening. Rice was this close to dying and I was begging mud to save her. Maybe this was my crisis of faith. Then again, maybe it was that stupid idea I was looking for. What had I got to lose? Rice for one, and my sanity for another.

Did I believe the ochre could save her? It had done things that in my book were not only unbelievable but also unthinkable.

One of the larger jars glowed, the ochre slowly rising to the rim. This was my answer. I scooped the mud into the palm of my hand, taking a moment to close my eyes and offer a silent prayer of thanks. They had obviously thought my plea was worthy of an answer.

I wasted little time contemplating the act that had just taken place and ran up the stairs to the first floor and Rice's room. The tableau I left hadn't changed. Beri was still on her knees next to Rice's bed while Grit and her healers were busy mixing a potion in the mortar. I crossed the room and knelt next to B.

"Wait! What are you doing?" one of the healers asked.

"I'm saving my kid's life." I lifted my hands above Rice's face, painting her lips with the unadorned ochre. "Come on, Rice honey."

I pried open her lips and stuck my finger in, running the ochre on her tongue. "Swallow."

Grit appeared behind me holding a shallow bowl. I took it from her and gently lifted Rice to take a sip. "Here you go, shortie. Take a drink."

Would she do it? Could she do it? I dribbled the water on her lips and her tongue poked out to touch it. Her mouth opened slightly and I allowed a drop or two to fall. Rice's eyes opened slightly and she gazed at me as she tried to smile.

"Mama?" she croaked.

"She's right here with me, Rice. We're both here," I whispered. "We love you."

"Wuv," she said back, before her eyes closed once more. That was all she said for some time.

"Now what?" Beri asked.

"Now, we wait."

"What did you do?" Grit was confused by my actions.

"I gave her some of the ochre from the mine."

"But the herbs—"

"Grit, it was time to put my money where my mouth was." Grit's perplexed expression nearly made me laugh. Now was not the time for joviality. "I mean it was time to put my faith in the ochre."

"Faith? You?"

"Shocking, isn't it?" But would my faith be rewarded? I was hoping so. "The gulacca root was our only hope, but that option was no longer available." Now was not the time for fancy explanations. "We had no more root so I tried the only other thing I could think of."

"But why just the ochre? It has never been used that way before. We have always used herbs and plants."

"There are things you don't know about this ochre. Things that in time you will come to appreciate," I said enigmatically.

"You cannot tell us?"

"I suppose I could…"

If you do, you are betraying everything.

"…but for now it's best kept a secret."

"But–" Jama said.

Grit laid her hand on the woman's arm to stop her talking. "Ratha knows best."

My eyebrow rose at the statement and I exchanged a glance with the old woman. That was one for the books. Ratha knows best. We both knew what that was worth.

I moved to the wall and slumped to the floor, leaning my back against the wall.

"Come here." I opened my arms to Beri. "It's going to be a while." Beri joined me and accepted the cuddle. Her head lay on my chest and I closed my eyes for a moment.

Little Rice. I remember clearly the moment she was born. She had a set of lungs on her even then.

✝

"Come on, B. Like Grit said, push!" I knelt beside Beri's bed and acted as her one-girl cheering squad.

"You push!" she growled at me.

I'd never been part of a natural birth before and Beri was turning out to be quite a tigress.

"Do you want me to call Gorin?" I offered. I knew the old man would have all the up-to-date techniques involved in birth.

"You bring him here and I'll kill you!" Beri stared at me. Oh, yeah, she meant it.

Grit continued her chanting above Beri's spasming body. Fen was positioned at Beri's head, while Epi knelt at her feet.

"How much longer?"

"As long at it takes, Ratha."

"Just great," I mumbled.

"You've got somewhere else you have to be?" Epi asked.

"If it means B stops screaming at me, then yeah."

Epi chuckled. "Who'd have thought you'd be scared of an iddy-biddy baby."

"It's not the baby that's worrying me, it's her." I pointed my finger at the writhing figure in front of me. *"She's scary."*

Epi laughed loudly. *"This is something I've got to remember."*

"And I have a clear memory of a mountain top. Do you want them to know your secret?" I challenged.

Epi stopped. *"Er, no. You are no fun."*

"And I thought the Noorthi didn't believe in fun."

"When you two stop chatting, I could use your attention." Grit looked at us sternly and we looked suitably chastised. Beri let out a moan and I forgot all about the conversation.

"How long is this supposed to go on?"

"As I said, it will take as long as it takes. The child will not be rushed."

"Is B supposed to be in pain like that?"

"That has always been our way."

I have to admit that I found it upsetting seeing her suffer that way, but Grit didn't seem concerned about her progress. Who was I to tell her how to deliver a baby? My experience was non-existent. I'd always been told an hour with the medtech and it was all over. B had been having this baby for more than five hours. I think I was in as much pain as she was and it was making me cranky.

"Hell-o! I'm right here!" I heard the irritation in Beri's voice.

"I know that, dear."

"I don't like being talked abou-wow-wow!" Another contraction hit. *"Sweet mother of all that is holy!"*

I gasped. *"Is that cussing I hear?"*

"This is all your fault!"

"You're the one who wanted this baby!"

"You had to go and touch me, didn't you!"

"I didn't know what I was doing!"

"You got that right. Who else did you get pregnant?"

"Now, B–"

"Will you two stop it!" Grit yelled. *She closed her eyes and breathed deeply. "This is not our way," she murmured. "Do you want Ratha to leave?"*

"By the Mother, no! If I have to suffer, she's got to suffer!"

"And what am I supposed to do?"

"You sit there and be the focus of her wrath," Grit said. *"The rest of us can then do our work."*

"Great," I mumbled and slumped back. My knees were killing me. Now Beri was going to finish me off. My hand crumpled under Beri's firm grip. *"Ow! Ow! Ow!"*

"Now what? She's just holding your hand." Epi seemed way too amused at my situation.

"You hold her hand."

"I'm not the one who got her pregnant."

"This is all a conspiracy, isn't it?" I'm sure this was Noorthi karma coming back to bite me in the ass. *"Kick poor old J while she's down."*

"I would never kick you, at least not while you were conscious."

I gave Epi a withering glare. Beri flexed her hand again and I'm sure I felt something give in my fingers. For a holy woman, she sure was strong.

"Now it is time."

"Time for what?" I asked stupidly.

Grit stared at me. *"You can push, Ashaltea."*

"You mean she wasn't before? What was all that wailing and grunting about?" Now I was confused.

"Practice," Epi answered.

I grinned at her evilly. Maybe I should drop her off on top of the plateau and let her deal with her fear of heights for a while. Epi's smile dropped. While we were bantering, Beri grunted and let out a howl. A second later the grunting stopped and Epi and I turned our attention to the squirming bundle in Grit's hands. Carn, she was so small... and wet... and wriggling around ready to take on the universe. That was my kid. My kid. Our kid. I had a kid. Oh...my... Carn.

"What's that?" I pointed to the cord sticking out of her stomach that seemed to be attached to Beri.

"That is the blessed union. The mother and child are as one until the child is born."

"Then what? My kid is going to walk around with that thing hanging off her?"

Before I had finished my question a knife appeared in Grit's hand and she flicked it quickly, cutting the cord.

"What the Carn are you doing?" I reached for Rice, but Grit batted my hands away.

"She is fine, young pup. This is the way."

"Yeah, the way to kill them both."

Epi came up to me and prodded her finger in my chest. "You do not question the way," she said seriously. It seemed I had reached the line in the sand where my comments were blasphemous. I never thought Epi would stand up to me. It seemed that I was wrong.

"My apologies." I stood back. I always had a smart remark for whatever befell me without thought of who it offended. Now I knew how far I could push Epi before she pushed back.

"J," Beri croaked.

"Yeah," I stumbled to her side.

"Water."

"Oh, sure." I scrambled to the work bench and poured a cup of water. I was in a bit of a daze with everything that happened and all, so my journey of a few steps back to her was instantly forgettable. Gently I lifted Beri up to give her a drink and I felt her tremble. "It's over."

The baby cried loudly, the sudden sound causing me to juggle the cup in my hand.

"No," Beri said quietly, "It's just beginning."

†

I hadn't realized that I had been smiling, but Beri's comment made me realize that I had.

"What's so funny?"

"Nothing. I was just remembering when Rice was born."
These are memories?
Very special memories.
"That wasn't funny."
"No, not for you."
"You thought it was funny?"
I heard the edge in Beri's voice. "Er, no."
"But you were smiling."
"I was remembering you cussing at me."
"I... do... not... cuss," Beri said succinctly. "You cuss."
"I sure do, but when Rice was being born you cussed at me."
An Ashaltea would not do such a thing.
Believe me, Book, she cussed.
"I have no recollection."
"You were sort of busy at the time, as I recall."
"I did not." Beri's voice rose in volume.
"Maaa."
"I'm telling you, B. You cussed in your own way."
"And I'm telling you, I'm incapable of doing such a thing."
"Raaa."
"What!" I barked. It took a second for me to realize where the sound came from. "Oh, Carn!" I crawled from my seated position to the bed in a moment. "Hey there, honey. How are you feeling?" I felt Beri's presence beside me. "See? Mama's here too."

"Ow," Rice complained, her hand rubbing her tummy. Grit lowered the blanket and Rice's torso was smeared with an oily black substance.

"What the...?" I stood and grabbed Grit's arm. "Get a sample for Malt," I whispered, "and don't let anyone see you."

"Why?"

"I think she was poisoned."

"Poi—"

"Please, Grit, just do as I ask." I returned to Beri's side.

"What just happened?"

"The ochre has cured her."

"But how?"

"I'll tell you later. Believe me, it worked."

"Believe? You believe?"

"Don't be so surprised. I discovered a thing or two that changed my mind." I could say that again. I leaned in to Rice's ear and whispered. "Thank you, guys."

Rice giggled. "Funny."

"Feeling better, huh?" Rice nodded. "That's my girl. Now hold still while Grit cleans you up." But asking Rice to stay still was like asking me to give up breathing. It was impossible. She giggled and squirmed as the wet cloth wiped away the black slick on her chest.

When Grit had finished she sidled up to me. "This is truly a miracle. Is this Noorthi doing?"

"It sure is. I'll tell you how later."

"Why not tell me now?"

"Because I don't want Clea to find out."

"Is this not something for all Noorthi?"

"No. This is why you were scattered to the far reaches of all universes, *memesh*. It's something that, for now, must remain a secret."

"As you wish, Ratha."

I felt that Grit gave up too easily, but knowing her she'll probably ambush me later on and pinch the truth out of me.

"Ratha?"

"Yes?" I hadn't recognized the voice at first, but I certainly knew the dimples. She offered me a drink and I took it. "Thank you, Delphan." Her dark eyes met mine and she smiled.

"Delphan?" Beri looked at me, then at her. "How do you know her?"

"Jealous?" I raised my eyebrow at B.

"We Noorthi do not possess such shallow emotions."

Yeah, right. "Fen was talking to her earlier down in the basement." Beri looked at me as if trying to decide whether I was lying or not. "You can ask Grit if you don't believe me."

"No, I believe you."

"No, you don't. You just want me to think that you do."

"I do not lie."

"Fine."

197

"Maaaaaa!"

Little Rice didn't like not being the centre of attention, so she made her presence known.

"Yes, Rice." Beri leaned in and gave her daughter a hug. It was so damned cute to see Rice's tiny arms fling around Beri's muscled arms enthusiastically and try to grab on with all her might.

"I was just being polite... honest." I stood and moved back a few steps to allow Beri time with Rice. I waved Grit to me. "Delphan," I whispered. "If she asks to come with us, say 'yes'."

"Yes? Why?"

I just knew she'd say that. "She has been chosen." I tapped my forehead.

"How do you know?"

I tapped my forehead again. "She is your successor."

Why are you telling her after I said not to tell anyone?

Grit already knows about you, or have you forgotten? Someone has to know otherwise she could get left behind.

Maybe that is the way of things.

I'm not coming back.

That may not–

I... am... not... coming... back.

"Why do you look like you have indigestion?" Beri asked.

"You're right. Something disagreed with me." I handed her the cup and she took a sip before she strolled to Rice and offered her a drink.

Rice greedily drank the water until she emptied the cup. "More."

"Delphan, do you mind?" I asked. The young woman happily complied, refilling the cup from a jug. She smiled at me again and I saw the confusion in her eyes. She didn't know why she found me interesting, but I was like an itch she had to scratch. Somehow I didn't think that leaving Delphan behind was going to be a problem.

The room shook. Beri looked at me. "What? It's not my fault."

"Should we be worried?"

I glanced at Grit and thought about it. "Nah. It's the Great Mother talking, remember?" By the look on B's face I think she really didn't believe that. Despite her heritage, my B was not stupid.

Clea stepped into the room, her smile turning to pursed lips when she saw Rice sitting up in bed. The smile re-appeared just as quickly. "This is good news. Your child is well?"

"Yes. It seems she has recovered."

"I thought she was gravely ill."

Because of you, bitch.

Ratha, what are these evil thoughts?

You best close your covers, Book, because I'm going to be thinking a whole lot more evil words about this woman.

Such thoughts are counter-productive.

But it makes me feel a whole lot better.

But—

Book!

"Our *hedera* was able to find a cure."

"Is that so?" Clea turned her attention to Grit. I silently pleaded with *memesh* to agree, even though it was a lie.

"I... I..."

"She is humble about her abilities, Ashaltea-Sa."

Clea turned back to me and her eyes narrowed. I wondered what I had said, until I realized I had used her title instead of her name. I was mentally kicking myself for that one. "You got a problem with that?"

"No, but if she is that good I may just exercise my right and have her stay here."

Over my dead body. All my girls were coming home with me.

Why do you keep saying things that you cannot possibly do.

You don't think I'd fight for Grit? I'd fight Jute for her, as I would Beri and Rice. They are my family.

Family. This concept is foreign to me.

You have a lot to learn.

I will consider your offer.

"I'm afraid we can't accommodate you, Clea. Our *hedera* has pressing commitments at home."

"But–" Beri started.

"No," Clea held up her hand, "I understand. Your *hedera* is too busy to see to our needs. That is fine."

I saw the deception, and I wondered if Grit could. "Thank you, Ashaltea-Sa. My sisters are in need of me." She did. I silently applauded her diplomacy.

Clea smiled sweetly and as she turned away I saw the edge of her lips turn down. It seemed I had won this round.

Chapter Thirteen

Confronting Issues

Once Rice was safe I went outside to contact Sasha. "Hey, Sash!"

"Yeah?" She sounded a little weary.

"Has Malt arrived yet?"

"I'm here, J."

"Are the artifacts and plants stowed away?"

"Yep. There's just me and that girl waiting around for something to happen."

"Where are you, Sash?"

"Both Malt and I are on the ground."

"And your buddy?"

"He's circling around upstairs."

"Great. Then, I think it's about time we make a move."

"What do you want us to do?"

"Stay put. I'll send out our Noorthi to meet up with you."

"J, that Noorthi girl's gone!"

"Malt, it was your responsibility to look after her!"

"She took off before I could stop her! She must have slipped out while I was in the hold."

"Stay put."

I hadn't seen the girl so I wasn't even sure if she had made it this far yet. Maybe Canthi had already arrived while I was seeing to Rice. If that was the case, then Clea would know where we had been. I ran inside and descended the stairs to the reflection room in the basement in case she had sought out her sisters.

The room was as I had left it. The Alengolan Noorthi were seated around the pool whispering to one another, in quiet meditation or praying. My Noorthi, less Grit of course, were still huddled in a circle. I approached them quickly and hunkered down. "I want you all to go outside. We're going home."

I didn't wait for an answer and quickly left. I still had to find Canthi.

I tried the first floor and she wasn't there. I heard a harsh cry and ran down the stairs to the entrance. I arrived just as Jute dropped Canthi's body to the ground. That, that... thing had snapped the poor girl in two, leaving Canthi's back bent at an obscenely sharp angle.

I saw red. Twice this had happened to me. Why couldn't I protect those around me? "Hey, you! Bitch!" Her black eyes focused on me while a smile touched her lips. "I'm going to cut your heart out!" I knew I couldn't because of that damned metallic mesh of hers, but the intent was there.

"I wish you good luck." Clea came up behind me. I assumed she had observed everything.

"Was that really necessary?" I nodded toward Canthi's fallen body.

"She had betrayed her sisters."

The Noorthi filed out and looked on with concern. Fen ran down the stairs to Canthi's still body.

From the contact I had with Canthi, I couldn't see the sweet girl betraying anyone. "I seriously doubt that."

"She revealed your evidence to me."

"Unwittingly," I added.

"Unwittingly, of course, but she revealed a secret that shouldn't have been uttered."

"I don't get it. All she knew was that I had visited Exeter and I was on my way back here."

"You are their protector. Is it not their job to protect that knowledge if it is for the benefit of all Noorthi?"

In an insane sort of way it made sense. "But it wasn't worth forfeiting her life."

I heard a cough and looked to see our conversation was being observed by the Noorthi, both Alengolan and Juno, who had gathered in the dusty forecourt. Beri had a sad sort of smile on her face. Yeah, I know. I said forfeited. It was too fancy a word for such a solemn occasion. I walked down the stairs to meet her.

"Clea, it's time to step down." I said loudly for all to hear. I seriously doubted she would do just that, but I had to ask.

"Jordana, is it?" She knew damned well what my name was, but I nodded just the same. "You are misguided in your assumption."

"Assumption? It's no assumption." I looked around at the assembled Noorthi. "You say you come from Peralis?"

"That is my home."

"There's no Noorthi on Peralis. I was just there."

"I was *born* on Peralis," Clea qualified. She looked me in the eye and dared me to answer. She smiled at me in triumph.

"Not so fast, sweetheart." The Noorthi gasped at my familiarity with their leader. "As you know, I also checked Exeter is where it was claimed your Noorthi sisterhood existed."

"And what did you find out?" She seemed unconcerned with what I would reveal.

"Oh, they'd heard of you. In fact, I found them cowering in the dark. And how convenient is it that you killed the one person who could verify the facts."

"I can verify them," Malt said.

"She is with you. What you say cannot be accepted."

"Then maybe this will convince them all." I held up the tiny disc that recorded our trip down the mine at Exeter.

"That can be manipulated."

"And how do you know that? From my contact with the Noorthi, they have no knowledge of modern aids. How could you possibly know what it is?"

"Jute showed me things."

"Right. A woman who can't talk explained to you what this is. No, the only way you would know is if you had lived in the universe before the Noorthi. I know for a fact that you are not one of them. Like me, you are an adopted Noorthi."

Erica Lawson

"Prove it."

"Your mother didn't want you!" I yelled. "You were left abandoned with a group of women who couldn't give you the love that you so desperately wanted. It was beyond their understanding. So when you were old enough, you took your revenge. The Ashaltea suddenly became ill, as did her successor."

I paused and waited for the information to sink in. There were hushed whispers. "You then offered to step into the role of Ashaltea."

"I did what any responsible Noorthi would do, offer myself to serve the greater good."

"Oh, you served all right. Jute arrived on Exeter and the Noorthi were nothing more than your servants. The one thing you didn't count on, however, was the delay in the ochre falling into the chasm. Exeter is safe from an explosion."

"You lie!"

"Are you calling me a liar?" I smiled gleefully at her. "I dismantled the makeshift bomb myself, as you will see on this recording. You had finished with the Exeter Noorthi and were moving onto bigger things, so you left a little surprise for them. Unfortunately, for you, it didn't happen. You're nothing but a fraud."

"Sisters, this *human* is nothing but a pretender. She is not one of us and therefore has no say in our lives."

Grit stepped forward. "I beg to differ, Ashaltea-Sa. Jordana Laren is our anointed Ratha and she has proven her worth. She is one of us in spirit."

"*Hedera*, she has bewitched all of you. She cannot be trusted."

"And you cannot be trusted!" I called out. I was getting sick of this ranting and raving. "How about we show them your chambers, eh? Then you can explain to them why you have a universal star map on your wall with the locations of the ochre mines throughout the various star systems." I pressed my case. "And then explain to us why you need to know this information. Why do you think your distant ancestors sent the sisterhood out to the far reaches of space? It was always the opinion that the Noorthi

204

secret was too dangerous for any one person to know it all. They splintered their group for the good of all.

"And now you want to undo all of that. But to what end? What can you possibly gain by knowing this secret?"

I really didn't know what to expect of her. All I had was speculation and partial truths. Unless she was prepared to reveal all, the only thing I could prove was that she wasn't a true-born Noorthi. Would that be enough to usurp her power?

"Jute. This pretender has worn out her welcome. Please show her off this planet."

So, she had called my bluff. "Aren't any of your concerned that she lied to you? In my three years with the Noorthi I have never known them to lie. They are not capable of lying. Yet lies roll off Clea's tongue with practiced ease."

She says she is from the Exeter Noorthi, but they quiver at her name. She says she is the daughter of an Ashaltea. Is she lying about this also? She has already told you one lie. How hard can it be to tell another? If each of you looks into your heart you will see that I'm telling the truth."

Jute approached me and shoved, sending me sprawling onto the ground. "See? She uses someone who is no stranger to violence, someone who is not worthy to bear the sign."

I stood and held up my wrist for all to see. I was doing my own bit of grandstanding, but I didn't expect the reaction I got. The Alengolan Noorthi dropped to their knees and bowed to me.

"Oh, for crying out loud!" I was exasperated. "Why do they keep doing that?" I asked Grit.

"You are the chosen one." It was a rhetorical question, but Grit answered it just the same.

"That is so corny." Then I had a thought. "How come you didn't do that?"

"We knew better."

And I suppose that was it in a nutshell. My Noorthi were more at ease in the universe, and I loved them dearly. They viewed life with a lot of optimism, humor and practicality. It was something that the Alengolan Noorthi were sadly lacking.

205

"You seem to forget, Jordana, they have no one else to turn to. I am their only choice for Ashaltea-Sa." Clea had a point.

"Then maybe it's time for a change." I saw Grit's jaw tighten as I said it. Was this her great upheaval? "Maybe the succession of Ashaltea shouldn't be solely based on who your mother is. If there is a woman amongst you who shows some leadership ability, then she should be your Ashaltea-Sa."

"Why don't you understand that I am the Ashaltea-Sa? No one here will support your cause besides your own Noorthi."

"Why? Are they too scared to speak up because of you? It wouldn't surprise me."

"Jute, I think it is time to act."

Jute's eyes glittered. This was not good, at least for me. "Come on, Jute. You don't have to do this," I pleaded.

"Scared?"

"No, but I'll try the peaceful way first." I couldn't go in fighting right away with all the Noorthi watching. However, that didn't stop Jute from charging at me. It was like hitting a brick wall. My body slammed into her hard frame and it felt like the front of my body was trying to go through the back of my body. I groaned. It was a habit that I would have to lose if I was to remain a hero in Grit's eyes.

Jute lifted me above her head. Again. This was really getting old.

"Keep her busy, J!"

I glanced sideways and saw Malt and Sasha dragging something heavy to the edge of the forecourt. Jute body-slammed me to the ground. "No problem," I groaned. I rolled out of the way just as her foot came down, but I could do little about the kick to my midriff that followed.

"I just need a couple of minutes."

I didn't think I had a couple of minutes, but if that's what it took I'd just have to find the time from somewhere. "Great."

"I wouldn't try that if I were you." My gaze shifted to Malt's position and I saw Sasha holding off Tikka. "Get on with it, Malt."

I had no idea what Malt was up to, except that it would probably save my ass. Jute approached me with no fear. She was expecting me to capitulate, I suppose, and while it was a viable option it was not one I wanted to use. I was the Noorthi Ratha and my job was to protect.

My foot shot out and swept Jute's feet from underneath her. She thudded heavily to the ground, giving me the chance to stand. Not that the fact that I would be standing would help my situation, unless I was planning on running away. I moved to the edge of the clearing and grabbed a branch. Well, it had worked once.

But not this time. Jute was already on her feet and her two massive hands grabbed the branch and ripped it out of my hands with ease. She batted me away with it.

"Hurry up, Malt!" I was running out of ideas.

I pulled myself upright and instantly regretted it. Jute's image swam in front of me. When I could finally gain some focus there was three of her. Which one was the real one? What the craz? I picked the middle one and hoped for the best. With some luck, I could swipe either side of me and hopefully get all three Jutes at once.

"Believe!" Grit's voice rang out. I glanced at her and she gave me a stern look.

"Believe… right," I muttered. Was fear holding me back? Grit had been right in so many things. Was she right this time, as well? I looked at the scar on my wrist. It was there for a reason, just as I was here for a reason. Believing meant that I would have to accept that I was some sort of anointed avenging angel for the Noorthi. To right wrongs. To protect. To be a hero.

Time had passed for me to hide behind my fears. I had to step up to my responsibility or admit defeat.

"Your time is done, Jute." The words tumbled from my lips. Did I mean it? Yes… yes I did. I had let go and now stepped into the shoes only I was supposed to wear.

Her shoulders bobbed and she snorted. I think she was trying to laugh. Clea made the sound for her, laughing at my ridiculous statement. When I stared at her she stopped, her confidence replaced by indecision. "Kill her."

If the Noorthi doubted her sincerity, Clea had condemned herself with those two words.

"Your power is gone, Clea. Now you will join Jute in her fate."

Jute was already lumbering toward me. I bellowed, allowing all the pent up anger and frustration to fuel my resolve. I charged at Jute, dropping my head and leading with my shoulder. The hard contact was jarring, but I continued to push forward. My run had slowed to a walk but I persisted, taking one step at a time to push her back. I swiftly withdrew and Jute stumbled forward. I took the opportunity to jump on top of her, rolling her so that I was sitting on her chest. I pinned her arms with my legs and began to hit her with my fists. It was like trying to hit Bessie, not that I would, but the woman's metal-embedded skin was resisting my fists.

I ignored the pain and kept hitting her. One strike broke her nose and I heard the crack. Jute stared up at my in surprise and I smiled. It drove me onward. My fists were bloodied and torn, but I paid it no mind. Jute was on the defensive and I had to keep her there.

A smear of blood painted her lips, but I suspected it was more from biting her tongue that any actual damage. Still, a visual sign of damage to her invulnerability was as good as the crack to her nose.

"Ready, J!"

Was I ready to give up my position as attacker? Jute's expression changed from surprise to one of anger. She was about to dish out some serious pain. Yes, I was ready.

"Go!" I yelled as I rolled off the top of her and out of the way.

The hum was faint as first, slowly building in volume as Malt increased the power. I wasn't sure what she had in mind, so I took a step or two backward. Jute's face wrinkled in confusion. Suddenly, she started clawing at the dirt as her body moved slowly toward Malt's whatever-it-was. The sound increased and Jute moved a little faster across the courtyard, finally ending upright and immobile on the board Malt had erected. Jute struggled to get free, but she seemed to be stuck fast.

I walked up to the board but Malt called out, "Stay clear."

"Why?" The question was quickly followed by a tug on my belt buckle. The pull was enormous and I felt my boots slide across the dirt. "Oh, craz." My progress was stopped abruptly as I hit the board. Now I understood.

"Good work, honey," I said with my face mashed against the metal sheet.

I imagined Malt's smile was electric. But it was the only image was I was going to get from my position against the board.

"I could use a hand to get off this."

It took Fen, Beri and Grit to pull me off the thing, while Sasha stood guard over the machine. I was going to end up with a massive bruise across my back from where the belt dragged me, but it was worth it. We had stopped Jute. Now I had to decide what to do with her.

"Watch out!"

My attention was drawn to Beri as she called out and pointed her finger at Jute. I swiveled on my foot and brought my fists up ready to continue the fight. But it wasn't Jute I had to worry about. Clea had pushed Malt to the ground and had the small console in her hand. "Jute, I want you to tear her into little pieces." Her thumb rested on the slide control and pushed it viciously upward.

"No!" Two of Malt's hands shot into the air. "Too much!"

The energy in the air hit me in waves as the panel increased its pull. There was a harsh gargling sound coming from Jute and her face was contorted in agony. Her body was covered in huge pits, her skin pulled taught as the board tightened its grip on her.

Malt wrestled with Clea for possession of the console pad, the air beating heavily with the vibration. Suddenly there was a squelching sound and a collective gasp. I didn't want to look. Clea stopped resisting and allowed Malt to take the controls. The vibration stopped and the air was silent. It was an eerie sensation.

Okay, I looked. Jute slid down the board, leaving behind a bloody smear. Her body was riddled with holes where the metal mesh had been torn away. It seemed that Malt's magnetic field had been pushed to maximum and Jute's metal mesh didn't stop until it reached the plate. "Someone cover her up," I said.

I heard a sob and saw movement in my peripheral vision. It was Malt. I glanced at Grit and silently pleaded for her to join me. This was going to need some delicate handling. Maybe Fen would have been better for the job, but I suspected that Malt looked up to the old woman. Grit may be ornery at times, but her bearing spoke of wisdom and experience, and Malt could certainly use some of that right now.

I slowed my pace to stay with Grit.

"Don't you think you can handle this?" Grit asked.

"Yes but, then again, my life has a lot of violence in it. I think she needs a reassuring word from you, *memesh*."

She grunted, which I assumed was a 'yes'.

It took several minutes for us to find Malt. She didn't move as we approached. Despite everything, I think the kid was glad that I came after her. "Hey!"

Her tear-stained face looked up at me from her position on the ground. "I killed her!" The tears flowed unheeded.

I sat down beside her while Grit looked on. "No, you stopped her. Clea killed her."

"But my machine—"

"Malt, listen to me. This is not your fault. You saved my life... again. You stopped Jute from killing me. You made her immobile. You are not responsible for Clea's actions."

"Ratha is right, *Reekaskti*."

"What? What is that?" Malt gazed up at Grit.

"I suppose it means 'she who plays with toys'. We do not have a word for toy, or for play, but that is what I meant."

"See? Only special people get cool names like that," I jumped in.

"Does that mean I'm one of you?"

I looked up at Grit and asked, "Does it?"

Grit smiled. "I suppose it does. She has proven her worth, Ratha."

"You have the Noorthi seal of approval, so that must mean they don't believe it's your fault either."

"Do I get a tattoo?"

"A tattoo? Now wait just one minute..."

210

"You've got a tattoo. Why can't I have one too?"

"You're too young to have a tattoo. Next you'll want to take Bessie out every other night."

"A-hem!" Grit said loudly.

"Do you feel better to go back now?" I stood up and extended my hands.

"A little. As long as I don't have to see her."

"I think that can be arranged." Malt took my hands and allowed herself to be pulled to her feet. "Can I drive Bessie for an hour or two when we get back? I promise I'll be careful."

"Oh, brother." Was I this bad? Worse, I think. Suddenly I felt very, very sorry for my dad.

We wandered back slowly to the Noorthi house and Malt used her sleeves to wipe her face.

"How did you get the magnetic thing ready so quickly?"

"It was the same thing I used to get you to the ship. Don't you remember?" Did I? I was pretty much out of it at the time.

"I'd been working on it for a while. I figured if you were going to confront the giant you'd need my help, so Sasha helped me carry it to the clearing." Malt sniffed.

I slung my arm over her shoulder. "That was pretty smart. Good work."

Malt looked up at me with red-rimmed eyes. The tears had stopped for now. I had found that time was a good healer, and considering that Malt was young I knew her mind would be on something else soon enough.

"Grit has something for you to look at back home."

"What?" Malt looked from Grit to me.

"The poison?"

"Poison? What poison?" Malt's curiosity had already started.

"There was a black slick on Rice's body. I asked Grit to take a sample for you to study. I think it's poison, but I want you to make sure."

"Okay."

We arrived back at the Great House where Beri stood by as the cleanup began. Jute's body had already been taken away and the metal board was in the process of being cleaned.

"Cosu akti noor Reekaskti!" Grit summoned her Noorthi together.

"What's going on?"

"It seems that Grit has deemed Malt is worthy to be a Noorthi," I announced proudly.

"Really? And what does *Reekaskti* mean? I haven't heard that one before."

"She who plays with toys."

Beri threw back her head and laughed.

"I thought it was very inventive." Although I thought it was hilarious too Malt wouldn't catch me laughing in front of her. "Now she wants a tattoo."

"A tattoo."

"She's too young for a tattoo...." I began.

"You've got a tattoo."

"No, that's a scar. Besides, I got that only three years ago. I was much older than she is now."

"J, she's a Noorthi...."

"Can't she be a Noorthi without the tattoo?"

"What is your problem?" Beri was quite amused about my stubbornness.

"If she gets a tattoo, then there'll be another one, then getting her body pierced. Where will it end?"

"You're afraid she won't need you anymore."

Beri was right, although I wouldn't admit it to her. "Where did you get that idea? I just think..."

"You just think you're going to lose this one." Damn the woman. "She wants to belong, so we'll let her belong."

Beri drew me to the circle seated on the ground. In the middle of the circle sat Grit and Malt. Grit took one of Malt's hands and held it in her own. She started the incantation, murmuring softly so her words couldn't be heard. Delphan stepped through the circle and handed a small parcel wrapped in soft cloth to Grit. She bowed and stepped away.

Malt looked up at Delphan and stared. Well, well... The two girls gazed at one another for a long moment. There was some confusion in that look but there was something else, something that was going to condemn Malt to hours and hours of sleepless nights.

The ceremony continued much as I remember it, except for the slight chuckle when Malt's name was mentioned in English. I watched her face as Grit applied the tattoo. I had to give it to her. She barely flinched with the needle pricks. She was probably too much in awe of the whole situation, and while there were the sparkling lights at the end of the ceremony, I seemed to remember my lights were of a more robust nature. It was probably my imagination remembering the event a little differently, considering where that initiation led me.

Everyone stood and there were hearty congratulations from the Juno Noorthi, while the Alengolans were a little more reserved in their happiness. These women were truly boring.

I had a sudden thought. "Where's Tikka?" She had been missing from the confrontation. As if to answer my question the ground shook. "Oh, she didn't." There was another tremor. "She did." There was no time to lose. "Malt! Get to the ship and tell Sasha to get the freighter down here!"

"I'm on it!" The tattoo ceremony seemed forgotten for the moment as Malt grabbed Delphan's hand and dragged her away.

"What's going on?" Beri found me. She had collected Rice from a Noorthi minder and the kid was sitting on B's hip.

"I think the planet is about to explode."

"Plode?" Rice cried.

"Yeah, honey. A big bang."

"Oooh, bang."

"Not now, Rice," Beri scolded her. "You have to be quiet."

Rice stuck a finger into her mouth and batted her eyelashes at me. She was such a manipulator.

"Tikka's missing. I think she's trying to carry out Clea's plan."

"What plan?"

I sighed. "Didn't you listen to anything I said?"

"I was busy watching Jute."

"Why?"

"I just wanted to make sure she didn't attack before you knew about it." She did care, I knew it, but it was going to make the arrangement all the harder to bring up.

"To cut the story short, Clea was going to blow up this planet once she had the information she needed. I think I wrecked her plans."

"I don't get it—"

"Do we have to discuss this now?" My gaze slipped over her head. "Grit!" I called out, "Find the artifacts from the Great House and assemble here. Let our sisters find all the Alengolan Noorthi. We have to leave."

Then there was chaos. The ground rumbled in defiance, the soil ripping open in pain. There was a roar as the surface buckled and heaved. I reached for my comlink. "Sasha! We need that transport now!"

"I'm on it," Sasha replied.

A few minutes later Bessie appeared overhead, slowly lowering to the ground. The ramp was already emerging and the hatch door opened. "You need to leave," I said.

"You're coming too," Beri pleaded.

"I have to make sure everyone gets out of here." I was already pushing Beri toward Bessie. "Go." Rice fussed and wriggled in Beri's arms. "Get her on board." I kissed Beri on the forehead and mussed Rice's hair. "See you soon, shortie."

"Raaa!" she squealed. Rice knew something was wrong.

I saw Fen helping an elderly Noorthi. "Fen, time to go. Where's Grit?"

"She's still in there." Fen nodded in the direction of the Great House.

"Back in a minute. Keep loading, Malt." I took the staircase two steps at a time. Grit was at the far end of the hall, wrestling with Clea. "Grit! We've got to go!"

I started running down the corridor toward the two women when the roof collapsed. "Grit!"

They had both disappeared. Oh, Carn. I vaulted over rock to get to her.

Please, Book, save her. I'm not ready for her to go yet.

If it is her time, then so be it.
Not if I can save her.

I was not going to have some damned book tell me what I could and couldn't do. Grit would live to see another day, damn it! I felt each and every bruise I earned climbing over the rubble and figured that I would benefit from an ochre soak after this. My little ochre buddies could rub their asses off on my skin to soothe the ache.

"Grit! Craz, woman, where are you?" I didn't even realize that I was nearly screaming.

"Do you have to yell so loud?" She seemed almost calm in amongst the devastation.

"Don't scare me like that."

"I am pleased to see you too, child." She smiled gently, holding up the tiny statue that had nearly cost her her life.

"Where's Clea?"

Her eyes flickered to one side and I followed her gaze. All I saw was an arm sticking out of the rubble. While I was glad to see the end of her, I felt that the Noorthi were cheated out of their retribution. No, not retribution. That was not their way. Knowing them as I did, they would probably have forgiven Clea. I chuckled.

"What is so funny?" I saw that Grit thought I was laughing at her predicament.

I started moving the stones holding Grit in place. "I was just thinking that if Clea had survived what punishment you would have meted out."

"Punishment? That is not our way."

"I knew you would say that." I kept moving the rocks. "But I figured you would probably talk her to death. You and your incessant discussions."

"We do not discuss—"

"*Memesh*, please. I'm trying to rescue you here."

"Then hurry up."

The crotchety old woman was telling me how to rescue her. Some people were never happy.

Finally, I removed the last rock and I reached in to offer my hand. She took it with surprising strength and I pulled steadily until she was able to find her feet. I looked back over the rubble to the entrance and I knew Grit wouldn't be able to climb it. "Get on my back."

"I beg your pardon?" The earth rumbled again and more of the roof caved in.

"Don't argue. Get on my back and I'll carry you out."

She did as I asked and I heard her snicker in my ear. "I hope you will put me down before we reach the end."

"Afraid of being caught?" I asked.

"Of course not."

I said no more because I knew I was right. Like me, she had a reputation to uphold, and being carried out like an invalid was not an image she wanted to present to her fellow sisters.

I started over the rocky surface, taking one unsteady step at a time. Alengola continued to self-destruct, the tremors wracking the planet almost continuously. My footing was tenuous at best and a couple of times I landed on a bruised knee. This hero business was tough work.

"No time to think of yourself, young pup."

"That's not nice to be spying on my thoughts."

"What else is there to do when you take so long to travel such a short distance?"

"Oh, yeah? Well, you try it sometime!" I snapped.

She didn't seem to mind my answer and she laughed.

"What's so funny?"

"You are so easily offended."

I hadn't realized it at the time, but she was distracting me from my task as I had easily negotiated the obstacle course to the front door. It was another one of those mysterious Ratha moves that astounded me.

"You can put me down now," Grit whispered in my ear.

"You're welcome." I knew it was as much of a thank you as I was going to get. "Now get on Bessie and head for home."

"But—"

"My job isn't done yet." I was already pushing her down the stairs toward the waiting ship.

Something wasn't right. Beri was still on the planet and yelling. I ran up to her. "What's wrong?"

"Rice!" She didn't need to say more.

I grabbed my comlink. "Malt! See if you can find Rice!" I grabbed Beri's shoulders. "Get on board. I'll find her."

"But—"

"Don't argue, just do it!" I pushed Beri hard, forcing her up the ramp. I watched as she reluctantly disappeared inside.

Grit came up beside me. "Go," I said quietly.

"Come back."

"I will, *memesh-kan*." She smiled at my very personal address then left me standing at the bottom of the ramp. "Malt, I want you to get out of here. Head for Covaris."

"No! I'm not leaving you here—"

"Sasha will get us out. Make sure the Noorthi are safe. It's important." Reluctantly, she agreed and drew in the ramp.

"And what about you?" she asked.

"I'm going to go find Rice and get the hell off this planet."

"If there's time."

"I'll make time." I wish. If I could do that, then rescuing Rice would be a cinch. "See you at Covaris."

Are we alive I now had to find my kid before the planet exploded.

Chapter Fourteen

A Moment Too Late

"She's heading through the undergrowth ten degrees to the right of the ship."

"Thanks, kid." I broke contact quickly because I didn't want to argue. As I headed in the direction Malt gave me, I heard something. It was faint at first, but it grew quickly in volume as I got closer.

This is your last chance to be saved, I said to the book in my head. I really didn't want to be the one to go down in history as the killer of the Noorthi spirit.

You doubt your ability to rescue the child?

No. I may get to Rice, but this planet may not hold together long enough for us to escape. Do you wish to die with me? Who was I kidding? This thing inside me probably couldn't die.

"Mama!" Little Rice's voice was panicked, not that I could blame her. The ground under my feet bucked and heaved in its death throes.

"Hang on, shortie!" I called out.

"Raaaaaa!" I heard her terror.

I ran full out through the vegetation. I had no idea what I was treading on or whether it was safe. My complete attention was getting to my kid. Suddenly I ran out of ground, and I was hard pressed not to fall into the chasm under one of my feet. My arms flailed about as I tried to keep my balance and one hand reached out blindly to grab something to hold onto. Instinctively, my fingers wrapped around a branch and I hauled myself back to safety.

"Raaaa! <hic> Raaaa!" The poor kid had the hiccups.

"I'm here, honey. Stay still." I looked down and Rice was standing on a ledge twenty feet down. Her tiny hands reached vainly for me. "I'm on my way down. You stay there, okay?"

"Otay <hic>"

Oh, Carn, she was breaking my heart. There were very few handholds down the rocky face and the vines seemed sparse, so I resorted to the only thing I could use. I caught the end of an overhanging branch and used my weight to lower me down to Rice. The earth heaved again and I couldn't stop my face from slamming into the wall, but I couldn't let go. If I did, the branch would spring up and we'd both be stranded on the ledge.

The branch reached its limit and I was about five feet short. Without even considering my options, I let go. Damned if I was going to leave Rice all alone at a time like this. She threw her arms around my leg and hugged tightly. Those adorable child-like eyes of hers looked up my torso to find my face.

I sat down and let her come into my arms. "Okay?"

"Otay," she said, smiling at me.

What is this you are feeling?

Love. Love of family. This is what is missing from your Noorthi.

Interesting.

Forever, I said.

"So, short stuff, you running away from Mama again?"

She giggled.

"It's not a game," I said sternly. The platform we were on shook violently, pieces of rock breaking off and falling into the chasm. I held out my hand to Rice to allow her to play with my fingers. It wouldn't be long now, but at least we were together.

You are not trying to escape.

I looked up the escarpment to see what crevices there were to hold onto.

I can't, not with Rice.

But you could save her.

Not enough time.

The rumbling was deep and threatening, and debris was showering down from above. "Not long now. Do you want to meet your grandpa?"

"Granna?" She looked up at me expectantly.

"My daddy."

"Leaf?"

"I don't know, honey. He might have a sugar leaf or two just for you." I touched her nose as I spoke and smiled. Rice stood up in my lap and put her arms around my neck. She planted a wet kiss on my cheek. "Otay."

"Okay." That said it all. As long as she wasn't alone everything was okay. I held on tight and didn't let her see the tears that I shed. "Sorry, B. I wish I could be there for you." I closed my eyes and waited for the inevitable.

The sound was almost deafening. A wind had whipped up and was spraying dust over us. I pulled Rice tighter to me to cover her face from the stinging sand. "Come on," I whispered. "Do your worst."

"Are you going to sit there all day or what?" Sasha's voice came over the comlink.

I choked out a laugh. "What took you so long?"

"I took the scenic route." Her words echoed mine of a few days before.

"What are you expecting me to do? Just float up to you?"

"That would be nice, you being Ratha and all."

"Well, it ain't gonna happen any time soon. Get your ass down here."

A small metal platform lowered from the bottom of Sasha's ship. "Climb aboard."

"I hope you're not taking us home on this." The comlink went silent for a moment. "Well?"

"Wait, I'm thinking about it."

"Sash!" I yelled.

"Hey! I can hear you!"

She maneuvered the platform to the ledge and I climbed aboard with Rice in my arms. "Get us the hell out of here."

"One more detour."

"Sash!"

"You really want to fly into space without a suit? I'd prefer all your gorgeous body parts in one piece, but if that's what you want...."

"I have Rice with me. Stop talking." I felt a blush coming on and Rice giggled. Her finger came up to my cheek and pushed. "Yeah, Ra's all embarrassed."

"Embow... Ra." Rice's attempt was just too cute for words.

Sasha moved her ship and we flew through the air. Now I knew what bleezarks felt when they soared high overhead. It was exhilarating in a way, and yet terrifying at the same time, but that may have had something to do with the fact that I knew I could fall and they didn't.

It was a short hop to the landing site and the safety of the interior of the ship. As soon as my feet touched the ramp Sasha started retracting it. She was not going to slow down for my benefit, and I couldn't blame her.

I slumped into the co-pilot's chair and buckled up. Rice sat on my lap and I wrapped my arms around her middle and held her tight. "This is going to get a little hairy."

"You think?" Sasha glared at me. She had the ship in motion and we were swooping over the treetops briefly before heading upwards toward the stratosphere. Large chunks of rock were hurtling in all directions, exploding out of new fissures in the ground.

Sasha's sensor alarm went off. "Incoming," I said urgently.

"I can hear." Sasha glanced at the screen and veered sharply to one side as a block roughly the size of her ship shot by at an amazing speed. It must have just missed, but I wondered how many layers of metal it scraped off in passing.

The trajectory upward was rocky. Sash swerved in all directions to avoid getting hit, and it made the trip longer and more dangerous. We needed to get as far away as possible in the shortest time we could. The rock storm coming from the planet was making the job very difficult and I began to wonder whether we had enough time.

As if to answer my question, the planet exploded. "Hit it!"

Sasha slammed her vessel into full speed, trying to outrun the massive percussion wave following us at enormous speed.

"Jump!"

"But we could slam into—"

"Craz it, do it or we die!" I realized that I had cussed in front of the kid. I just hoped she didn't repeat it in front of B.

Sasha shoved the drive into hyperjump and we hoped for the best. It was either get shaken to death off Alengola, or we slam into a random planet, sun, star or asteroid field. In any of those events, at least we wouldn't know what hit us. It was in Carn's hands now.

✝

"Are we alive?"

"Don't know. You're still here."

"And what does that mean?"

"Well, in my version of the hereafter, you're there." Sasha winked at me. "Besides I'm still in this damned ship. If I'd died, I'd at least ask for my old ship back."

"Raa!" Rice barked.

"See? She doesn't like the way the conversation is heading."

"What? She's got no idea."

Rice looked up at me and we exchanged looks. "Do you really believe that?" My kid was smarter than anyone was giving her credit for.

"Oh, come on. She's two years old."

"So? How old were you when you noticed what your parents were talking about? I don't want her repeating anything to Beri."

"Have you talked to her yet?"

"Are you listening to yourself? In case you haven't noticed, I've been a bit busy trying to rescue everyone."

"Since when did that stop you?" She grinned at me. "I'm joking."

"No. I still haven't made my mind up." She looked almost disappointed. "It's not you, Sash. It's me."

"How do you feel right now?"

"What has that—"

"Just answer me," Sasha asked, "How do you feel? Excited that you escaped death? Adrenaline running through your system?"

"Yeah, I suppose it is." Where was she going with this?

"And when we get home, what are you going to do?" She had a point. "Beri can't help you. Are you going to go back to your trusty right hand?"

"Please, Sash!" I covered Rice's ears. "She's going to remember this!"

"Well?" Sasha looked at me seriously. "How much longer are you going to ignore this? You need to get it out of your system one way or another."

"Sash, I can't think of you as a convenience. You are my friend. I'm not going to use you when I have a need. It doesn't work that way."

"I know that!" Sasha cried. "It's a situation that I wish was different, but it isn't. And it's a situation that isn't going to change any time soon." She studied the holomap and calculated the distance left. "We should finish the jump in about three minutes."

"Where will we end up?"

She looked at the readout. "I picked a random destination. It looks like its Stereng."

"Could have been worse." I knew she didn't have the time to work out a destination, so we could have ended up anywhere.

"Yeah." I heard the wistfulness in her voice. She thought the conversation had ended. But she was right. It was a decision I had been putting off because I had reservations, but was it right for all concerned? I knew every moment that I hesitated made Sasha feel even more worthless. "Look, Sash—"

"No, it's okay. It was just a suggestion."

"My problem is that I don't know if I can keep this arrangement from just being an arrangement."

"I suppose that is a possibility," she said cautiously. "So what does that mean?"

"I wish I knew."

What do you suggest? I asked my book.

Noorthi sisters have no need for physical comfort.

223

So? Make some sense.

Ratha, there is no need to ponder this. Physical contact and emotional contact are not mutually exclusive.

Oh, but it is. It's what makes us human.

But we have evolved past that. Physical attraction is but a distraction to the spirit.

Then you're missing the best part. I suddenly had an epiphany.

"Sash? I'll talk to Beri and we'll see how she reacts."

Sash smiled at me. I had said something right.

†

We met up with a relieved Malt in orbit around Covaris. This planet was starting to grow on me. Now it wasn't the planet of my near demise, but the planet where I was reunited with my family. For a moment Beri didn't acknowledge my presence because her attention was on her child. I didn't take offense because I would have done the same.

"Why did you do that, Rice?"

"Scawed."

"That was no reason to run away." Despite her words, I could hear the tremor in B's voice.

"And she's sorry. Aren't you, squirt?"

"Otay." Rice ran to her mother and threw her arms around her leg. Beri scooped her up and hugged her tightly. Over Rice's head she mouthed *thank you* to me.

I mouthed back, *you're welcome*. I had never felt so scared in my life when trying to find Rice in the jungle of Alengola when the planet was disintegrating. Alengola no longer existed. It had now passed into the realm of myth. I only hoped we had rescued enough of it to ensure the continuation of its inhabitants and culture.

Grit came up to our little group and placed her hand on my arm. "Do you doubt it now?"

"No," I said, then chuckled. "I've given up trying to fight it."

"That is good." Grit turned and left me. She didn't mince words.

You have done well, Ratha.

Thank you, er, Book. What do I call you?

You do not have to call me anything. Who else are you going to talk to in your head?

I've had the occasional visitor from time to time.

Then we will discuss it when that happens.

Where do we go now? Do you answer my questions when I think them?

Yes, we can do that, but a lot of knowledge will come to you when it is needed.

My brain is going to be full of junk? I barely keep track of what I know already. I thought I heard a sigh in my head.

It will be available to you when you need it. You will just know.

Okay, but if I forget Malt's birthday or something, it's all your fault.

"Are you all right?" Beri prodded me.

"Yeah. I was just thinking. Wondering what we were going to do with the extra Noorthi."

"They can come back with us."

"It's not that simple, B. We'll be doubling the size of the Noorthi, plus mixing two different tribes. There's going to be arguments."

"We do not argue."

"Yeah… right. You don't argue like I don't cuss." Beri kept her mouth closed because she knew if she opened it she'd be proving my theory right. "They can come back temporarily until we can relocate them to somewhere safe." She didn't look happy. "B, it won't work. You live your lives very differently. I've just gotten used to you, and I don't want you to change under the influence of them. I'm sure they feel the same about themselves. No, it's only temporary."

Beri nodded and walked back to her Noorthi sisters. She knew I was right.

"And how are we going to get them back to Heaven?"

225

I reached for the comlink. "Sash? Contact your dad and get him to bring the transport to...." I didn't want him to have to travel all the way here, so where could we meet? "Any suggestions?"

Sasha was quiet for a moment. "How about Valos?"

"You are a troublemaker."

"What's wrong with Valos?" Beri looked at me.

"If you want your sisters to get a real education about what humans can do, then Valos is the place to go."

"Did someone say Valos?" Malt leaned out of the cockpit doorway. "You have my vote."

I laughed. "Of course, I would. You're hoping that cute brunette is still hanging out for your return."

"What brunette? What's wrong with Valos? I don't understand."

I placed my hands over Rice's ears. "It's a place where you can get drunk and have sex any way you want it."

"I thought that was what Telgan was for."

"It's like Telgan, only ten times bigger."

"I don't mind. I've noticed you've been getting a little edgy lately."

Edgy? I would have said downright horny. "Sash? Tell Rales to meet us at Valos, and bring some credits with him, plus a thousand extra. Tell your buddy to take the freighter to Valos. When your dad meets us, give the guy the thousand and say thanks for the rescue. We'll stay there for twenty-four hours for some recreation if anyone wants it." I heard Malt's whoop of joy and smiled. At least someone was happy.

"You know...." Beri said.

I had a feeling now was the time to bring up the arrangement. "Can you give Rice to Fen? I'd like to talk to you in private."

Beri glanced warily at me but she disappeared for a moment, returning empty handed. I held out my hand for her to grab. "Come on." I drew her into the cockpit, nudging Malt out of her seat and out of the room. I sat down and took the controls.

"Should I be afraid?" Beri looked at me uncertainly.

"No. Something's been on my mind for a while." Where did I start? "I have a dilemma."

"And I'm part of it?"

"Yes." The fact that she asked the question gave me hope that there wouldn't be a long, drawn-out explanation of my dilemma. "I'm wondering if we'll ever get together."

"Together?"

"As in physically together."

"You mean…"

"Yeah. In three years we've gotten to a kiss. I suppose I want to know, will it go any further? Am I hoping for something that may not happen?"

"No, it won't happen."

Hearing Beri say it was like at stab to my heart. While we had avoided the subject there was always a distant chance she would say 'yes'. Now that dream had died.

"That's how it must be, J."

"But I thought—"

Her hand came up to my lips. "I care for you more than you'll ever know, but I can't give you what you want. I am a Noorthi and I have responsibilities."

"Don't you think I know that? Hasn't everything that's just happened illustrated that point?" I stood up and paced. "But I don't know if I can go on this way, B. You and I have different ideas about this relationship."

"Relationship?" she said quietly, looking up at me. "We had a child, Jordana, not a lifetime commitment."

"But–"

"Sit." She waited patiently while I stood there glaring at her. I finally relented and sat back down. "If I do what I know you want, I will betray my Noorthi beliefs. We do not seek the weakness of the flesh. Ours is a spiritual attainment."

"Don't preach to me, Beri. I know what's involved. We've been together for three years…"

"And I'm happy with that. I have your companionship and nurturing support."

"But you don't want sex," I said flatly. It wasn't a question because I already knew the answer.

"Not from what I've seen in your mind, no." She smiled at me, and I know she was hoping for an answering smile. Craz, the woman was infuriating.

"So where does that leave us? I don't think I could handle being celibate for the rest of my life."

"You could pray."

"Very funny. Me pray." I looked down at my clenched hands and willed myself to let them go. My thoughts wandered to Sasha. Carn only knows why, but she was amenable to a relationship of sorts. It wouldn't be like me and Beri, but she said she would figure it out. Hell, I couldn't.

"What do you want, J?"

Now that was the million credit question. What did I want? Ideally, I wanted a sexual relationship with Beri, but that just wasn't going to happen. Could I survive without sex for the rest of my life? Not unless I wanted to wear down my right hand to a stump, no. It was either a compromise or walk away. I focused my attention on Beri, but I didn't see tension or apprehension.

"I'm stuck between an asteroid field and the Consortium." Beri's head tilted to one side. "I either find a compromise or I walk away, both of which are not my first choice."

"If you wish to seek another's...," she hesitated as she searched for an appropriate word. "Comfort to ease your pain, I will not stop you."

That wasn't the same as saying, 'I give you my blessing'. "I wish I didn't have to do that, B. Damn it! Why can't I be like you and live without these urges?"

"Because you're not like me, or my sisters. You are uniquely you, Jordana Laren. That is why we chose you. You have the resolve to do things we cannot, and yet you have the compassion to not overstep the boundaries of human empathy." Her hand rested on top of mine. "I give you my blessing."

I knew it. She listened in on my thoughts. *No fair, B!*

"I have to use every advantage I have, J, just to get around you. I can see what you are troubling about. If Sasha is amenable, you both can have a relationship."

"But I feel like I'm betraying you."

"How can you betray me with something I have no use for?"

"I know that, but it doesn't make it any less wrong."

"Then don't do it." Beri was beginning to irritate me. "No, I'm kidding. Our relationships are on different levels. I hope that you will still be there for me because I don't know if I can do what I have to do without you."

Could I compartmentalize each relationship? I seriously doubted it. At some point in the future I knew something would change and there would be conflict. Did I want to risk it all? I could have gone to a perfect stranger for the same thing, but then look where that got me. Besides, having sex is so much nicer with someone you actually know.

"Do you want me to talk to Sasha?"

Okay, that was really weird and made me feel uncomfortable. "Er, no thanks." Having one girlfriend talk to the other about sex? No thanks. "So that's it then? You've planned out my sex life?"

"Sure, if that's the only problem you have." She stood up, then leaned and planted a kiss on my cheek.

"Don't do that," I said quietly. Beri pulled back and looked hurt. "No, you can do it, but just not now. It makes the betrayal all the more heinous."

"You really need to lighten up, J. And leave the fancy words at the door, okay?" She walked out, leaving me alone with my thoughts.

"What have you done?" An aggravated Grit stood in the doorway.

"I didn't do anything. What are you talking about?"

"Our Ashaltea does not look happy. It can only be because of you."

"Why is everything my fault? Maybe it was Rice, or even Fen. Did you ever think of that?" But Grit just glared at me. "All right, it was me."

She plopped herself down in the chair vacated by Beri. "Well?"

"I asked for something and she wouldn't give it to me. She said she had her duty." I said duty like a spoiled child.

"You do not understand."

"How can I understand if you don't explain it to me?" Damn it! I wished they would just say what they mean.

"Beri has made a great commitment to you."

"Really? She could have fooled me." Grit sat there calmly studying me. "Grit, please! Spit it out!"

"Spit? I will not spit."

I sighed deeply. "Why won't she have sex with me?" After I said it I realized it sounded both selfish and crude, but if I didn't ask a pointed question I was not going to get a straightforward answer.

"We must keep the body pure."

"But that was for having a baby. She's had the baby, so what's stopping her now?"

"Why is everything about you, young pup?"

"It's not about... why?" Maybe it was the exasperated look on my face that made Grit answer.

"To us, the ultimate expression of this thing you call love is Beri's commitment to be with you."

"But why is making love so abhorrent?" Great, now my speech skills were ganging up on me.

"Abhorrent?" Grit thought for a moment.

I grasped for a Noorthi equivalent. "Neeshka."

"Ahh. Have you ever thought that it might not be wouldn't but couldn't?"

"Couldn't?" My mind zeroed in on the one possibility. "Is she missing... something?"

"Something?"

This was going to be a tough conversation. By the sounds of it Grit had no idea of what I was referring to. Without a visual demonstration I doubted I would get my meaning across to her. "Are the Noorthi human?" I started with something simple.

Grit smiled. "Ah, she finally is on the right path."

"Well, she is asking you. Are you human?"

"Not like you, Ratha. We are *keentanka*."

My mind sought an answer. "Evolved?"

"What does that mean?"

"I suppose it means that you are now something more than human."

"Our Order has been in existence for thousands of years, each generation a step closer to our destiny."

"And when will you reach that destiny?"

"We will know when we reach it."

"Oh, come on. You are able to see the future. You must have some idea."

"This is the one truth I cannot see. There are so many paths to choose, so many decisions not yet made."

"You mean me." I had expected her to tell me not to be so self-centered, but she didn't.

"Our whole future is in the hands of the powerful few. You have begun the great upheaval, my friend. Your destiny is now linked with ours. Do not abandon Beri because she will need your strength and resolve."

"What?" I grabbed Grit's arm. "Is she...?" I couldn't say it.

"No, of course not. She will have her trials, as will you. You both will find strength in one another."

I sat there contemplating what was in store.

"We have no need for physical displays of affection. Take comfort that she has not bound you to our ways. She has given her blessing to you to seek comfort elsewhere and I, for one, am happy to see that your search has not strayed too far from our midst."

Did that make me feel any better? Grit had also given her consent to my relationship with Sasha. It seemed that I was the only one who had reservations about it.

"I'm worried that things might change. That I will come to feel more for Sasha than I had planned. I don't want to cause a rift between Beri and myself."

"Then I will be here to remind you." Grit said the last two words with purpose. She would kick my butt if I let things get out of control. "While Sasha will be your *pallexis*, remember that Beri is your chosen."

"Yes, ma'am. After all, you're the *hedera*."

Well, that was it. Everyone agreed to this. My love life was now something for public record.

†

We had been on Valos for an hour. The Noorthi had been housed in a local hotel for the twenty-four hour layover. I couldn't leave them floating around in space while we all had fun down on the planet. Malt had already begun her search for the brunette and I sent Sasha along to make sure she didn't get into trouble.

I couldn't use the opportunity presented to me to satisfy my own needs, so I played babysitter to one hundred Noorthi. They ran me ragged. How many times did I have to fetch water and food? Couldn't they order all at once?

Rales came up to me and laughed out loud. "You look tired."

"Why did I ever agree to this?"

"Because no one else would do it?"

"They were smart." I found a seat and sat down. "How are things back at Heaven?"

"Fine. That sertech fellow fixed up everything. Thank Carn he was there."

"Yeah, thank Carn."

"What's wrong?" Rales took a seat next to me.

"You don't want to know." Talking to Grit about it was one thing, talking to someone who you considered a surrogate father was something else.

"You mean between you and Sasha?"

My jaw must have been hanging open because he laughed again. "Where did you hear that?" I asked.

"You're kidding, right? There are one hundred women upstairs. How could they possibly keep a secret like that?"

I wasn't going to tell him they had kept a really big secret for thousands of years.

"You don't seem upset," I said warily.

"It's none of my business."

Yeah, right. Of course it was his business. His two girls there thinking of doing something that was unthinkable. "Don't you think it's just a little bit creepy?"

"I wouldn't say creepy. Unusual maybe."

"Unusual? You mean you don't mind this?"

"Of course I mind this, but I know you girls and I believe that you will make the right decision."

"So you're saying I shouldn't do this."

"No."

"I'm confused."

"If I said 'yes', you'd think I was a little bit crazy."

"You got that right," I mumbled.

"I may not give you my blessing, but I do understand. Sasha always did have a soft spot for you."

"It was the first I'd heard of it."

"Then you're not very observant. Do you have a problem with Sasha?"

"No. She's a great girl, but I did consider her family."

"You hardly saw one another. Sasha was always off world when you were around. I thought you knew."

"No."

"Do I have to point out that you're not related?"

"But—"

"Are you worried about what people will think?"

"It seems it's a bit late for that," I mumbled. "I was more worried about what you would think." Sasha walked up to me.

"Well, I'll go and see if the ladies need any assistance." He made his excuses and left.

"Don't ask if they want water!" I called.

"Hey," Sasha said quietly.

"Hi. Where's Malt?"

"She found a brunette. I don't think it's the one she was looking for but she seemed happy enough."

"Sash! I wanted you to stay with her so she's not taken advantage of."

"The girl has four arms. The brunette has her work cut out for her."

"But–"

"J, she doesn't want me watching over her shoulder."

"But does Malt know what she's doing?"

233

"She has to learn sometime." Sasha inched closer to me. "So...."

"So...." My voice pitched higher than normal. I reached for Sasha's hand. "Sasha, this is a good thing you're doing for me."

"I was hoping it would be for us."

"I'm sorry I'm being an ass about this." I let go and clasped my hands together. "You'd think after everything I've done, this wouldn't be a problem."

"And it is?"

"Only because I'm afraid of someone getting hurt."

"I'm a tough girl."

I chuckled. "I mean getting hurt emotionally. I care a lot for you, Sash."

"I know what I'm letting myself in for."

"Do you know that the Noorthi have already given you a name? You're my *pallexis*. I found something similar, an old Earth word which sort of means concubine, or mistress." I glanced at her to see her reaction. "It seems they already know where your place is."

"I see."

"Are you afraid of being known as that? They mean no disrespect. It's just their way of fitting you into the hierarchy of the sisterhood."

"You've given the arrangement some thought."

"Just about every waking moment, when I'm not rescuing the Noorthi, defeating Jute or saving Rice."

Sasha grinned. "I think I can live with that." She held up her wrist. "Does that mean I get a tattoo?"

"Not you, too. See Grit because I don't want to know."

"Are you ready to test out this new relationship of ours?"

"If you don't mind, I figure one of us had better be paying attention while we're here, otherwise we'll get robbed blind."

"Oh."

"But once we're back on Heaven, I think I can squeeze you into my busy schedule." I winked at her and grabbed her hand, lacing my fingers with hers. "Oh, Carn. I hope this works out."

Chapter Fifteen

Good Night Sweetheart

We arrived back at Heaven exhausted and pleased. It was late in the day and there was a lot of organization needed to find a hundred places to sleep. As expected, the Noorthi took in their own, which was fine by me. Work had begun as soon as I contacted home from Valos, but it wasn't until the last light of the day that we had managed to put up enough temporary covering in case it rained. It was going to be a long few weeks ahead.

On the morning of the second day, Grit sought me out. "I was looking for you." I glanced up from what I was doing. "We have some unfinished business."

"We do?"

"The ochre..."

"Ah." In all the rushed activity to get the new Noorthi settled I'd forgotten about the artifacts. I reached for my comlink. "Malt?"

"Yeah?" Her weary voice mirrored what we all felt. Tired.

"That stuff I asked you to look after. Where is it?"

"In the alcove in the landing bay."

"Thanks, sweetie."

"Sweetie?" Malt laughed. "You must be tired."

"Tell me about it." I signed off and curled my finger at Grit. "Follow me."

"All I asked—"

"I know what you want to know, *memesh*, but this is also important." She followed me along the path to the cave. I proceeded through it and along the passageway until we reached the landing bay on the other side of the plateau. A few steps before

I reached the small alcove carved out of the rock I stopped. "You want to know how the ochre saved Rice."

"I have never seen that before."

I lowered my voice. "It's all to do with the secret." I moved forward. "Come." I threw back the covering Malt had flung over the artifacts to keep curious passers by away.

"By all that is holy!" Grit stepped forward slowly, dropping to her knees in front of the small statues, bowls, baskets and urns. "Where… where did you find these?" She looked up at me with tears in her eyes.

"I found them in the ochre mine. It was revealed to me."

"Revealed… to… you? How?"

I think she already had an idea about what I was going to say, but I knew she needed to hear it. "I found the Great One, *memesh*. She spoke to me."

"S-s-spoke to you?" Her eyes widened and I thought for a moment she was going to faint.

"If you stop repeating everything I said, I'll tell you." I waited for Grit to compose herself. "This ochre," I grabbed the jar that had been my friend and held it up, "is alive."

I gently shook the jar and the ochre glowed. "There are microorganisms living in the ochre–are part of the ochre–and they are able to manipulate it."

"I am not sure—"

"This is the ochre of legend. It's able to change into whatever you want it to be. I gave Rice some of this and asked it to cure her. The organisms expelled the poison through her skin. That was the black oily substance."

"Ahh. But she spoke to you. What did she say?"

"What you've been telling me from the beginning."

"And did you accept what she said any more than you did with me?"

"Well, she did better tricks than you did." That earned me a pinch. "Ow! Don't you ever get tired of doing that?"

"You are talking about the Holy One. You do not speak of her this way!" Grit held out her hand ready to pinch me again if I so much as opened my mouth.

I risked it anyway. "I saw her face in the mud."

"What did she look like?" Grit's voice was tinged with wonder.

"I don't know! Mud-like." I backed away quickly before she could reach in and grab me.

"She has meant no harm, *hedera*."

Grit stopped and looked. She blinked rapidly then flung herself to the floor.

"Oh, for crying out loud. Get up." Grit's prostrate form would gather spectators if she wasn't careful.

"Oh, Great One! Please excuse her insincerity."

"*Hedera*, I am well aware of Jordana's...." The mud hesitated for a moment. It was obviously looking for a word to describe me. A number of them came to my mind, plus a few more, less flattering ones.

"But she has a good heart," Grit said.

"I know that, Grit."

"Oh, she knows my name."

"Scary, isn't it?" I said. It looked like the Great One got out of having to put a name to me. I, for one, was rather glad of that. I had an urge to touch the urn and before I could stop myself I did.

Oh, Great One.

Ahh, my friend. I see that your transition is complete. Teach her well.

It is my duty, Great One.

We are now linked.

I just knew it. Now they were congregating in my head. Was there no rest for me? *Excuse me, but do I get a say in this?*

There were two voices and they spoke in unison. *No.*

"Jordana has done me a great service," the Great One spoke out loud.

"Ratha?" I think Grit was still in a state of shock.

"Hey! Are you questioning my ability to do something good?"

"Of course not, but the Great One—"

"Listen, are you saying I'm not smart enough to take pre-emptive action?"

237

Grit's mouth opened.

"Don't look so surprised. You gave it to me."

Grit got up from the floor and threw her arms around me. "Thank you," she whispered in my ear.

"While you're in a good mood, I suppose now is the time to tell you I also st... liberated some plants, as well."

"You mean you stole from the Sacred Garden?"

I felt another pinch coming on. "If I didn't, those herbs would be long gone."

"But the garden..."

'Grit, you'd have no herbs left. None of you would."

Grit's mouth opened and closed. I know she couldn't condone what I did because I stole them, but I knew she knew I was right. "Don't do it again."

"I think that might be a bit hard to do now."

"Well, then..." Her eyes narrowed and I knew she was scolding me.

Hedera is right. You did a bad thing.

Book, sometimes I have to do a bad thing to do a good thing.

"You're welcome."

"And now I think it's time," I said.

"Time? For what?"

"Time that this rock had an ochre mine," I said. Grit scowl disappeared. "But only you and I know about *her*."

"It will be difficult."

"The more people I know, the greater the danger is to all of us."

"You could have kept this to yourself," Grit argued.

"You had a right to know." I smiled sweetly at her. "You had carried the secret for so long you deserved a reward."

"That is no reason—"

"*Memesh*, can't you just accept it gracefully? Why do you have to argue about everything?"

"I do it because you do it. If you would just agree with me there would be no need."

"Please!" The mud in the jar vibrated wildly.

"Sorry," I mumbled. "We'll search in the next few days for a suitable location and we'll let the ochre do its thing."

"'It's 'thing', as you call it, is a sacred tradition," Grit said.

"Hell-o, you only knew about it ten seconds ago."

A huge sigh echoed in the landing bay.

"What?"

"Centuries I wait for you to arrive, and its come to this."

"Aren't you glad you picked me now?"

The mud remained silent. It had no one to blame but itself.

†

The past few days had worn me down, so I took refuge at the only place I considered mine. The plateau. It was there that Epi found me.

"Hi, stranger. Trying to avoid me?"

"Not at all. There's just been too much to do."

"So I hear." Epi sat down next to me. "So, how did it go?"

"I'm sure you already know, so what do you want to know?"

She leaned back on her hands and looked at me. "What makes you think I need to know anything?" I raised an eyebrow at her. "Grit seems awfully happy."

I lay back on the grass and put my hands behind my head. "Fancy that."

"I was just curious." She lay back on the ground next to me.

"And you want to know what's making her happy."

"Yeah, something like that."

I let that one slide past me. "Did you ask her?"

"Yeah. She said to ask you."

"Coward," I whispered.

"Did you say something?"

"No. She's just happy to get out alive and save some of the artifacts from Alengola."

"That's it?"

"Yep." Well, it was true. That's what I showed her. Artifacts from Alengola. It just happened to be more than she had actually thought she had.

239

"That's boring."

"You are a gossip."

"A… a what?" Epi leaned on her elbow. "What did you call me?"

"A gossip. It's an old fashioned Earth word for someone who likes to hear all the secrets and news then pass it on to others."

Epi opened her mouth, then closed it. She couldn't argue with that one.

"What have you heard?" I asked.

"You and Sasha, er…."

"Yeah, we'll be erring any day now." I was sick and tired of being the subject of such gossip, but if Epi knows then it was only a matter of time before everyone would know and I could finally put the whole matter to rest.

"That's good to know." She smiled at me, the smug woman. She put her hands behind her head.

"Is there anything else the sisters need to know?"

"No, that's enough for now." She giggled.

"What's so funny?"

"You. You're not really what I expected for our savior," she said seriously.

"I could say the same about you. I've now seen Alengolan Noorthi and Exeter Noorthi. It seems to me you're the odd ones out. Why is that?"

"I don't know. Maybe it had something to do with our rugged life on Rigeus. Is that a bad thing?" She glanced at me uncertainly.

"Actually, no. The other Noorthi are stuffy. No fun at all."

"And us?"

"You're argumentative, ornery and stubborn." My words didn't comfort her. "I love you guys."

"Really?"

"Three years ago I couldn't wait to get rid of you, but now…I couldn't wait to get home. I haven't had a home since my dad died."

"And now you think we're your family."

"And now we're all a family. We care for one another. Look out for one another. Love one another."

240

"Love. Care. These are foreign to us."

"That's what I'm here for. Tomorrow the lessons begin."

I heard a huge sigh. "Oh, boy."

†

The next morning I intercepted Gorin before he had a chance to leave. "Trying to get away before I could thank you?"

He smiled at me. "I haven't had the chance to do any real medicine for a long time. Maybe I should be thanking you."

I grabbed his hand and shook it. "You saved more than a hundred people's lives, my friend. I won't forget it."

"Ah," he grumbled. "Glad I could help."

"Glad you were nearby to help." I laughed. "It's funny how friendships evolve from the worst of circumstances."

"I nearly killed you."

"As you know, I don't die that easily."

"No. Extraordinary." He hesitated. "Well, I'd better be going."

I let go of his hand. "How are things at the Consortium? Did you ever find the traitor?"

"After Grimm died, things have been quiet. I have my suspicions, but so far he hasn't done anything to reveal himself." He swiped his brow. "I'm getting too old for this sort of thing."

"You're always welcome here, you know that." He stopped and I wondered whether he was thinking about taking up the offer.

"Maybe later." He looked over the valley. "This would be a nice place to end my days."

"Yeah, it's the sort of place you can lay back and say craz to the rest of the universe." He laughed. "I do it every day." I didn't really, but it sounded good.

"Ah, Jordana, don't ever change."

"I don't want to, but these damned women are trying very hard."

The smallest ship in our fleet emerged over the top of the cliff and landed on the plateau. "Garrett will take you wherever you want to go." I extended my hand again, but this time Gorin

241

grabbed me and pulled me into a hug. I relaxed and let him have his moment. "Keep well, Gorin."

"You too, Jordana." He let go and turned to leave.

"Will there be any problem with the missing medicine?" I called.

"No, I just told them there was a medical emergency on Sigma Three."

"And if they decide to check it out?"

"The tiny colony was destroyed by a meteor storm two days ago."

"Oh, sorry. It must be painful to do all that work and have it wiped from the universe by a natural disaster like that."

"You'll never know." He gave me one last look and smile and walked up the ramp.

The hatch closed and the ship took off. I gave Garrett a wave and the ship left, smoothly accelerating into space and out of my sight.

As I stood watching the small ship ascend, Beri came up beside me. "Is there a problem?" I asked.

"No. In fact I have some good news."

"I could use some." The fiery trail from the ship disappeared into the darkness and I turned my attention to our little village in the valley.

"You have been allowed to see to Rice's bedtime each night."

I turned and grabbed Beri around the waist, twirling her around in circles. "Woo hoo!" I yelled, drawing the looks of those below. I held up my hand to stop any concern. My heart thudded painfully in my chest. "Why?"

"You are our chosen one, J. The Great One has blessed you. If we can't do this then we are going against her Word."

"I'm ecstatic that I can see her, but I think you're doing it for the wrong reason. I should be allowed to see her because she is my... our child. She should know both her parents. Family is strength, B. The Noorthi don't know family. Maybe they should learn." I kissed her on the lips. "But I'll take the concession."

"What do you want to do?"

I remembered back to my early days with my dad and I grinned. "I think I have the perfect thing in Bessie."

Beri looked at me curiously. I saw she was wondering what she had agreed to.

†

I entered the Noorthi compound with a tablet under my arm. It took forever to reach Beri's abode because every single sister wanted to stop and say 'hello', 'thank you' or 'bless you'. While I found it endearing to start with, after the twentieth 'hello', I was ready to push them aside. They were cutting down my time with Rice. Finally I stood outside Beri's room and I cleared my throat to announce my arrival. Beri met me at the door and I entered behind her. The quiet was broken by the squeal of "Ra!" Rice jumped up and down on her bed and I saw why the Noorthi were reluctant to allow me access.

"Hey, squirt. Shhhh." I kept my voice low in the hope that Rice would copy me. "You have to be quiet."

"But Raa," she yelled.

"Quiet," I repeated solemnly.

"Otay." She put her finger to her lips. "Ssssssss."

I tried really hard not to laugh at her antics. "If you're good I'll tell you a story." I wasn't above trying a little bribery.

"Stowwy?" she squealed.

"Shhhh. Into bed. If you're really, really quiet." I sat down on the mattress and patted the space next to me. Rice settled for my lap instead.

"Stowwy?" She looked up at me with guileless eyes. Rice had a way of just melting my heart. I moved the tablet to Rice's lap and activated it.

"Once upon a time…," I started.

"What's that?" Her tiny finger poked a hole in the holographic image. I grabbed it and pulled it away.

"Once upon a time," I repeated. "There was a tiny princess."

"Ra! Me!" she said excitedly.

243

"Well, you know what? She does look like you. Are you a princess?"

"Pwinceness? What?"

"Okay, how about a tiny Ashaltea? Do you know Ashaltea?" Rice nodded vigorously. "A tiny Ashaltea called Rice."

"Me!" she squealed. I put my hand over the tablet, making the image disappear. "Ra!" she complained, trying to pull my hand away.

"No, quiet Rice. Shhhh."

"Sssssss." She cupped her hand over her mouth.

I removed my hand and continued the story. "One day she met Ratha." My image joined the tiny Ashaltea in the scene. Rice pointed at me and was about to call out when she remembered the game.

"Good girl." I stroked her hair and kissed the top of her head. "Ratha was her protector."

"Prow?"

"Ratha would make sure that Rice was safe. A big bad neomite tried to take the tiny Ashaltea away...." The image of a large beast stood in front of the little girl and the tall woman, roaring at them. "But Ratha scared it away." My image waved her hands in the air at the creature and it ran away.

I continued the story for another five minutes and Rice oohed and aahed as the tale unfolded. Beri stood leaning against the door while I entertained Rice and I saw her approval in my peripheral vision.

"Time for sleep, Rice." I tried to put her to bed, but she refused.

"More! More!"

"It's time for sleep, honey. If you don't sleep they might not let me come back tomorrow to tell another story."

I had never seen Rice move so quickly as she scrambled underneath the blanket.

"You want another one tomorrow night?"

"Pweeese," she begged.

I looked at Beri and she nodded. "You be a good girl at school tomorrow and I'll come back and tuck you in at night. All right?"

"Aww wight."

I stood and leaned to kiss Rice on the forehead. "Good night, sweetheart."

"Raaaa," she said tiredly.

I moved out of the way and allowed Beri to tuck her in. I watched mother and daughter together and I felt a pang of jealousy. I didn't experience that interaction much in my young life. Granted I had a very attentive father, but in some aspects he couldn't fill the void left by my mother's death.

Beri steered me out of the room and into the compound. "That was sweet."

"It's part of being family, B. Sharing."

"I'll encourage the sisters to continue your visitation rights."

"Good night." I kissed her lightly on the cheek and walked away. I sighed. I had a long way to go with these women.

†

The next morning the dip of my bed woke me. I looked over my shoulder and saw Sasha asleep behind me, her arm draped over my waist. But Sasha wasn't on the side the dip came from. On the other side of me sat Beri, watching me.

"Er, hi," I said sleepily.

She smiled down at me. "You look a lot more relaxed."

What I felt was a lot more uncomfortable. "Why are you here?"

"Just to see if you're all right."

"Okay." I felt sick to my stomach. B was sitting there expecting that Sash and I had had sex. "Do you want a report or something?"

She looked at me and blinked.

"Sorry. That was uncalled for."

Beri remained silent.

"We decided to start out slow. Sash and I fell asleep together. I just wanted to cuddle." I don't know if that's what she wanted to hear or not.

"You didn't have to tell me."

"No? Why else would you be here?"

A wave of nausea rolled over me. Damn it! I shouldn't have a hangover. I didn't even drink any more.

"I've been given good news."

"Did Grit tell you?"

"Yes, she did."

"So, when are you due?"

"Due for what?"

"When will the baby be born?"

"Oh, no," Beri said. "It's not me, it's you."

"M…m…Me?" She must have been mistaken. "Are you sure you heard Grit right?"

"Well, she definitely said it was you."

"I'm going to kill her," I growled. Another wave rolled over me. "So now you get the chance to be the daddy."

"Oh, no."

"No?" Suddenly I felt light-headed. "Do I ask who?"

Beri smiled. This was a smile that sent a shiver through me. "Grit."

"Grit?" I yelled, and immediately regretted it. I held my head as Sasha jumped up in bed.

"What? Who? Where?"

"Jordana is pregnant."

"Pregnant?" Sasha laughed, long and loud.

"And Grit is her spirit partner."

Sasha laughed even harder. In fact, she laughed so hard she rolled off the bed and landed on her ass on the floor.

And you didn't tell me?

Congratulations? We will have a new hedera.

Just great.

At that precise moment I leaned over the edge of the bed and threw up on Beri's boots.

Then I passed out.

About the Author

Erica Lawson

Erica Lawson is a "dinky di" Aussie, born and raised in Sydney, Australia, 58 years ago. She has worked as a secretary for most of her working life in a variety of interesting fields from a government scientific organization, the fire brigade, the film industry and finally, for the last 20 years, with a psychiatrist. Many of her friends will attest to the fact that she finally found her niche in the last job, gaining many helpful hints for her own state of mind.

Her first book, "Possessing Morgan", was released in December 2009. It is a winner of the 2010 GCLS award for best thriller/mystery novel. Her second book "The Chronicles of Ratha: The Children Of The Noorthi", a science fiction adventure, was released in December 2010 and a finalist in the 2012 GCLS Awards. Erica's third novel, "Soulwalker", released in 2012, won both the Rainbow A ward for Best Sci-Fi of 2012 and GCLS Best Speculative Fiction in 2013. Her fourth novel, "Reflected Passion" won Best Historical Fiction at GCLS in 2014.

Erica has two novels published with Affinity eBooks. "Miss-Match", co-written with A.C. Henley, in April 2013. Her first solo effort for Affinity, "Out Of Retirement", came out in April 2014.

Erica now writes solely for Affinity eBooks and her previous novels, first released through Blue Feather Books, are being reissued by Affinity. They are available through Affinity eBooks website, Amazon, Barnes and Noble, and Bella Books.

Romance type: Lesbian romance. I qualify that with adventure, thriller, science fiction and historical settings.

Erica Lawson also writes under the name "Aurelia" on online fan fiction.

Website Link:—http://www.ericalawson.com

Yahoo Group: Aurelia's Musings—
http://groups.yahoo.com/group/aurelia_fan

Publisher: Affinity eBook Press—
http://www.affinityebooks.com

Other Books from Affinity eBook Press

**The Chronicles of Ratha: Book 1 Children of the Noorthi—
Erica Lawson** Jordana Laren is a hard-drinking, hard-fighting womanizer, who works as a freighter pilot in her spare time. Her latest customer drugs her, steals her ship, and abandons her on a desert hellhole called Rigeus, infamous penal planet for the worst women criminals. Her chances of survival aren't looking good. She has no food, water, or weapons, and the nearest bar is a million miles away. Just when she's ready to write her last will and testament, Jordana is rescued by a group of barely-clad women. Has she found nirvana? Her own personal harem seems like a possibility, until the intercession of their enemy, the Velkren. Their leader, Vel, remembers Jordana well, and not fondly. But why is Vel on this planet, surrounded by murderers, thieves, and bad-tempered bitches? Jordana knows Vel isn't a prisoner, so why is her nemesis on Rigeus mining mud, of all things? Jordana knows only one thing. She has to get off the planet before Vel kills her. Unfortunately, the women who saved her reveal themselves to be holy. They are the Noorthi, and Jordana's dream of endless debauchery becomes a nightmare of eternal servitude. The Noorthi make her one of them, marking her with a wrist tattoo, and leaving her no choice but to protect them with her life. The last thing Jordana wants is to become involved in galactic politics or heroic actions. But the tattoo ochre in her body is suddenly giving her morals and scruples, not to mention a better vocabulary! And she really can't pass up a chance to outwit Vel, whose megalomaniac plans are endangering not only the Noorthi, but the civilized galaxy itself. But Jordana is torn. Does she stop Vel at all costs, or

does she get out from under the thumb of the Noorthi while she can? Some things were never meant to be easy...

Cowgirl Up—Ali Spooner When the new ranch hand, Coal Bryan, arrives at the MC2, the last thing she's looking for is love. Her co-workers are surprised when Coal turns out to be female. Coal, used to the reaction, quickly earns the respect of the crew with her work ethic and skill with horses. Coal uses the strenuous work and friendship of the ranch hands to try and forget her broken past. Melissa Conway, owner of MC2, offers Coal a place to live in her home. They both are shocked to find they are linked in a way neither of them imagined. Mary Leah, Melissa's sister, arrives at the ranch to recover from a recent tragedy. The attraction between Mary Leah and Coal is instant and mutual. Can the three women survive their personal dilemmas? The love and friendship they develop certainly helps but will it be enough to bring them together. Ride along with the MC2, for boot scootin', butt kickin', dirt eatin', rodeo adventures, with a love story thrown into the mix.

If I Were a Boy—Erin O'Reilly Katie McGuire appears to have it all. A devoted husband, a job she loved, and a comfortable lifestyle. Helen Swenson is a successful financial director of a prominent investment firm, with an unfaithful husband, and few friends. Their husbands' annual trip to Padre Island National Seashore to reunite with their air force pilot squad becomes a pivotal point for the two women. Their lives take on a completely new meaning when an undeniable magnetism between them draws them together. Passion and secrecy becomes the norm, as they have no choice but to succumb to their attraction. Can the vacation love affair continue? When they leave for their respective homes, will they regret what happened? Life is not that easy to change and the people around them are the hardest to convince. There is no more powerful motivation than love. Except hate and there are plenty of people who want to see their relationship destroyed. Will Katie and Helen be able to make a life together work or succumb to doubts and the pressures of family? This story will fill you with the thrill of passion and the tenderness of love.

Nesting—Renee MacKenzie   Macy Stokes, a divorced mother who is struggling with her sexual identity, jumps at a once-in-a-lifetime opportunity to help her friends. She doesn't foresee it will put her in jeopardy of losing her son, Jeremiah. Fresh out of high school, Cam Webber travels to Augusta, Georgia, to reconcile with her aunt. When she learns that's impossible, she determines to gain acceptance from her aunt's partner, Sharon. Meanwhile, Cam sets her sights on Macy, but Macy has other ideas. Kenny Brewer is a good old boy who loves his wife, Dorianne, even when he thinks she's gone totally off her rocker. Dorianne gets it in her head that a local woman is her long-lost half-sister. But soon, her obsession with that is eclipsed by medical problems that involve them all. Set in Augusta, Georgia, *Nesting* explores the age-old issues of guilt, regret, and redemption, and the part they play in driving people to create and protect family-at any cost.

Reece's Faith—TJ Vertigo   In the return of the main characters from the bestselling novel *Private Dancer*, we see the blossoming relationship of bar owner, Reece Corbett and actress, Faith Ashford. The two women explore new, uncertain territory together, using sexual intimacy as a glue of comfort, helping them become strong and whole. A trusting Reece shares with Faith the sordid tale of how she became *The Animal* and Faith finds herself newly empowered by Reece's ongoing trust and support. Jealousy arises when Faith has to kiss a man on her TV show and two amorous women stalk Reece. When Faith is outed on her television show, things get crazy. With the arrival of her parents on the scene, the craziness escalates. As Faith tries to justify her lifestyle and defend her love for Reece, she discovers that nothing about her parents is as she once believed. This, not to be missed passionate and erotic romance, will have you begging for more.

Starting Over—Jen Silver   Ellie Winters, a successful potter, is living on a remote hilltop farm inherited from her parents. Her well-ordered life is shaken apart when her past meets her present. Robin Fanshawe, Ellie's philandering long-term lover, has a fragile truce with Ellie. The arrival of women from Robin's present threatens to break that tentative pact. Charming Dr. Kathryn Moss, an archaeologist and an old lover of Ellie's, arrives on the farm searching for a new site to dig. When she discovers a previously unknown Roman settlement and ancient burial site on Ellie's farm, Ellie allows her to start an archaeological dig of the area. Will Ellie also allow the rekindling of an old romance or will she stay with Robin? Can that long term relationship, albeit tentative, recover from this collision or will an old romance trump everything she knows? Will Robin, seeing the interaction between Ellie and Kathryn, leave her womanising ways behind? Will she take a chance on giving herself wholly to the woman she loves? These questions and the mystery of whose royal resting place is disturbed at Starling Hill are answered in this classic romance of simmering passions, anguished loss, and the wonder of love.

Twisted Lives—Ali Spooner   A twist of fate leaves Bet and her daughter Kylie stranded at the entrance of the home of Alex Graves, as she flees the control of an abusive husband. When custom–homebuilder Alex arrives to find steam boiling from Bet's car and a beautiful child asleep in the passenger seat, her heart goes out to them. Alex offers shelter to the pair setting off a chain of events that bring both mother and daughter close to her heart and danger to her door. A heartwarming story of true love that will keep you smiling long after you've finished the book.

Malodorous—Del Robertson   Sequel to My Fair Maiden Something in Fairhaven stinks. Other than the mutton stew, that is. Gwen thought life after being a virgin sacrifice would be a bed of roses. Bodhi was just looking for a wench to bed. Neither less-than-dashing hero nor not-quite-so-pure maiden imagined they would meet again, much less be trapped together in a city the likes of the ill-named Fairhaven. There's a killer on the loose. Fairhaven's on lockdown, its citizens fearful for their lives. The local guards are corrupt. And, Bodhi's been accused of murder...

Desert Blooms—Dannie Marsden Luce's story continues in DESERT BLOOMS... When we last met Luce Velazquez in Desert Heat, she went through hell and back to salvage her soul and reputation. Hoping to get her life back on track with lover Beth Ryan, a woman who understands her pain and can relate on every level. Instead, Luce is in the hospital, and Beth in protective custody. Jessica Sullivan, Luce's friend and ex, has big doubts about the sincerity of Beth's love, and is in no hurry to release her from custody. Can Luce's new found happiness last, or is Jessica correct in her doubts? A heart stopping romance that will fill you with the wonder of friendship, anger of betrayal, and the everlasting vision of love.

Finding Her Way—Riley Jefferson Is it love or just great sex? After ending an abusive marriage, Jerrica Kerrison is finally alive and she's apologizing for nothing! She has a job with a financial firm in Boston, a townhouse in Newburyport, and a sports car she drives way too fast. Jerrica has everything except that indefinable emotion called love. Madison Jeffrey is a lost soul. A PR job in the south has always protected Madison from the pressures of her family. But one day, fate brings her back to New England, forcing Madison to face her long buried demons, and a sister who despises her. When a chance meeting brings Jerrica and Madison's separate worlds crashing together, the attraction is instantaneous. After one passionate night together, Jerrica retreats into the safety of her world, leaving Madison to figure out what happened. Will Jerrica open up her heart to the idea of love? Can Madison finally believe that she is worthy of unconditional love? Or will a devil hiding in the shadows tear them apart?

HER—Lisa Ron Fox has been looking for that one person who will make her feel complete-her perfect match. Together with her friends, Megan and Tree, Fox continues her quest while dodging exes and clingers, laughing a lot along the way. When she meets Madeline, she instantly knows that she has found HER. Madeline has her own problems-notably a domineering husband. Can Fox win her heart? Can they make a life together? This story will make you laugh, cry, and hold your breath as the story unfolds. With the right person love can conquer all.

Bayou Justice—Ali Spooner Hell hath no fury like a woman scorned. When Kara, Sasha's new lover is taken hostage as a diversionary tactic to allow the drug dealing Bellfontaine brothers to escape justice, Sasha springs into action. Kara is released physically unharmed, however her emotions and budding career in the District Attorney's office are left in shambles when she is held to blame for their release, Appalled by the failure of the criminal justice system, Sasha exacts her own brand of justice for the acts committed against her lover. From the Bayous of Louisiana to the jungles of South America, Sasha plots her revenge.

Out of Retirement—Erica Lawson Melanie Stokes was a doctor—a very good one, or so she hoped. She was calm and cool under pressure, and very little fazed her. Until…Caitlin Joseph ran a small retirement home for older women in need. The fact that everyone in the house was gay was a coincidence, although it did cut down the number of women agreeing to live there. Mel took up an offer to do some relief work for a local community center when their regular doctor was away on holidays. As soon as she arrived at the home she knew something was different about the place. Was it the little old lady chasing the paper boy down the street or the sign saying "Dykes Retirement Home"? But there was something about the place that also appealed to her. Sure, Caitlin was cute as a button, but it was more the fact that she took very good care of her charges despite their rather bizarre behavior. The older women seized the opportunity to introduce a woman into Caitlin's lonely life, using any means possible to keep Mel coming back. Their plans were boosted by the introduction of another woman into the house, who set hearts a fluttering and blood pressure rising. Now if she was a lesbian it would have been perfect...

Letting Go—JM Dragon A failed relationship puts Stella Hawke's life on the brink of chaos. When her grandmother falls gravely ill in Ashville, Stella ends her army career to take care of the woman during her last weeks. Little does she know that an old army comrade, socialite Reggie Stockton, whose family owns the local newspaper, also lives in Ashville. Will she allow herself to accept Reggie's help to turn her life around and let go of the past? This is a journey where both women re-evaluate what they want out of life. Will that path lead to happiness or to a parting of the ways?

Through the Darkness—Erin O'Reilly Becca Cameron is a loner—by choice. She lives in a hundred year old farmhouse built by her great grandfather. A tragic accident in her home a year earlier drove away her lover, and Becca tries to accept what she cannot change and hang on to the belief that love can conquer all. Chase Hunter had a meteoric rise in the Eastman Corporation and was, at thirty-four, the youngest vice-president. To Chase, her work was all consuming leaving little time for friends or lovers. There was simply no place in her life for anything but her job. When Becca and Chase meet at their work place, the attraction is spontaneous. Life begins to look brighter for both women as work takes a second seat to romance. Unknown to either woman, someone is watching their every move... Will passion outweigh doubt? Can love conqueror fear?

Beginning of the End—Alane Hotchkin What happens when life doesn't go exactly as you planned and you must protect others from your own fate? Escaping a horrific childhood, Nikki longed to find happily ever after in adulthood. What she found was Hell. Or did it find her? Finding the courage to break the cycle of betrayal, she opens her heart one last time. Alex lived a childhood others dreamed of. Her father never once denied the young rebel a thing. All her life she dreamed of protecting others; to follow in her father's footsteps. Soon though she learned sex and fists made the most powerful of weapons. Alex controls the women in her life through fear and sex, will breaking the cycle be too much to overcome? Will loving Nikki be enough to change her, or is Alex beyond help? Alex would give Nikki the world, but at what price? When a person's tightly controlled reality snaps, what then…? This is the Beginning of the End for one of them and the ultimate sacrifice for the other. But who is who in this game of life?

Galveston 1900: Swept Away—Linda Crist On September 7-8, 1900, the island of Galveston, Texas, was destroyed by a hurricane, or 'tropical cyclone' as it was called in those days. This story is a fictional account of Mattie and Rachel, two women who lived there, and their lives during the time of the 'great storm'. Forced to flee from her family at a young age, Rachel Travis finds a home and livelihood on the island of Galveston. Independent, friendly, and yet often lonely, only one other person knows the dark secret that haunts her. Madeline "Mattie" Crockett is trapped in a loveless marriage, convinced that her fate is sealed. She never dares to dream of true happiness, until Rachel Travis comes walking into her life. As emotions come to light, the storm of Mattie's marriage converges with the very real hurricane. Can they survive, and build the life they both dream of? This second edition of one of Linda Crist's best-loved novels maintains the original story, while incorporating some reader-pleasing passages that were cut from the first edition. As an added bonus, the short story "Something to Celebrate" is included at the end of the novel, detailing further adventures of Rachel and Mattie.

Rapture: Sins of the Sinners—A. C. Henley & Fran Heckrotte A serial killer is targeting young lesbians throughout the state of Texas. Texas Ranger Cochetta Lovejoy is assigned to the case. Convinced she knows who is committing the murders, Ranger

Lovejoy is willing to do whatever it takes to put the perpetrator behind bars--even if it means stretching the limits of the law by manipulating the judicial system. Detective Agnes Kelly-Elliott is one of Ft. Worth Police Department's finest investigators. When Ranger Lovejoy appears on the crime scene of a recent murder, Agnes fears a dark secret that, if revealed, could destroy her family ties and end her career. This is a dark, gritty, graphic tale of desire gone awry, and flawed characters looking for redemption in all the wrong places.

Absolution—S. Anne Gardner Games of the rich and famous, love, lust, and forbidden passions weave this tale that play out through decades and the world. The close ties the Alcalas have to the royal house of Spain provide them with an unspoken untouchable policy. Their passions and their secrets are about to come to light with a force that cannot be stopped. In this whirlwind is Cristina Uraca Alacala who is searching for a truth that has been denied to her most of her life and she must find. She is not unlike her family; Cristina does not stop until she gets what she wants. In the fog lies the truth that she must travel through to find. In this tale wealthy socialite Annais Francesca D'Autremond is a pivotal person of interest in Cristina's search for the truth. When these two women meet they find themselves drawn together by something greater than themselves. As the truth of a hidden past becomes clearer their passions grow beyond the realm of the no return instead of a status quo. Both tied together by destiny; will both survive the onslaught of past and present passions?

Denial—Jackie Kennedy Time spent in Somalia has Doctor Celeste Cameron accustomed to living and working in a war zone. Coming back home to America, Celeste is glad to see the end of the peril she has been in—or so she thinks. Danger seems to follow Celeste and she finds it in the shape of Amy. What Celeste feels for Amy scares her more than anything she has faced in war zones. Amy has the same feelings, but is in denial and vows to marry Josh, Celeste's twin brother, no matter what. When fate brings them together again, will they give in to their mutual attraction or will they once again deny what they feel?

Taming the Wolff—Del Robertson ONLY ONE WOMAN... As devastatingly beautiful as she is headstrong, noble-born Alexis DeVale abruptly finds her preordained life in upheaval. Abducted at sword-point, held for ransom, thrust into a maelstrom of lawlessness and piracy... HAS THE POWER... The strength of her passion, the depth of her love... TO TAME THE WOLFF... Mayhem. Brutality. Murder. These are the tools of the trade - and Kris Wolff is the master of her profession. Captain of the high seas, a roguish pirate, her heart hardened by life, her passion tightly controlled by the secret she's forced to keep. Faced with a new danger, The Wolff finds herself unable to guard her heart from the tumultuous desires that Alexis DeVale has awakened.

Private Dancer—TJ Vertigo Reece Corbett grew up on the mean streets on New York City, abused, used and in trouble with the law. Faith Ashford grew up wealthy, with all the creature comforts that money provides. When they meet fireworks begin.

Miriam and Esther—Sherry Barker Miriam thought her life would play out in the bustling metropolis of Dallas, but after a life-changing accident, she moves to the small town of Cool Lake, Texas to get her head on straight and regain her senses.

McKee—A.C. Henley Private Investigator Quinlan McKee has returned to Los Angeles after a three-year absence, only to find herself embroiled in a world of child slavery and police corruption.

E-Books, Print, Free e-books

Visit our website for more publications available online.

www.affinityebooks.com

Published by Affinity E-Book Press NZ LTD
Canterbury, New Zealand

Registered Company 2517228

www.ingramcontent.com/pod-product-compliance
Lightning Source LLC
Chambersburg PA
CBHW052024020726
47501CB00004B/1232